It s..itter
mo...his
abs..on-
sters? Some of them seemed barely human when he thought
about it. Faith had seen it, had expressed her grave concern,
but Slade knew best. He'd gone about his bloody business,
never thinking twice about what it might cost him.

She'd been kidnapped early on, by the same men who'd
killed Slade's brother, but he'd been in time to rescue her
and settle up Jim's score. Faith hadn't blamed him then, or
when he'd led a pack of murderous fanatics to her doorstep
later, working on another case. She'd fought beside him to
defend her home—the home they were supposed to share
when she agreed to be his wife.

All gone now, shot to hell.

Titles by Lyle Brandt

The Matt Price Gun Series

THE GUN
JUSTICE GUN
VENGEANCE GUN
REBEL GUN
BOUNTY GUN

The John Slade Lawman Series

THE LAWMAN
SLADE'S LAW
HELLTOWN
MASSACRE TRAIL
HANGING JUDGE
MANHUNT
AVENGING ANGELS
BLOOD TRAILS
RECKONING

RECKONING

— THE LAWMAN —

LYLE BRANDT

BERKLEY BOOKS, NEW YORK

THE BERKLEY PUBLISHING GROUP
Published by the Penguin Group
Penguin Group (USA) Inc.
375 Hudson Street, New York, New York 10014, USA

Penguin Group (Canada), 90 Eglinton Avenue East, Suite 700, Toronto, Ontario M4P 2Y3, Canada
(a division of Pearson Penguin Canada Inc.) • Penguin Books Ltd., 80 Strand, London WC2R 0RL,
England • Penguin Group Ireland, 25 St. Stephen's Green, Dublin 2, Ireland (a division of Penguin
Books Ltd.) • Penguin Group (Australia), 250 Camberwell Road, Camberwell, Victoria 3124, Australia
(a division of Pearson Australia Group Pty. Ltd.) • Penguin Books India Pvt. Ltd., 11 Community
Centre, Panchsheel Park, New Delhi—110 017, India • Penguin Group (NZ), 67 Apollo Drive,
Rosedale, Auckland 0632, New Zealand (a division of Pearson New Zealand Ltd.) • Penguin Books
(South Africa) (Pty.) Ltd., 24 Sturdee Avenue, Rosebank, Johannesburg 2196, South Africa

Penguin Books Ltd., Registered Offices: 80 Strand, London WC2R 0RL, England

This is a work of fiction. Names, characters, places, and incidents either are the product of the author's
imagination or are used fictitiously, and any resemblance to actual persons, living or dead, business
establishments, events, or locales is entirely coincidental. The publisher does not have any control over
and does not assume any responsibility for author or third-party websites or their content.

RECKONING

A Berkley Book / published by arrangement with the author

PRINTING HISTORY
Berkley edition / June 2012

Copyright © 2012 by Michael Newton.
Cover illustration by Bruce Emmett.

All rights reserved.
No part of this book may be reproduced, scanned, or distributed in any printed or
electronic form without permission. Please do not participate in or encourage piracy of
copyrighted materials in violation of the author's rights. Purchase only authorized editions.
For information, address: The Berkley Publishing Group,
a division of Penguin Group (USA) Inc.,
375 Hudson Street, New York, New York 10014.

ISBN: 978-0-425-25029-7

BERKLEY®
Berkley Books are published by The Berkley Publishing Group,
a division of Penguin Group (USA) Inc.,
375 Hudson Street, New York, New York 10014.
BERKLEY® is a registered trademark of Penguin Group (USA) Inc.
The "B" design is a trademark of Penguin Group (USA) Inc.

PRINTED IN THE UNITED STATES OF AMERICA

10 9 8 7 6 5 4 3 2 1

ALWAYS LEARNING   **PEARSON**

For J. B. Books

I

The lawman woke to agony and thought, *God-damn, I'm still alive*. He wasn't clear on why that should displease him, for a moment, other than the pain that racked his damaged body. Then, his memory began to fill the gap with grim, disjointed images like fragments of a shattered mirror that reflected only loss.

He saw a ceremony under clear blue sky, himself a part of it. There was a minister, all solemn-faced, but everybody else was smiling, so it couldn't be a funeral. He stood before the preacher, wasn't sure exactly why, until a soft touch on his left arm made him turn.

The woman was more beautiful than anyone he'd ever seen. The sunlight on her white dress nearly blinded him. The lawman recognized her, knew her name but couldn't think of it. Frustration and embarrassment shamed him. He had a sense that matters were about to go from bad to worse.

The urge to flee was powerful, but how could he escape with everybody watching him? And now the minister was speaking, leaning toward him with a pensive look, addressing him by name. Interrogating him.

2 Lyle Brandt

"Jack Slade, do you take this woman?"

I have, he thought, remembering, but knew that wasn't right. The clergyman and witnesses expected something else.

He tried the words for size. "I do. *I* do. I *do.*"

So simple, but the syllables defeated him. His mouth was dry, tongue withered, perspiration beading on his face. When had he stepped into a desert? He could likely manage, with a sip of water and a hat for shade, but as it was . . .

The sunlight seared him, threatening to bake his brain inside his skull. His lips cracked when they tried to utter the appropriate response. Half turning to the beauty at his side, he found her staring at him, mortified. He was humiliating her and couldn't help himself.

Sorry, he thought, but couldn't say that, either. Christ, his mouth was dry! It felt as if his teeth might crack at any moment. How hard could it be to say—

The crack of gunfire saved him, galvanized the lawman into action he could manage, spinning toward the sound and reaching for his Colt.

Not finding it.

Stupid! Of course he wouldn't wear a pistol to a wedding, least of all his own. His next impulse was to protect the woman, even if her name eluded him. He had to shield her from the mounted gunmen who were charging at them, scattering the wedding guests, their weapons blazing.

He was reaching for her, meant to place himself between her and the guns, when crimson spouted from the bodice of her snow white gown and sprayed his face, half blinding him. He followed through the move as panic's talons clutched his throat, threatened to strangle him.

The next shot struck him from behind, a stunning blow. They fell together, his last impulse driving him to cover her, protect her with his dying breath. If he could only speak her name, to comfort her.

"Faith! *Faith!*"

Thrashing, he tried to struggle out of bed but couldn't manage it. The sweaty sheets were tangled; they snared and hobbled him. His shoulder burned as if a red-hot blade was twisting in the flesh. His rib cage felt like broken glass. Hot, angry tears streamed down his cheeks where he'd imagined blood.

"Stop that," a woman's stern voice cautioned, as her hands restrained him. "You could tear your sutures out."

He opened grainy eyes and waited while they focused on the face above him. Freckles and a long nose, green eyes, frizzy ginger hair beneath some kind of square-cut cap. The woman wore a blue-striped pinafore over a slate gray, long-sleeved dress.

All wrong, unless his fever dreams deceived him.

"Faith?" he asked, voice cracking.

"You just rest now, Marshal," she replied. An unfamiliar voice.

Another woman—younger, blond, same uniform—appeared beside the first, regarding him with troubled eyes. The first one muttered from the corner of her thin-lipped mouth, "He's asking for her."

"Heavens," said the blond. "I'll fetch the doctor."

"Faith," he told them, softer than a whisper now.

"Just rest," the older nurse repeated. "Doctor's on his way."

Slade recognized the doctor, knew his name was Lucius Abernathy. They had never met professionally, but he knew some of the doctor's other patients, most of whom were still alive. The ones who weren't, Slade guessed, would likely still be dead, with or without his help.

"You're back among us, then," the doctor said, standing beside Slade's bed. He wasn't tall—no more than five foot eight or nine—but looking up at him, he might have been a giant.

"Back? I guess," Slade said.

"You had us worried. Touch-and-go," said Abernathy, "but you're tough."

"Where's Faith?" asked Slade.

Ignoring him, the doctor said, "You have two bullet wounds. One in your shoulder, here." Pointing at Slade's left. "It missed the clavicle, the scapula—all of the bones, in fact. That's lucky, but it took a bite out of the muscle, so you'll have some stiffness there. Can't say how long. Maybe for good."

Slade was about to ask for Faith again, but Abernathy forged ahead.

"The other shot—I can't say whether it was first or second—hit your seventh rib a glancing blow and cracked it, ricocheted up to the sixth, and then went out your back. Another lucky shot, considering. An inch or two toward center, and it would've drilled your liver. You'd be talking to Saint Peter now, instead of with Yours Truly."

"Faith," Slade croaked.

The doctor, seemingly oblivious, told him, "You should be up and mobile in a few more days. Nothing too strenuous for, oh, two weeks at least. You'll know when you can get to work again. I've spoken to the judge, of course. No problem, there."

Slade clutched the doctor's sleeve, wishing he could drag Abernathy to his knees.

"Goddamn it! Faith!"

The doctor blinked at him, looked stricken as he said, "She's in the Lord's hands now, Marshal. You need to concentrate on getting well, yourself."

Slade closed his eyes and felt the doctor move away, sleeve fabric slipping through his fingers. A minute later, something pricked his arm and chilled him, sent him plummeting through smoky darkness. Even falling, though, he still heard Abernathy speaking from a distance, to the nurses.

"I've administered a sedative. He should be quiet for the next few hours, but you need to watch him. When he comes around again, he'll want to see her. Call me if you need to. I don't want him agitated by the funeral."

Slade felt a scream building inside of him, but when he tried to let it out, only the whisper of a sigh escaped. The room was spinning, and he felt as if he'd drunk a quart of whiskey in a span of seconds, but it couldn't fill the aching void inside him.

How old had he been when he'd last wept? Slade fumbled for the childhood memory but couldn't find it. It had been decades, surely. He'd been tough, no one could fault him there, but it made breaking that much harder.

Why was he alive? What good was he to anyone when he had failed the most important person in his life?

Slade dreamed. A little slice of Hell on Earth.

He couldn't say where memory left off and fantasy began, as if it mattered. He saw Jim, his twin brother, the mirror image of himself at twelve, trying to talk him out of leaving home. Slade shoved him, ran—and found himself standing before a headstone with his brother's name inscribed in plain block capitals, the dates below it testimony to a life cut short.

He sought revenge but found a badge instead—and unexpected love, for all the good it did him. Lost, now, through his own damned negligence.

It struck him that a man should guard the things that matter most, instead of leaving them behind to wither in his absence. He'd been busy hunting men, or were they monsters? Some of them seemed barely human when he thought about it. Faith had seen it, had expressed her grave concern, but Slade knew best. He'd gone about his bloody business, never thinking twice about what it might cost him.

She'd been kidnapped early on, by the same men who killed Slade's brother, but he'd been in time to rescue her and settle up Jim's score. Faith hadn't blamed him then, or when he'd led a pack of murderous fanatics to her doorstep later, working on another case. She'd fought beside him to defend her home—the home they were supposed to share when she agreed to be his wife.

All gone now, shot to hell.

Slade dreamed their wedding, tried to see it through this time and break the curse. If he could make it through the vows, what was to say they might not have a happy ending after all?

Or if they couldn't, he recalled somebody telling him that if you died within a dream, you died in fact. A possible escape? Could he catch up with Faith before it was too late?

She's in the Lord's hands now.

Of course, and why should Slade suppose that he was headed in the same direction, with the life he'd led? Gambling and whoring until he received the telegram that told him of his brother's death, then hunting men to earn his daily bread. Granted, the hunting bit was lawful, but he had to wonder if the killing was excused.

By whom?

Slade hadn't cracked a Bible since he'd left his parents' house, had never met a preacher whom he fully trusted. Thinking of the last one he had dealt with, in a town called Jubilee, he pictured a fanatic filled with hate for other races and religions. Not the sort of man you'd trust to save your soul, assuming that soul saving was a matter of concern.

Slade drifted back into the wedding dream, facing the preacher. Not the crank from Jubilee, but someone else he recognized, although the face seemed blurry to him somehow, as if seen through a distorting pane of glass. And there was something odd about the preacher's voice, as well. An accent Slade knew he should recognize. Not eastern, like New York, and not a southern twang. Not British, but that brought him closer to the truth.

An Irish brogue?

"Dearly beloved," said the preacher, "we are gathered together here in the sight of God to join together this man and this woman in holy matrimony, which is an honorable estate, instituted of God in Paradise, and into which holy estate these two persons present come now to be joined."

Slade felt a welling of emotion in his chest, as if his heart could burst from happiness and sorrow all at once. The preacher smiled at him and forged ahead.

"Therefore, if any man can show any just cause why they may not lawfully be joined together, let him now speak, or else hereafter forever hold his peace."

A pause at that, the minister staring beyond Slade and Faith toward the audience, scanning faces for any who might raise an objection. When no one spoke, the preacher frowned.

"Nobody, then?" he asked, almost a challenge. "Well, in that case, I am bound to say . . . I take this woman for myself!"

The preacher burst out laughing, reached beneath the robe he wore—that had transformed itself somehow into a barber's apron—and produced a wicked-looking knife.

"Connor MacGowan at your service, Marshal Slade," he said—and lunged at Faith, thrusting the blade into her abdomen.

She may have screamed. Slade couldn't tell, amidst the shouting from the wedding guests, over the pulse that hammered in his ears. He clutched MacGowan's throat, strangling the preacher-barber as they fell, with Slade on top. Slade put his weight and all his strength into it, but he couldn't silence the Irishman's laughter or wipe the broad smile from his face.

"Think you've stopped me, Jack?" the grinning man inquired. "You haven't. No one can!"

Slade felt the blade rip through his shoulder, then withdraw and find a new target between his ribs. The pain was savage, but he wouldn't let it stop him. Squeezing his assailant's throat until his fingers met, the laughing face beneath his crumbling into ash, Slade shouted, "Die, you bastard! Die!"

He snapped awake with firm but gentle hands pinioning his arms. Slade strained against them, but the strength he'd felt a moment earlier had fled, leaving him weak and drenched with sweat.

"You're dreaming, Marshal," said the nurse with ginger hair. "You're safe now." Bringing one hand to his forehead then, she added, "And I think your fever's broken. Rest, now, while I call the doctor."

Exhausted, Slade lay still as she retreated, but he kept his eyes wide open. Worried that another dream like that might kill him.

Wondering why he was still alive.

The doctor came, told Slade he'd passed some kind of crisis point, then left again after he ordered broth for Slade. The broth came half an hour later, barely warm, but Slade was grateful to have something in his stomach, after how long?

When he posed the question to the nurse who fetched his soup bowl, she looked troubled for a second, glancing toward the doorway as if she expected someone to appear and chastise her for talking to him. Finally, frowning, she said, "This is your third day with us, Marshal."

"Third day?"

"You've been badly injured," she reminded him.

Three days lying on his back explained the stiffness in Slade's neck and joints, besides the pain that radiated from his wounds. Three days meant anyone who'd died the afternoon that he was wounded should be in the ground by now.

He replayed Dr. Abernathy's terse instruction to the nurses: *I don't want him agitated by the funeral.*

Slade didn't have to ask whose funeral. The leaden weight that had replaced his heart left no doubt on that score.

Judge Isaac Dennison arrived near dusk, according to the shadows on Slade's wall. He brought a walking stick but hardly used it, more as an aid to locomotion. His own wounds from another shooting incident were healed, and if they pained him much these days, Dennison kept it to himself.

"You're looking better, Jack," he said, in lieu of salutation. "When you first came in, I thought you were as good as gone."

"Three days ago, I'm told."

"That's right. A grim day all around, but you should know—"

"I missed the funeral," Slade interrupted.

"You've missed all of them," the judge corrected him.

Slade grimaced. "All? How many?"

"Four, all told," said Dennison.

"Four dead."

"Counting the raiders," Dennison replied. "They didn't rate a service, but we planted them."

"And Faith."

"Now, that was touch-and-go," said Dennison.

"Was it . . . ?" Slade choked on the question, couldn't ask if it was quick. Settled for, "Did she suffer?"

Dennison frowned, as if uncertain how to answer that for Slade's sake. Finally, he said, "I guess you'd have to ask her when she comes around."

"Ask her?" Despite the fact that he was lying down, Slade felt a sudden dizziness. "What do you mean, *ask her*?"

"Well, now, perhaps I should have said *if* she wakes up,

but thinking positively never hurt—" He stopped, then said, "Good Lord! Did some fool tell you that she died?"

Slade thought he felt the bed—maybe the room itself—shift underneath him. "Nobody's told me anything," he said, at last. "I just . . . I . . ."

"Just assumed the worst," said Dennison. "I see I'll need to have a word with Dr. Abernathy on the subject of his bedside manner."

"He said that she was in the Lord's hands," Slade replied. "I thought he meant . . ."

"Of course, you would. Damned fool." Slade wasn't sure if Dennison meant him, the doctor, or a bit of both. Before he could inquire, the judge continued, "What he *should* have said is that she's still unconscious. Comatose. From what I'm told, she could wake up at any time . . . or not."

From giddiness at learning Faith was still alive, Slade felt his spirits plummet. "There was no head wound," he said. "I would've seen it."

"The doctor should be trying to explain this," Dennison complained, but then pressed on. "It's something about shock and blood loss interfering with the brain. I haven't studied medicine, you know. Pin Abernathy down, next time you see him."

"Right," Slade said. "I will. About the shooters . . ."

"Time enough for that, later," said Dennison. "I'm under doctor's orders not to agitate you, and it seems I've overstepped. Damned fool! You rest now, Deputy. I need you back in harness."

Slade's last visitor, as daylight crept through his window, was Ben Murphy. He looked dusty from the trail, with two days' stubble on his jaw, his forehead pale above the line drawn by his hat. The badge had turned a little on his vest, its star off center.

"Hey," he said. "They told me you were back among the living."

"Barely," Slade replied. "You've been out hunting?"

"For the pricks that put you here," said Murphy. "Haven't found 'em yet, sorry to say."

"They got away," Slade said, not asking. One more blow.

"Well, most of them. Left two facedown at Miz Connover's place, before they ran. Gene Braden, out of Texas, and a Hoosier named Ike Weems. We're looking for his brother, Joe."

"How many others?" Slade inquired. "I didn't get a count."

"That's no surprise," said Murphy. "No one else was counting, either, but there must've been a dozen, give or take. Two down leaves nine or ten to go."

"You have their names?" asked Slade.

"Aside from Weems, a few," Murphy replied. "Judge says he'll fill you in on all of that when you're up and around."

"I'm up now."

"Doesn't seem so, to me," Murphy said. "It's an order, all right? He hears that I riled you, I'm out on my ass."

"Damn it, Ben!"

"I can tell you that everyone's looking, from here down to Texas and up into Kansas. Word's out, Jack. We'll find those we know, and they'll give us the others."

"While I just lie here."

"What choice have you got? You can't walk, much less ride."

"I'll be out of here soon," Slade replied.

"Glad to hear it," said Murphy. "There's bad men enough to go 'round."

"I want these."

"Sure you do. But you won't mind if we bag a few, while you're healing?"

"You know about Faith?"

Murphy nodded. "It's lousy, but don't count her out. She's a fighter, I hear."

"Those shooters," Slade said, changing subjects to relieve the sudden blockage in his throat. "When you catch up with them—"

"Don't even say it," Murphy cautioned him. "We all feel that way, and the judge has issued special orders. Bring 'em back alive, or come with witnesses who'll swear we shot in self-defense. The old man wants to see 'em swing for what they done."

"He said four funerals," Slade suddenly recalled. "Who were the other two?"

"A couple of Miz Connover's hired hands," said Murphy. "Hanes and Murdoch."

Art and Ed. Slade knew and liked them both. It was a stretch to picture either of them dead, but unfortunately he'd have to get used to it. How many other friends and casual acquaintances had Slade lost to the violence that dogged him? And how many had he killed himself?

Too many, some would say.

But if you looked at it another way, with vengeful eyes, it still wasn't enough.

Murphy was right: he wasn't fit to hunt the bastards who had plunged Faith into darkness, killed her men, and nearly claimed Slade's life. At least, not yet. But finding them would take some time, particularly if they'd scattered to the four winds, running for their lives.

He'd heal. And on the first day he could travel without falling off his horse, Slade would be after them. Whether Judge Dennison approved or not was irrelevant.

Slade would pursue them as a lawman or without the sanction of a badge. The only way for Dennison to stop him would be holding Slade in jail until the final member of the raiding party was accounted for. And being pledged to serve the letter of the law, how could the judge accomplish that?

"Rest easy now," said Murphy, as he took his leave. "I'll see you later on."

"Right. See you," Slade replied, distracted.

Hearing Murphy's words again: *The old man wants to see 'em swing for what they done.*

No problem.

Slade would gladly bring the killers back to hang, if they submitted to arrest. But if, as he suspected, they should choose to fight it out . . .

Well, he could always hope to have a witness handy when the smoke cleared.

Or, if all else failed, he knew the way to Mexico.

2

Slade was ready for the doctor when he came around next morning, day four since a storm of lead had torn Slade's life apart. When Abernathy stepped into the room, he found Slade sitting upright, more or less, his meager breakfast finished and removed, a look of grim determination on the lawman's stubbled face.

"You're feeling better, I surmise," said Abernathy.

"Might be," Slade suggested, "if I wasn't being lied to, left and right."

"What's that supposed to mean?" the doctor asked him, frowning, primed to take offense.

"I asked you about Faith," Slade said. "You left me thinking she was dead."

"I beg your pardon?" Now the doctor looked confused.

"Beg all you want," said Slade. "But don't tell someone that his bride-to-be is in the Lord's hands, when she's lying in a bed unconscious, fighting for her life."

"I didn't mean—"

"I don't care what you meant," Slade interrupted. "All I

want to hear is what happened to Faith, and when I should expect her to improve."

"Marshal, there's such a thing as doctor-patient confidentiality."

Gritting his teeth, Slade eased one of his legs out from beneath his bedding, braced as if to rise. "Don't make a sick man kick your sorry butt," he warned.

"All right, just calm yourself," the doctor said, "before you have a hemorrhage and ruin all my work."

Slade sank against his pillows. "I'm waiting."

"As you know, Miss Connover was shot." The doctor's tone was professorial. "One bullet struck her in the upper chest, above her left lung. I was able to remove it and confirm that it did not directly damage any vital organs. Still . . ."

His hesitation set Slade's teeth on edge. "Still *what*, Doctor?"

"Your fiancée lost a great deal of blood," said Abernathy. "Even without the severance of any major artery or vein, an injury like that is bound to bleed significantly. One of Miss Connover's employees understood the need for putting pressure on her wound, but with the battle going on around him, it was hit-and-miss. Then, when the raiders were repelled, more time was lost transporting both of you to town."

Slade thought about the three-mile ride from Faith's ranch into Enid. He could almost see himself lying beside her in the wagon, one of Faith's hands crouched above her, pressing on her wound and trying not to let her die.

"I hope you took her first," he said to Abernathy.

"I assessed your injuries and started with the case I deemed most urgent. If it helps you, Marshal, that *was* Miss Connover."

"It doesn't help me," Slade replied. "What did it do for her?"

"She survived removal of the bullet, but the operation—as with any surgery—resulted in a further loss of blood." After a moment's hesitation, Abernathy said, "So, I attempted a transfusion."

Slade frowned. "That's where you take one person's blood and give it to another?"

Abernathy nodded. "In this case, the donor was a nurse, Miss Kathleen Eddowes. I transfused one pint."

"Was that enough?" asked Slade.

"There are inherent risks for both the donor and recipient in a transfusion," Abernathy said. "Of course, we cannot bleed a donor dry to help the patient. As it is, surveys conducted over forty-some-odd years in Europe and America show beneficial outcomes in approximately half of all transfusions."

"And the other half?" Slade asked.

"In most of those," said Abernathy, "the results are negative."

"Meaning?"

"The patients die. Whether because of their original disease, or from some problem with the donor's blood, we just don't know enough to say with any certainty."

"But Faith's alive," Slade said.

"Alive and comatose," said Abernathy. "And again, I can't say why. If the transfusion's not responsible, it may be that she simply lost too much blood or replenishment began too late. Another possibility, for all I know, is that she fell and struck her head when she was shot. I found no evidence of an external trauma to her head, but I can't rule it out."

"So, you can't tell me why she's still unconscious," Slade summed up, "or if she'll ever come around."

"Regrettably, that's true," the doctor granted. "As a rule, chances of a full recovery decline the longer a coma persists."

"When you say full recovery . . ."

"I mean with all the patient's physical and mental faculties intact," said Abernathy.

Slade had never thought about the matter. Now, he asked, "How does a person in a coma eat and drink, or . . . you know."

"They require attentive care," the doctor said. "A liquid diet is the norm, fed through a tube in small amounts. As for the rest—"

"All right," Slade said. "Enough. You're telling me it's damn near hopeless."

"Not at all," the doctor said. "But there's no point in fostering false hope, either. In a majority of coma cases, we expect to see at least some small degree of brain damage. A slowing, if you will. In some cases, the damage is profound. As for the rest . . ."

"They die," Slade finished for him.

"Yes."

"The care she needs," Slade said. "Is this place good enough to handle it?"

The medic didn't seem to take offense. "We're adequate," he said, "but not superior. I won't pretend we lead the field."

"She'd have a better chance, then, in a bigger hospital," said Slade.

"A more advanced facility, of course," the doctor said. "Regardless of its size."

"But moving her's a risk, I guess."

"It could go either way," said Abernathy. "If you made it through the application process and could cover the expense, you'd need at least one nurse to travel with her, in sufficient privacy to cope with all her needs. And yes, the trip could still have serious adverse effects."

Slade gave up thinking of escape. "I need to see her," he told Abernathy. "Now."

• • •

It wasn't far to travel—just a few yards down the hall—but
Slade prepared for the short walk as if he was embarking
on a weeklong ride to track some outlaw in the badlands.
Every move he made was painful, but somehow it didn't
seem as bad as the day before. Slade didn't know whether
his wounds were actually mending overnight or if he was
just distracted by the information he'd received concerning
Faith.

In fact, he didn't care.

When he demanded clothes, the nurse with ginger hair
demurred. Dressing would risk reopening his wounds, she
said. When Slade insisted that she bring him pants, at least,
to keep his buttocks covered in the backless johnny gown
they'd given him, she vanished for a quarter hour, then
returned with someone's old high-water trousers. They were
baggy in the waist, requiring Slade to clutch them with one
hand, but after struggling a while to put them on, he didn't
mind. In place of boots, he slipped into a pair of
moccasins.

Thus clad, with the nurse beside him all the way to brace
him when he tottered, Slade proceeded down the hall to Faith's
room. Shuffling like an old man to avoid the jarring pain of
proper strides, it seemed to take forever, but he guessed that
it was only minutes after all. His escort made approving noises
when they reached Faith's doorway, as if Slade had scaled a
mountain pinnacle unaided, in the middle of a blizzard.

And he felt that way.

Slade's first shock was how pale Faith looked against the
bed's white sheets and pillowcase. Her raven hair, so lustrous
in sunlight, seemed to leech the color from her face here in
the sickroom. For a frozen heartbeat, Slade thought she had
died while he was hobbling down the hall, but then he saw
the rise and fall of Faith's chest underneath the blanket.

She was breathing on her own, but that was all.

The nurse waited outside while Slade approached Faith's bed. It seemed a longer trip than coming from his own room, but he made it, stood, and studied her as if he was examining a marble statue in a gallery of some museum. Slade couldn't count the times he'd lain beside Faith, watching as she slept, but she had never been so deathly still.

He forced himself to touch her cheek with anxious fingertips, almost surprised to find her warm and soft, instead of cold and hard like porcelain. His touch had no effect—another first—and Slade felt something coil around his heart.

Dread, maybe. Or a simple killing rage.

He had no idea who was responsible for this, beyond the names Ben Murphy had provided. Gene Braden and Ike Weems, already dead; the other Weems brother still living. None of them meant anything to Slade. They'd never crossed his path, as far as he knew. As for Faith . . .

One thing his job had taught him in the past few years: it didn't take a grudge to prompt a killing. An urge produced by simple greed or lust could lead to tragedy. Some killers couldn't even tell you why they used a gun or knife. It felt like something they could get away with, so they did it.

Simple.

Slade knew such men—had dealt with one of them quite recently, in Jubilee. He never quite got used to them, but understood that there were only two ways to control them: lock them up for life among their own kind where they couldn't injure decent folk, or put them down like rabid dogs.

He bent down, almost kissing close to Faith, and whispered to her, so the nurse outside the doorway couldn't hear him. Slade wasn't ashamed of anything he had to say but valued privacy where raw emotions were concerned.

"I love you," he told Faith. "You know that. And I'm counting on you to come back. Whatever happens, though, rest easy on the men who did this. I'll take care of them, I promise you."

Slade brushed her forehead with his lips, then straightened up—another lance of pain between his ribs—and made a point of taking longer steps as he rejoined the nurse. It hurt, but he was healing. And he needed to regain his strength as soon as possible.

Slade found the doctor waiting for him when he got back to his room. The nurse left them alone as Slade moved toward his rumpled bed.

"It's good for you to get some exercise," said Abernathy, "but you can't be too aggressive with it. Even in a rugged individual, the flesh takes time to heal."

"I hear you, Doctor," Slade replied. "Now, when can I get out of here?"

Judge Isaac Dennison craved a cigar, but with his doctor in the room he managed to suppress the impulse. There was something to be said for sweet anticipation.

"So, he wants to get out of the hospital," said Dennison. "That's only natural. I know the feeling very well myself."

Doc Abernathy nodded. Said, "But you were wise enough to heed professional advice."

It was a year and counting now since fanatical gunmen from Dennison's past had tried to kill him at the federal courthouse where he conducted trials for the western half of Oklahoma Territory. He'd been badly wounded—nearly died, in fact—and Abernathy had saved his life.

Jack Slade had hunted down the men responsible for the attack. Another job well done.

"He's hurt and angry," Dennison replied. "It goes against his grain to lie in bed and watch the world go by his window."

"Isaac, we both know exactly what he wants. These sons

of bitches shot the girl he loves at their wedding, for God's sake! He wants to destroy them."

"Who wouldn't?" asked Dennison.

"Right. That's my point. You're his boss. It will be up to you to control him."

"Assuming I can," said the judge.

"He's your deputy. Give him an order."

"There's giving, and then there's enforcing," said Dennison. "You know the difference."

"He's a lawman sworn to follow your directives," Abernathy said.

"Unless he gets fed up and quits. I know you've heard of the Emancipation Proclamation, Doc. I can't force anyone to work against their will, unless they've been convicted of a crime."

"What Slade's considering could be a crime," said Abernathy.

"Oh? Confided in you, has he? Did he fill you in on the conspiracy?"

"Damn it, I'm serious!"

"And so am I," said Dennison. "We know he wants revenge, the same way you or I would. But I can't arrest a man for *wanting*, even if he had the strength to get up out of bed and do something about it."

"Which he will," said Abernathy.

"Maybe, maybe not. He isn't on his feet yet, and you have him riding off on a vendetta."

"Do you doubt he'll go?"

"I question your ability to see the future," Dennison replied. "We can surmise his feelings with a fair degree of accuracy, but a number of events could interrupt the outcome you're predicting."

"Such as?" Abernathy challenged him.

"Such as his bride-to-be awakening," said Dennison. "In

which case he might feel obliged to hang around and nurse her back to health."

"I wouldn't bet the farm on that," the doctor said.

"You're giving up on her?" asked Dennison.

"Hell no! But I've got nothing left to offer, either. I'm a useless spectator from this point on."

"Try praying," Dennison suggested. "Meanwhile, there's a fair-to-good chance that my other deputies may find the trash who did this thing and bring them in, dead or alive."

"All of them? I was told they'd scattered," Abernathy said.

"That doesn't mean they've gone invisible. If they exist, they can be found."

"You trust a lot to luck, Isaac."

"I trust my men—including Slade."

"And you just said he might jump ship on you, if you restrain him."

"The operative word is *might*," said Dennison. "You keep mistaking possibilities for certainties. I would suggest you stay away from poker tables, Lucius."

"I'm no gambler. You know that."

"So stop betting against my man."

"I'm simply telling you—"

"Doc, tell me something useful. How long have we got before he's up and moving?"

"He was up this morning," Abernathy said. "That's why I'm here."

"When you say up . . ."

"He questioned me on Faith's condition, then insisted that I let him see her."

"And?"

"He made it down the hall and back without collapsing," Abernathy said.

"It's not exactly riding off to track a gang of killers," Dennison replied.

"He'd try it, though, if someone put him on a horse."

"I'll make damned sure they don't."

"For how long?" Abernathy pressed him.

"When will he be fit to ride?"

The doctor thought about it. "Sutures out inside a week," he said. "He'll still have pain. The shoulder will be stiff for who knows how long, possibly for good. Say he could ride within a week, ten days. That won't mean that he's fit to face an able-bodied murderer, much less a gang of them."

"I'll think about that when the time comes. Now, unless there's something else, I have a trial beginning in—" He checked his watch and said, "Eleven minutes."

"More killers?" Abernathy asked, as he was rising from his chair.

"A pair of ordinary horse thieves," Dennison replied. "Assuming that they're guilty."

"Right. I'll leave you to it, then."

"Appreciate you stopping by," said Dennison. "Just close the door on your way out."

He couldn't argue with the doctor's take on Slade, particularly since they'd met when Jack was hungry to avenge his murdered brother. Then, the young drifter had listened to reason and put on a badge to do it the right way.

And this time?

Dennison was no more psychic than Doc Abernathy, but he knew the urge for vengeance would be strong in Jack—and stronger still, if Faith Connover died. In that case, it was anybody's guess whether or not the judge could manage Jack. And if he failed, then what?

A grieving lover on a killing spree was bad enough. A lawman on the same errand was worse. If Slade turned outlaw, he would have to pay the tab, assuming that the other deputies who served Dennison's court could find him.

Would they even try?

Too many questions for a day when there were lives at stake before his bench. Wishing he still had time for that cigar, Dennison took his walking stick and left his chambers, heading down to court.

It was mid-afternoon when Slade awoke to find Judge Dennison standing beside his bed. He pushed himself upright and grimaced at the pain it cost him but refused to whimper.

"Judge," he said.

"I hear you've been up and about, Jack."

"Not far. I just went to see Faith."

"How's she doing?"

"The same."

Dennison took a chair from the corner and brought it across to Slade's bedside, then sat. "I thought it might be time," he said, "to brief you on what's happening, and what we know about the men who put you here."

Slade nodded. "Good."

"I understand Deputy Murphy told you some of it already," said the judge.

"Not much."

"About the dead men?"

"Right."

"Gene Braden came from Texas, where he'd done some time at Huntsville for a robbery. Murder suspected, but they couldn't prove it. He escaped two years ago. I get a feeling that the Rangers didn't make much effort to retrieve him once they heard he'd left the state."

"Export the problem," Slade replied.

"It works," said Dennison. "For them, at least. Isaiah Weems—or Ike, as he preferred—was Indiana born and raised, for what it's worth. He and his brother, Joseph, have been in and out of trouble since their teens. They always work together, so we're risking the assumption that Joe Weems is one of those who got away."

"Ben says there were a dozen, give or take," said Slade.

"We haven't pinned it down, but that's approximate," said Dennison. "Faith's men identified another of the gunmen as Burch Thornton. It appears he worked around the place until they caught him stealing from the other hands and peeping in her windows after dark. She fired him, which I'm thinking may have motivated him to join the raid—or even pitch it as a plan to someone else."

"Thornton," Slade repeated, but he couldn't put a face to it. "Who else?" he asked.

"Two others that were recognized from town," said Dennison. "A pair of drifters, Tommy Garrity and Charley Fox. I never heard of them, myself, but one of Faith's men recognized them from the Paradise Saloon."

"Do they have records?"

"Nothing federal," the judge replied. "No paper on them that we've found so far. I'm having posters issued."

"That leaves five or six still unaccounted for," Slade said.

"It does," the judge agreed. "We're working on it, Jack. My guess is that the first one of these characters we catch, he'll spill the other names."

"To save himself," Slade said.

"It's hypothetical," said Dennison. "If one of them can nail the others down, and if he'll testify, I'd bargain down to life without parole for him alone."

"And hang the rest?" asked Slade.

"If they're convicted, absolutely," Dennison replied.

"Seems like a lot of trouble," Slade observed. "They'll probably resist arrest."

"It's possible, of course," said Dennison. "Under the circumstances, I'd require eyewitness affidavits to an act of self-defense."

"That's what I heard."

"We're all sworn to uphold the law, you understand," said Dennison.

"Yes, sir."

"In any case, I'm hoping that we'll have this all wrapped up before you have to think about it."

"I'm already thinking," Slade informed him. "Has the doctor told you when he plans to cut me loose?"

"A week or so, before he pulls the stitches," Dennison replied. "As for resuming any duties, it depends on how you feel. What you can handle."

"I'll be fine," Slade said.

"We'll see. I can't send out a one-armed deputy to make arrests."

"I've got both arms," said Slade.

"And one of them effectively disabled at the moment," Dennison reminded him. "And then, your ribs."

"The bullet only nicked them."

"Nicked and cracked," said Dennison. "On its way out your back, as I recall."

"It missed the vitals," Slade insisted.

"And we're thankful," said the judge. "But you'll be slower than you were, Jack. For a while, at least."

"I'm a right-handed shooter, Judge."

"That's only part of it," said Dennison. "You have to mount and ride, pitch camp and break it down on trips away from home, be able to secure a rowdy prisoner who doesn't call for shooting. If I send you out before you're fit, I've signed your death warrant."

Slade recognized the truth in that but also understood that Dennison was worried about sending him to find the men who'd wounded him and put Faith in a coma.

Burch Thornton. A thief and Peeping Tom.

Slade couldn't wait to meet him.

But he said, "Don't worry, Judge. I'm not in any rush to try my hand against ten guns."

"I hope not, Jack," said Dennison. "I'd hate to lose you, one way or another."

3

Burch Thornton shifted in his saddle, trying to get comfortable on the piebald mare he'd borrowed from a Cherokee who wouldn't need it anymore. A mile or so in front of him, a barn and farmhouse nestled in a ring of trees with tilled fields stretching off on either side.

"I don't know," he said. "It could be trouble."

"Trouble's what we do, *amigo*," Sabiano de la Cruz replied, smiling. "Here, take a closer look."

The spyglass Sabiano handed to him was an old one, tarnished brass. There'd been some leather on the fattest section of it, once upon a time, but most of it was gone and what remained was worn down paper-thin. One of the lenses—Thornton couldn't tell which one—was also scratched, which made him want to swipe at an imaginary hair, but otherwise the view was clear.

What Thornton saw was one man working with a jumpy horse in a corral beside the barn, some chickens pecking in the dooryard, and a boy of ten or twelve splitting short logs for firewood. There was also movement in the house, beyond an open door, but Thornton couldn't make out any details.

"There's a woman for you," Sabiano said. "For all of us."

"I ain't exactly in the mood," said Thornton.

"No?" The leader of their outfit shrugged. "Ho-kay. That's more for us."

The other seven men besides Thornton, that meant. They sat strung out along the rise on stolen mounts, armed to the teeth and going nowhere in particular—except to Hell, Thornton surmised, if they got caught. Two down already, since he'd joined the bunch, and while they might have called it his fault, nobody except Joe Weems seemed too upset.

Losing a brother had to sting, Thornton supposed, but couldn't swear to it from personal experience. He'd lost a daddy, years ago, but hadn't missed the drunken, raging bastard for a minute since.

There'd been a few tense moments, granted, when they rode away from Faith Connover's spread without a thing to show for it except a pair of empty saddles. Thornton had expected some kind of reprisal, but the others seemed to take it all in stride. Sometimes you win a hand, sometimes you lose. Joe Weems wanted to call him out, of course, but Sabiano put a lid on that, reminding Joe of one time he and brother Ike proposed a bank job that had nearly finished all of them.

High times.

Now they were looking at another spread that didn't seem to pose a threat of any kind, if they were slick about it going in. One man, one boy, likely a woman in the house. Maybe a daughter, learning how to cook at Mama's knee.

Why not?

Thornton wondered whether he was getting gun-shy, running with a pack of killers bonded by a common lack of interest in tomorrow. As the only one of them who hadn't served a stretch in prison—just a few nights here and there, in local jails, for cutting up when he was drunk—Thornton felt like the virgin little brother of the family.

Except, he knew this family would leave his carcass rotting on the roadside in a heartbeat, giving no more thought to him than to Gene Braden or Ike Weems.

"All right," he said at last, pretending Sabiano gave a damn for his opinion. "How we gonna do it?"

"Ride down there and take it," Monty Stofer said. "How else?"

"They've got a mile to see us coming," Thornton said. "That's plenty time to shut themselves inside the house with rifles."

"Says the guy who had the great plan back in Enid," Tommy Garrity put in.

"Okay," Thornton replied. "You want to line up for a turkey shoot, it's fine by me."

Still smiling, Sabiano said, "So tell us how you'd do it."

"Send six or seven off and circle 'round behind them," Thornton said. "Stay out of sight until it's time to rush the house. When they're in place, then two or three—the best hands—ride up to the front door. Try to draw the man out, anyway."

"That's pretty smart, *hermano*." Sabiano calling him a brother now, as if it meant something.

"You likely thought of it already," Thornton said, knowing it never hurt to kiss ass when the man in charge could kill you without losing any sleep.

"Maybe I did," said Sabiano, pleased to know how wise he was. "We do it my way, then. Ho-kay?"

"Somebody's comin', Pa. Three riders."

Abel Crawford turned away from the cremello stallion, trusting it enough to show the horse his back, and followed

Jubal's pointing finger toward the eastern skyline. He was right, of course; no faulting Jubal's vision at that age.

Three riders, still the best part of a mile away, approaching with no hint of stealth or urgency. Which didn't make them safe, by any means. One thing that farming in the Oklahoma panhandle had proved to Crawford, early on: no stranger could be trusted at first sight.

That they were strangers Crawford had no doubt. He couldn't see their faces, but his only neighbors to the east were Paul and Molly Fielding, with their brood of kids, farming a spread eight miles away. They had no hired hands, and their boys weren't big enough to be mistaken for grown men. They didn't have three horses, either, come to that.

He studied and disposed of all the other possibilities in seconds flat. A peddler would have had a wagon, and he likely would've been alone. A posse hunting outlaws should have numbered half a dozen men, at least, if there had been a town nearby—which there was not.

So, drifters.

Crawford frowned and told his son, "Go on inside the house."

Jubal ran for it, calling, "Ma! Hey, Ma! There's riders comin'!" Likely getting Leta and his sister all stirred up.

Crawford saved ten or twelve seconds by scaling the corral's fence, rather than walking back to its gate on the side near the barn. Not much time, but better than nothing. His wife was in the doorway when he got there, brushing back a strand of golden hair that had a tendency to stray and getting flour on her forehead in the process.

Any other time, he would have teased her, maybe licked it off to make her shiver, but today he drew her back inside the house and shut the door. Securing the latch, he told Jubal to close the window shutters all around.

"Yes, sir!" his little soldier said and hastened to obey.

Crawford got down his Centennial model Winchester

from its place above the mantelpiece. It was sixteen years old but still deadly accurate with its .45-70 Government rounds. He could score consistent hits on man-sized targets at three hundred yards, which ought to keep an adversary out of pistol range.

"Abel, who are they?" Leta asked him.

"If I knew that," he replied, "I wouldn't need the Winchester."

"I don't want any trouble, with the children here," she said.

Or you, he thought. And said, "Nobody does."

A bald-faced lie, of course, since drifters often carried trouble with them like the plague, infecting everything they touched. Crawford spent more time worrying about his family in the hands of strangers than he did about coyotes, rattlesnakes, or broken bones—a threat almost as prominent as vagaries of weather to his crops.

But they'd been lucky, until now. The few drifters that happened by—no more than one or two a year, and commonly alone—were satisfied to beg a drink of water or to ask if there was any work available. Three men set Abel Crawford's teeth on edge and filled his mind with images that made him cringe, thinking of Leta and their eight-year-old Arlene.

Because some men were savages, and if he had to use the rifle, Crawford wouldn't hesitate.

Jubal came back to join his parents and his sister in the living room, saying, "All finished with the shutters, Pa."

"Good boy," Abel replied. "Now, fetch your twenty-two."

"Yes, sir!" Sounding excited at the prospect of a fight, but nervous, too.

Jubal was back a minute later, with his Stevens single-shot, the break-top model chambered for the .22 Long Rifle round. Abel saw worry on his wife's face, trying to ignore it as he told their son, "Load up, but don't get anxious."

"Yes, sir. I mean, no, sir!"

"You'll be covering that window," Abel told him, pointing to the left of the front door. "Don't show yourself, and don't do *anything* unless I'm shooting first. You hear me, Son?"

"I hear you, Pa."

"All right, then. Leta, you and Arlene stay back in the kitchen. May as well keep working on that stew, before it burns."

"But, Abel—"

He stepped in to kiss her, smothering her protest, then moved toward the door, trailing an empty promise.

"We'll be fine," he said. "Just wait and see."

Every morning that he woke up, Sabiano de la Cruz was half surprised to find himself alive. No one who knew him as a youngster would've bet he'd get to twenty-one without a bullet in his brain pan or a noose around his neck, but here we was, still kicking—and the leader of his own outfit, at that—a week short of his twenty-ninth birthday.

Some kind of miracle.

The odds had been against him, growing up in El Paso del Norte on the Rio Grande. Texas Rangers had killed his *padre* when Sabiano was five, whereupon his *madre* turned to whoring as a means of self-support. She hadn't lasted long—*las putas* never did—but Sabiano was already on his own before a drunken vaquero beat her to death with his empty tequila bottle.

Theft was easy for a *niño* fast on his feet, and Sabiano had soon learned to fight for his loot. When fists failed him, with older and stronger *muchachos*, he switched to a knife— then a pistol he stole from a gringo who left it unguarded. The first time he'd used it, to ward off an old man's unhealthy interest, he'd known there was no turning back.

So, here he was, almost eighteen years later, leading a couple of locos to see what a stranger was made of, how far he would go to protect what was his. The other six had split up as he'd ordered, three off to the north, three south, to come around behind the farmhouse and its outbuildings.

Burch Thornton's plan, although he hadn't minded giving Sabiano credit for it, with the others listening. A sly one, that *pinchazo,* still worried that Sabiano or some of the others might blame him for prompting their move on the spread outside Enid, where two of their men had gone down. It was a fact that Sabiano had been disappointed by their lack of profit from the raid, but at least he'd had the chance to kill a gringo.

As for losing Weems and Braden, Sabiano cared no more for them than any other *presidiario* who joined his gang. They came and went like stray dogs, marked for death before he met them. There were always more where those came from.

Before they started toward the farmhouse, while his men were still riding around to flank the spread, he'd seen the farmer send his boy into the house, then follow up and shut the door behind him. Closed the window shutters, too, anticipating trouble—which was smart, but wouldn't save the little family.

Even if there were four or five of them inside, each old enough to use a gun, they were already trapped. Their only source of water was a well between the farmhouse and the barn, now hopelessly beyond their reach. All Sabiano had to do, if he had been a patient man, was sit outside and wait for them to die of thirst.

But he had never been a patient man.

When Sabiano wanted something . . . well, he *wanted* it. He didn't like to wait—for money, liquor, women, anything at all. Particularly, in this case, he did not want the farmer's wife to die inside the house before he had a taste of her.

It would be one thing if she sold her life resisting Sabiano and his men. He could respect her then, and count the loss a lesson for the future. But to sit around for days until thirst claimed her?

No.

He'd burn the place before that happened. Flush her out into his waiting arms.

"They're ready for us," Thornton said from Sabiano's left, at sixty yards.

"You thought they'd all come out and welcome you?" Miguel Fortunato inquired, from his right.

"Shut up and let me handle this," he ordered them. "And don't forget to smile."

"They all have guns," said Leta Crawford.

"I'd expect that," Abel answered her, "riding around out here. We don't know if they plan to use 'em, though."

"Don't trust them, Abel," she advised.

"There ain't much chance of that," he said and smiled, as if to put her mind at ease.

Leta didn't think about it, normally, but now she wished they had more guns. She was a fair shot with the Winchester, but that was Abel's, and she didn't want to cause a ruckus at the moment, taking Jubal's twenty-two away from him. Instead, she clutched a long knife from the kitchen, not that it would do her any good.

If it came down to knife fighting, she reasoned that their cause was lost.

Their uninvited visitors were scruffy-looking men. She might have called them saddle tramps, but that implied a drifter seeking work. These three looked more like outlaws, in her very limited experience. Pistols and knives and faces that would seem at home on wanted posters. Two of them were Mexicans, maybe mestizos, while the third—sitting his horse to Leta's right, facing the house—looked more like poor white trash.

All right, the Bible told her not to judge, and she was working on it, spiritually, but you had to make some hasty judgments on the frontier, if you wanted to survive.

Like now.

"They can't come in," she said. Not asking Abel now.

"It never crossed my mind, darlin'," he said. And called out to the riders, as they reined up in the yard, "What do you want?"

"Some water for the road," the middle man replied. "Maybe some *alimento*, eh?"

"I don't know what that is," said Abel.

"Food," the spokesman for the three translated. "That smells good, what you got cooking."

"Draw your fill of water from the well behind you," Abel answered. "We can't spare you any food right now."

"Right now?" the seeming leader of the group echoed, smiling. "You mean, we come back later and you feed us?"

"Nope," said Abel. "Not today or any other time."

The Mexican put on a sad face, then. He said, "I guess you not a Good Samaritan."

"I'm no kind of Samaritan," Abel replied. "I look out for my family." And as he spoke, he cocked the Winchester.

"I hear that," said the Mexican. "You want to shoot a man because he's hungry?"

"What I want," said Abel, "is for you all to turn around and ride away. There's nothing for you here."

"Not even water, now?" the Mexican responded, almost teasing.

"Changed my mind," Abel informed him.

"That's not neighborly, you know?"

"You're not my neighbor," Abel answered, sighting down his rifle's barrel. "And there's nothing left to say. Get off my land, and stay off."

"Ho-kay, amigo. You say go, we go. Don't shoot me in the back like a *cobarde,* eh?"

Leta saw him begin to turn his grullo gelding to his right, her left, giving a small nod to the other Mexican. Then the first man was tumbling from his saddle, had a pistol drawn and fired it once before he landed crouching on the ground.

Abel squeezed off a shot and missed—or maybe stung the horse without a rider, since it bolted, kicking like a bronco. Jubal followed with the Stevens .22, his shot a high-pitched snap beside the louder Winchester's report. Leta could not have said what he was aiming at, but all three gunmen in the yard were still alive and moving, firing at the house.

"Get down!" Abel commanded, then he fired again. Another miss, while Jubal fumbled to reload his single-shot. Arlene was wailing, scared to death, and Leta clapped a hand over her mouth to keep her from distracting either of their men.

The house was built from stout logs, but the door and shutters weren't as thick. Bullets were punching through, buzzing like wasps whose sting could kill. One hit the stew-pot on the stove, a plunking sound, and supper splashed across the wall.

Keeping one hand over her daughter's mouth, the other white-knuckled around the smooth grip of her carving knife, Leta began to pray.

God, help us! Help us, please!

Burch Thornton fired a wild shot toward the house, then wheeled his mare off toward the farmer's barn, looking for cover. If he'd needed any further proof that Sabiano was a crazy man, the Mex had shown it to him when he drew against a rifleman concealed behind stout walls.

And now, what?

There were two guns firing at them from the house—one small, a .22 or .32 at most, the other with a solid kick behind it that would absolutely knock you down and keep you down. Thornton was wishing that they'd never seen the farm, but it was too late to go back and reconsider.

He had two choices now: pitch in and fight, or slip around the barn and ride like hell away from there while Sabiano and the rest were tied up fighting with the farmer's family. It stung him to consider running, being thought a coward by the other members of the gang, but what were they to him? Not friends, in any sense that mattered. More acquaintances—or say it plain, accomplices—who'd likely stab him in the back without a second thought if it procured some kind of personal advantage.

Thornton owed them nothing, and he didn't seriously think they would come looking for him if he rode away. What stopped him, safe within the shadow of the barn, was thinking of the lonely road ahead, no one to talk to or to back his play in case of trouble.

Damn it!

He dismounted, tied his reins off to a slat of the corral fence, shielded from the house, and made his way back to the southwest corner of the barn, where he could watch the action in the dooryard. Sabiano and Miguel had both found cover, de la Cruz beside the well and Fortunato peering from behind a privy on the far side of the house. Their horses, loosed, had circled somewhere out of sight.

Where were the others? Shouldn't they have been in place by now?

As if in answer to his thoughts, a storm of gunfire broke around the farmhouse, peppering its rear and flanking walls. Thornton could see a couple of the other riders now—or spot their gun smoke, anyway—and knew that it was over for the homesteaders. They might hold out a few more hours, until nightfall, but with darkness they were finished. De la Cruz would fire the house to rout them if he had to. Shoot the man and boy as they came out, and save whatever females he could find alive.

This was the way it should've gone at Faith Connover's spread, taking her hired men by surprise and wreaking havoc, grabbing the boss lady as a prize. There'd been surprise, all right, but how could Thornton know they'd ride up in the middle of a wedding ceremony, everybody on the place assembled, plus a passel of their friends from town?

They'd been outnumbered and outgunned, but still had caused some damage. He had personally seen those nosy bastards Hanes and Murdoch—who'd humiliated Thornton, prompting Faith to fire him—drop with bullets in them. That was worth the risk and effort, even if they somehow managed to survive.

But this place? It was nothing to him. He was simply excess baggage. Still, since he'd decided to remain, Thornton knew he must be seen to do his part.

Starting right now.

He suited thoughts to action, bolting from the cover of the barn and weaving as he ran across the dooryard, diving to land belly down at Sabiano's elbow. It felt crazy and exhilarating, sprawling in the line of fire, and better still when Sabiano turned to face him with a crooked smile.

"I thought you run away, amigo," said the Mexican.

"My horse was trying to," Thornton replied. "I talked him out of it."

"Maybe you make a decent outlaw, after all. *Un proscrito fuerte*, eh?"

"I'll think about that later," Thornton said. "Right now, you have a plan to get inside that house?"

"I always got a plan, amigo," Sabiano answered. "What you say we smoke 'em out, or roast 'em if they choose?"

"Suits me," said Thornton. "Must be something in the barn that we can use to start a fire. Maybe a lantern."

"Go and see," the Mexican commanded. "And be careful one of them don't kill you, eh? *Vaya usted!*"

4

On day six, Slade got up and went to visit Faith again. This time, he managed it without the nurse, although she scolded him, then scurried off somewhere, presumably to tell the doctor Slade was acting up.

Faith hadn't moved. She lay as pale and still as something chiseled by a sculptor. She was breathing, but beyond that Slade could not detect a sign of life. It made him wonder what would happen if he pinched her. Would she flinch? Was there some trick to waking people out of comas that Doc Abernathy was afraid to try? Or something new he hadn't learned in school?

Slade didn't know a great deal about medicine. If called upon to name the vital organs, sketch the major bones and arteries, he would have done all right. Those things were handy for a lawman, either in a fight or patching up a wound until a sawbones could be found. The rest of it was all beyond him, and he had to take what medics said on trust— up to a point.

How did a doctor know if people lost in comas dreamed or not? If they could make out spoken words? Were they insensible to pain or simply paralyzed? Could Faith be screaming in her mind for help, right now, while he stood at her bedside doing nothing?

Slade had heard stories of people who seemed to be dead but were really alive. Some were buried prematurely, a horror that Slade could scarcely imagine. Old George Washington himself had feared that prospect so much that he had made his servants vow to hold his body twelve days after doctors had pronounced him dead, in case he proved them wrong.

What if Doc Abernathy might make the same mistake with Faith?

With that image in mind, Slade had to touch her cheek again. Still warm. The blanket draped across her breasts still rose and fell with shallow respiration.

No one would be calling for the undertaker yet.

From Faith's room, Slade went back to find the nurse. Walking caused him a bit less pain today, as he supposed it would each day thereafter, dwindling until simple actions felt normal again. As things stood, though, he couldn't wait another week or two before he got up and around.

Each wasted hour gave Burch Thornton and his killer cronies a longer head start. More time to run or find a hiding place. It had been six days since the raid, and Slade knew a decent rider could've reached the Rio Grande by now, if he held his horse to a trot for ten hours each day. At a gallop, riding only five hours a day, Thornton might have been in Mexico four days after the shooting at Faith's ranch.

Long gone.

Or maybe the killers had split up and scattered. Why not?

No one knew yet who most of them were, and sticking together would make them stand out in a witness's mind. Riding apart, in different directions—even if they went by twos and threes—they'd break the pattern of a large gang on the run.

Slade realized it could take months or years to find them

all. Judge Dennison had deputies already on the hunt, but they'd be constantly distracted by the normal course of crime throughout the territory. None could spare a month— much less a year or more—to hunt a single group of outlaws. Only Slade could claim that kind of dedication.

And it might mean turning in his badge.

So be it. He would do what must be done, and short of throwing out the U.S. Constitution, there was no way Dennison could stop him until Slade had actually crossed the line by committing a crime.

Even then, the law would have to catch him first.

Slade recognized the incongruity of his peculiar situation. He'd originally met the judge—and Faith—while seeking vengeance for his brother's death. Now, Faith was comatose and maybe dying, while Slade contemplated turning outlaw to avenge her.

And what then?

If he could pull it off *and* Faith recovered with her faculties intact, they'd never spend another day together. Slade would be running or locked up in jail, maybe waiting to hang. He didn't relish the idea of a tearful parting on his way to mount the gallows, but he wouldn't risk letting the men who'd shot Faith get away scot-free.

He'd take it one step at a time, beginning with a change from borrowed duds to clothing of his own. Which, since his keepers wouldn't bring them to the hospital, meant going to his room at the hotel.

For stepping out, Slade turned his johnny gown around to wear it as a shirt of sorts, and tucked its dangling tail into a stranger's baggy pants. He'd nearly reached the exit when he met the nurse with ginger hair. "What do you think you're doing, Mr. Slade?" she asked.

"I'm going out to get some air," he said.

She looked alarmed but managed to compose herself, saying, "I'm sorry. That's not possible."

"I beg to differ," Slade replied.

Her face was set in opposition. "I cannot allow—"

He interrupted her to say, "Nobody asked you, ma'am."

"I beg your pardon!"

"No begging required," said Slade. "I do my best to be a gentleman, where ladies are concerned, but you'd be wise to get out of my way."

Slade's hotel and the hospital were two long blocks apart. He took his time, getting the feel of freedom, even pleased to smell the dust and horse manure from Main Street, loving the sunlight on his face where awnings didn't shade the wooden sidewalk. Folks who knew him seemed surprised to see him out in public, gawking at his curious attire and greeting him as they might welcome someone who'd returned home after years away.

Slade felt self-conscious in his strange getup, worried that someone might accost him and demand his trousers back. He didn't have a clue where they had come from, why the nursing staff had access to them, and it nearly made him cringe to think of it, hoping a corpse had never worn the pants. The sooner he was out of them and into clothes he recognized, the better.

Turning into his hotel, Slade startled the receptionist, a young man with his hair slicked down and parted in the middle, eyes gone wide behind his steel-rimmed spectacles. The man edged back a step as Slade approached his desk, then caught himself.

He said, "Good morning, Marshal. No one told us you'd be coming by today."

Us being *him*, presumably, since there was no one else in sight.

"You're not the only one surprised," Slade said. "I'll need my key."

"Of course." The young man—Clifford Something, Slade had never learned his surname—fetched the key and handed it to Slade. It was a blessing that he didn't offer help getting upstairs.

Speaking of stairs, they proved to be a challenge. Slade went slowly, took the best part of two minutes getting to the second floor, and spent another minute on the landing there, to catch his breath. The short climb hadn't winded him, exactly, but he'd broken sweat and there was no denying that his ribs hurt.

Never mind.

Slade reached his room, opened the door, and was relieved to find most of his things where he had left them. Better yet, someone had brought his hat, gunbelt, and boots back to the room and left them on his bed while he was in the hospital. He made a mental note to ask around and thank whoever did it, then got down to business.

Undressing pained him, most particularly taking off the johnny gown, which taxed his wounded ribs and shoulder most. The pants were easier. He simply had to drop them, kick out of the moccasins, and survey his reflection in a mirror mounted on the wall. His wounds looked raw, inflamed. It hurt him more, somehow, to see them, so he turned away to dress himself.

Slade assumed the long johns he had worn under his wedding suit were shot to hell and stained with blood, but he still had another pair. He left the top alone to spare his shoulder, slipping on the bottom half before he found a pair of pants that fit and pulled them on. A long-sleeved shirt resisted him at first, but Slade persisted, cursing through clenched teeth, until he had it buttoned up and tucked into his pants.

Stockings and boots were relatively easy, after that, letting his right arm do most of the work. When he was dressed, Slade gave the mirror one more chance and satisfied himself he was presentable. He buckled up his gunbelt, with its heavy Peacemaker. Put on his hat, but left his vest and badge behind.

Next stop, the livery, to see his horse. That meant traversing six blocks, from his hotel to the stable, but he thought the walk would do him good. Or maybe kill him, if he wasn't strong enough to make it after all.

Ben Murphy caught up to him, halfway there. He said, "They told me that a crazy man was loose in town. I see it's true."

"Just going for a stroll," said Slade.

"The way I hear it, you escaped from custody," Murphy replied.

"Funny," Slade said. "I didn't know that I was charged with anything."

"You've got the old man troubled, Jack."

"No need for him to be. I have to stretch my legs sometime."

Murphy glanced toward Slade's hip and asked, "You plan to exercise your trigger finger, while you're at it?"

"Not today," Slade said. "But pretty soon."

"Judge wants you back," said Murphy. "Hell, we all do. But he's worried that you might be getting ready for a hunting trip."

"It's what we do," said Slade.

"I know, and I've been tryin' to imagine how you feel right now. Thing is, if you go vigilante, I could wind up hunting *you*. I'd hate for that to happen, Jack."

"Same here."

"So, if you can't stay out of it, at least think twice. Okay?"

"I'll go one better," Slade replied, "and think three times. How's that?"

"All I could ask," said Murphy, trying to appear relieved. "Where are you headed, anyway?"

"Down to the livery. Make sure my animal's been taken care of."

"You mind some company?"

Slade would've rather been alone but couldn't speak the words to Murphy's face.

"Sounds good," he lied and forced a smile.

On day seven, Slade retraced his path from the hotel to the livery stable. His roan mare had seemed pleased to see him the day before, and it was mutual. The hostler had been taking special care of her and took a tip from Slade, reluctantly, but kept it, all the same.

Slade had meant to spend time with the horse, but Murphy's presence made him feel self-conscious, awkward. Even as he cursed himself for giving in to the sensation, Slade had folded, told the horse he would return tomorrow for some exercise.

"You up to that?" Murphy had asked him as they left the livery.

"I have to start sometime," Slade had replied.

He'd tried to be polite when Murphy trailed him to Anderson's, a restaurant Slade liked to patronize, but wasn't sure he'd managed it too well. He wound up telling Ben that he was strong enough to cut a steak himself, and Murphy left him to it. Later, wondering if he had wounded Murphy's feelings, Slade decided that he didn't really care.

He'd passed a restless night at the hotel, sleeping by fits and starts. Besides the tenderness of slowly healing wounds, Slade was disturbed by dreams and an oppressive sense that he was wasting precious time. The men who'd gunned him down—who might have murdered Faith, in fact—were moving farther from his grasp with every passing day. The more time that he wasted getting well, whatever *that* meant in his present state, the more likely it was that he would never find them all.

And Slade wasn't convinced that he could live with that.

So day eight was a test, not only of his physical ability but of his will. It started when he took his long guns from the hotel room, with ammunition in a saddlebag. Slade draped the saddlebag over his injured shoulder, pushing it, and held a gun in each hand as he walked along Main Street.

Both shoulder guns were Winchesters. The rifle was a lever-action model 1873, chambered for the same .44-40 cartridge Slade used in his Colt Peacemaker revolver. The other, also lever action, was a model 1887 shotgun twelve-gauge, that he'd taken from one of the Ku Klux Klan assassins who had tried to kill Judge Dennison last year. That shooter didn't need the weapon anymore, but Slade had put it to good use.

Saddling the mare was Slade's first major test. Eddie, the hostler, offered to take care of it, but Slade was adamant. There'd be no one to help him on the trail, and it was damned sure that he couldn't leave his horse saddled night and day, for personal convenience. So he did it all himself, nearly dropping the saddle on his first attempt as pain spiked through his wounded side and shoulder. Worried that he'd torn his stitches by the time he got it right, Slade felt around inside his shirt and was relieved to find no leaking blood.

The next test: mounting up. Slade never had been sure why riders always mounted from the left side of a horse— something about the swords they wore in ancient times, he'd heard—but there was no good way to do it with a pair of holes drilled through his body. Sticking with tradition, using both hands on the saddle's horn, he managed on the first try, but it cost him. By the time he settled in the seat and got his right boot in its stirrup, Slade was sweating like a man who'd run five miles.

"Your turn," he told the mare. "I'm tuckered out."

He rode south out of town, the opposite direction from Faith's ranch, nodding and greeting folks who waved or called to him along the way. As on his walk, the day before, there weren't a lot who publicly acknowledged Slade. Most residents of Enid likely recognized him—when he wore the badge, at least—and all would be at least vaguely aware of what had happened on his wedding day, but in a growing town of thousands, there were definite priorities in choice of friends.

And Slade was never one to court a crowd.

It felt good, riding on his own, after so much time spent in bed with people fussing over him and telling him the things he couldn't do. He let the mare run for a while, rising a little in the stirrups to reduce the jolting of his injured side, but thought the fading pain a decent trade for fresh wind in his face.

Five miles outside of town, Slade found a swale with trees along its rim and water trickling through it in a clear stream, over rocks. He left the mare in shade, to graze and drink its fill, and took his guns a hundred feet along to where the bank was highest. He had brought no targets with him, but gnarled roots protruding from the soil served just as well.

Slade started with the shotgun since it had the stronger kick and took less skill to aim. Five rounds in relatively rapid fire, pumping the lever-action with his right hand as the twelve-gauge boomed and bucked against his shoulder. Slade was firing birdshot, cheaper than the buckshot rounds he used when hunting men, but with the same demands on flesh and bone in terms of managing the gun.

It left Slade with a vague sense of vibration as he shifted to the rifle, taking his time now to aim as he emptied the tubular magazine, squeezing off fifteen rounds in succession. He rated his aim above average but knew it could still use some practice. His right arm did most of the work, but his left still supported the piece, and he caught himself starting to flinch from the promise of pain as he fired.

The Colt came last, simply to satisfy Slade that he'd given all his weapons equal time. His draw was smooth, a bit slower than normal as he favored his left side, but it would come around. When he had put six rounds within a decent ring on his imaginary target, he began reloading each weapon in turn, preparing for the ride back into town.

Tomorrow, Slade decided, he would go to see the judge and talk about returning to full duty. Failing that, he would consider striking off alone, minus the badge or any other semblance of authority, to do what must be done.

Day nine since the wedding massacre. Slade rose at half past five and was the first in line at Anderson's for breakfast when they opened, thirty minutes later. When he'd fortified himself with food and coffee, he walked down to visit Faith and found no change, except fresh linen on her bed.

Slade missed her smile, her touch, and silently reviled himself for focusing on his emotions when Faith's life was hanging in the balance. His depression seemed a miserable self-indulgence. Angry with himself and unsure what to do about it, Slade departed from the hospital and moved along Main Street past shops just opening their doors for business, to reach the courthouse.

Judge Dennison was in, of course, always in chambers and reviewing cases well before the first was scheduled to convene before his bench. Dennison's clerk—a young replacement for the one who had been killed in the attack that left the judge wounded and close to death—initially had tried to get the jump on his employer, timewise, but had finally surrendered when the judge kept turning up ahead of him, regardless of the hour. Nowadays, the clerk showed up promptly at eight o'clock, with trials beginning at ten.

It was seven thirty when Slade climbed the courthouse stairs to reach the judge's chambers, footsteps echoing in the deserted corridor. Reaching the door, he knocked and heard Judge Dennison say, "Enter."

Slade went in, closed the door behind him, and took his hat off as he crossed the room to stand before the judge's massive desk. He noted no surprise in Dennison's expression, as he raised the hand that held a pen and gestured toward a nearby chair.

Slade sat and was about to speak, when Dennison remarked, "I heard that you were back among the living."

"More or less," Slade said.

"It's opportune, considering the news I got this morning," Dennison continued.

"News?"

"It may—and I stress *may*—concern the men responsible for your condition and Miss Connover's," said Dennison. "That's unconfirmed, but there's enough to prompt suspicion that they haven't run as fast or far as I expected."

Nodding woodenly, Slade said, "I'm listening."

"Two things," said Dennison. "First, I'm informed there's been a murder on the reservation. White men shot a Cherokee who'd gone out hunting, and they stole his horse."

"How many white men?" Slade inquired.

"The agent, Berringer, was vague," said Dennison. "A gang, he says, but since he didn't witness the event, it's his interpretation of a statement he received."

"There was a witness, then?" asked Slade.

"Apparently, another hunter heard the shots and found the wounded man in time to speak with him, before he died. He did not see the gunmen personally, but reported back to Berringer that there were 'many' horses. Berringer interprets that as meaning nine or ten."

"It fits," Slade said.

"If accurate. Then, we have something else," said Dennison.

"All right."

"The Cherokee was killed two days ago," Dennison said. "Frank Berringer allowed himself to be distracted, so the word only arrived this morning. By which time, there'd been another . . . incident."

Silent, Slade waited for the judge to spell it out.

"A family was slaughtered," Dennison continued. "Crawford, I'm informed the name was. Twenty miles or so beyond the reservation, to the southwest."

"Heading off toward Texas," Slade suggested.

"Headed somewhere," Dennison agreed. "I won't predict the actions of such animals."

"They're people," Slade corrected him. "No animal would act this way."

"You're right, of course," the judge agreed. "Which means they can't simply be shot on sight, like rabid dogs. You take my meaning, Jack?"

"I hear you," Slade replied.

"And you agree?"

Hope quickened in him, then. "Does that mean that I get the job?" he asked.

"I seem to be short-handed at the moment," Dennison replied.

"Then, I'm your man," Slade said.

"You haven't answered me," the judge reminded him.

Slade frowned, nodded. Surprised himself by saying, "Truth is, I'd prefer to see them tried and hanged. It's slower. But a bunch like this, certain to swing for what they've done, you know they won't come easy."

"I anticipate some difficulty there," said Dennison. "But, Jack, you must be circumspect. Observe procedure and obey the law from first to last."

"Okay."

"And I'll require a witness to confirm all necessary acts of self-defense."

"No problem, Judge," said Slade. "I'll need to have a tracker with me, anyhow."

"You have someone in mind?" asked Dennison.

Slade smiled and said, "I might, at that."

5

On day nine, Slade stopped in to visit Faith once more and found her still the same. It was more difficult to leave her this time, since he wasn't sure how long he'd be away from town or whether she would be alive when he returned.

If he returned.

There was no point in dressing up their present situation, turning it into some kind of happy-ending fairy tale. Faith's doctor couldn't offer any honest words of hope for her revival, and the hunt that Slade was undertaking for the men responsible involved substantial risks that he'd have seen the last of Faith and Enid once he rode away from town.

And it was time for him to start that ride.

He'd left most of his gear in the small lobby of the hospital, behind the desk where a young woman greeted new arrivals. She'd seemed anxious about sitting next to guns but offered no complaint after she recognized Slade's badge. Leaving, he got a little smile from her but couldn't tell if she was sad or just being polite.

What did it matter, either way.

Slade's roan didn't appear to mind the added weight of the saddlebags he'd stuffed with spare clothes, ammunition, corn dodgers, and jerky, plus a little coffeepot he carried when he traveled. Add a full canteen, a coil of rope, and Slade was ready for the trail. Whatever lay in front of him, he'd meet it head-on, with his eyes wide open and a grim determination not to fail.

Which didn't count for much against a well-aimed bullet, truth be told.

The last time Slade had visited the Cherokee reservation, he'd been looking into claims that renegade tribesmen had raided white homesteads and murdered the settlers. An overly aggressive army officer had been prepared to launch reprisal raids, and maybe start a war he couldn't finish, when Slade proved beyond any doubt that the killers were white— and had been at their trade for some twenty-odd years, forgotten since fleeing an inn they had once run in Kansas. Travelers there who stopped for supper or a night's sleep with the Bender family rarely saw the next sunrise, but once their bloody business was exposed, the killers had eluded posses and escaped to take their murder racket on the road.

When Slade thought back to that investigation, he admitted it was mostly luck that he'd unmasked the Benders. And they would've had him, even so, if not for the assistance of a Cherokee who'd been regarded as a suspect in the killings.

Little Wolf.

He'd been there when Slade needed him, had literally saved Slade's skin, and they'd joined forces to avert a racial slaughter in the making back at home. It had been touch and go, some people on both sides anxious to see blood spilled, but they had pulled it off together. Now, Slade was returning to investigate another crime, hoping he might obtain assistance from a tribe that owed him nothing and had no reason to wish him well.

Slade hadn't met the latest agent assigned to the Cherokee

rez by the Bureau of Indian Affairs in Washington. His predecessor in that post had been a pompous ass, convinced that Indians were simpleminded people with a touch of lunacy that sent them off on random sprees of rape and murder if they weren't kept firmly underneath a white man's thumb. His attitude, in Slade's experience, was condescending at the best of times, and often hostile to the people in his charge. After the Bender slayings and the narrowly averted war, he'd been recalled—and likely elevated to a higher post, the way things worked in government.

Today, Slade didn't care if he was dealing with a rabid missionary or a lazy diplomat just marking time until retirement. Either way, he had a job to do, connecting murder on the reservation to the men he sought and getting help to track them down.

Slade was a seasoned man hunter by now, but there were tricks to every trade, and tracking men or horses by the little signs that most white eyes could never catch required assistance. Slade was not too proud to ask for help, and he'd been authorized to pay his chosen guide a dollar per day from the federal purse.

But first, he had to find a guide who suited him.

Slade didn't know if his first choice would be available or willing to accommodate him. He had made no effort to keep track of Little Wolf, had no idea if the Cherokee brave had settled down to raise a family or left the reservation altogether. He would remember Slade, if he was still around, but as for joining in another expedition, that was anybody's guess.

Slade wasn't sure exactly when he crossed the line dividing open range from reservation property, but two riders found him soon afterward. They came toward him slowly, Winchesters in hand, while Slade unhooked the hammerthong on his holster. Closer in, he saw the tin stars on their shirts that marked them as Cherokee tribal police. They saw

Slade's badge, as well, and stopped some thirty feet away, holding their rifles with the muzzles pointed skyward, silently observing him.

Slade broke the ice, saying, "I need a word with Agent Berringer, about the killing that you had out here."

Still without speaking, his two escorts turned and led him westward, toward the small town he remembered as the reservation's centerpiece.

"Frank Berringer," the agent said, giving Slade's hand a solid double pump before he let it go.

"Jack Slade. I'm here about the killing you reported to Judge Dennison."

Slade saw no point in mentioning the two-day lapse between the murder and the agent sending his report to Enid. There was nothing to be done about it now, no point in making Berringer his enemy before they even had a chance to talk.

"It came as something of a shock," said Berringer. "I was forewarned about a certain level of hostility between the homesteaders and tribesmen on the reservation, but I'd hoped we would be left alone by hooligans."

Slade nodded. "Your runner said there was a gang involved?"

"So I was told," said Berringer. "You understand, the shooting wasn't witnessed as it happened. Two young men, Sparrow and Strong Horse, went out hunting deer. They separated, to improve their chances, but stayed close enough to hear gunfire and come to one another's aid. As Sparrow tells the story, he heard pistol shots and knew there must be trouble, since the only handguns on the reservation are carried by tribal police."

"And he found . . . Strong Horse, was it?" asked Slade.

Berringer nodded. "He was dying when Sparrow reached

him, shot five times. His horse and rifle had been taken. Sparrow brought him in, then took our officers out to the spot. They counted tracks from nine, perhaps ten, horses and pursued the killers, but you understand they have no jurisdiction off the reservation."

"And the settlers hereabouts might take it badly, seeing Indians chase white men," Slade suggested.

"I suspect that's right," said Berringer.

"I don't suppose you have a coroner out here," said Slade.

"Nothing like that," the agent said.

"So, you confirmed five shots but have no way of telling whether different guns were used?"

"We aren't equipped for autopsies," said Berringer, "nor would the Cherokees permit it. They're particular about their funerary rituals, as you may know."

"I haven't made a study of it," Slade replied.

"A week of solemn mourning is required," said Berringer, "with fasting for the most part. If a person dies at home, the tribal priest destroys whatever personal belongings are presumed to be contaminated by the death. That wasn't necessary here because the killing happened at a distance from the victim's home. Still, there is an immersion ritual for family survivors, at the nearest river, said to help a loved one's spirit make its transit to the afterlife."

"I'm more concerned about the living," Slade replied.

"Of course. I understand," said Berringer. "If you intend to question Sparrow, I should warn you that he doesn't speak much English."

Slade considered that and asked the agent, "Is it likely that he'll add to what you've told me?"

"I doubt it," Berringer replied. "He didn't see the killers, after all."

"No point in bothering him, then," Slade said. "I'll need to see the place where Strong Horse died, and go from there."

"You plan to track the men yourself, from here?" asked Berringer.

"Fact is, they've struck again," Slade said. "Or someone has. A homestead, twenty miles or so beyond the rez, southwest."

"More murders?"

"What I need to do," Slade told him, "is to catch their trail from where it's freshest. See if I can follow up and overtake them."

"Yes, I see," said Berringer. "You're doing this alone?"

"That brings me to the other thing," Slade said. "I'm hoping you can spare one of your men to help me with the tracking part of it."

Berringer frowned at that. "As I mentioned, Marshal Slade, tribal police have no authority beyond the reservation's borders."

Slade reached up to tap his badge and said, "Don't worry. I've got all the law we'll need, right here. Besides, I wasn't thinking of your officers."

"Excuse me?" Now the BIA man looked confused. "I'm sorry. I don't understand."

"You've got a man here—had one, anyway, I hope he's still around—who helped me with another case I had, before your time. We got along all right, and I was hoping I might ask him if he'd ride along and see this through."

"This man wasn't a tribal officer?" asked Berringer.

"Not when I knew him," Slade replied. "He would've made a good one, though. I'm sitting here today because of him."

"Meaning?"

"I was an inch away from being gutted when he helped me out."

"I see. And you'd assume responsibility for his behavior, off the reservation?" Berringer inquired.

"My pleasure," Slade assured him.

"Well, it's irregular, I must say. But considering the circumstances, I'm agreeable. His name was . . . ?"

"Little Wolf," Slade said.

And watched the agent's face go slack. "Oh, *him*," said Berringer. "I have to disagree with you, concerning his potential as an officer."

"Why's that?" asked Slade.

"Because," the agent said, "your Little Wolf is sitting in our jail right now."

The reservation's jail was actually a stockade made out of logs, about thirty feet on a side, surrounding a small hut or cabin. One of Berringer's tribal policemen opened the gate and stood back while they entered together. Catching a look as he crossed the pen's threshold, Slade wondered what would happen if the Cherokee chose to lock up the white men for fun.

Instead, the same two officers who had escorted Slade to meet their agent stood beside the stockade's open gate and waited, rifles tucked beneath their arms, while Berringer and Slade approached the hut within. Up close, its size and structure put Slade in mind of a smokehouse or tool shed more than a cabin. There'd be room to stand and pace a bit inside but nothing more. The three sides Slade could see from where he stood were windowless.

During their walk to the stockade, the BIA man had explained why Little Wolf was caged. There'd been an argument over a certain female member of the tribe—encouraged by the lady, Berringer suggested—and the quarrel had turned to violence. It didn't seem that Little Wolf was the aggressor, but he'd been the last man standing, and the BIA's regulations called for punishment of any intertribal homicide, including self-defense. Frank Berringer, presiding over what passed for Little Wolf's trial, had sentenced him to sixty days.

"He still has three weeks left to serve," said Berringer before his knuckles drummed a tattoo on the jailhouse door.

Slade frowned, belatedly examining the door for locks and saw that there were none. The door opened slowly, fading daylight entering the hut to grant a first look at the Cherokee who'd saved his life.

"Marshal," said Little Wolf. His voice was soft and had the dusty sound of one that hasn't exercised for weeks on end. His face and tone were neither welcoming nor hostile.

"Little Wolf, you have a visitor," said Berringer, stating the obvious. "Under the circumstances, I'll remind you that he must be treated with respect."

"We never had a problem there," Slade interjected, then asked Little Wolf, "You want to talk in there or step outside?"

Instead of answering, the prisoner emerged. The eighteen months that had elapsed since their last meeting hadn't left a mark on Little Wolf, in terms of aging, but he had some fading bruises on his face. Slade didn't have to wonder where they'd come from, and he had no urge to see the other guy. Before he had a chance to speak, Frank Berringer pressed on.

"Are you aware of what has happened while you've been confined?" the agent asked.

"I know that Strong Horse has been killed," said Little Wolf. "By white men."

"That's correct," said Berringer. "They've also murdered settlers and perhaps committed other crimes. Now Marshal Slade, whom I believe you know, is looking for the men responsible."

Straight-faced, the Cherokee replied, "They are not here with me."

"No, Little Wolf, we didn't think . . ." The agent caught himself, cheeks coloring, and said, "The marshal has a proposition for you to consider. Marshal Slade?"

"I need a tracker who can help me find these men before they do more damage," Slade explained. "When I heard about the murder on the reservation, here, I thought of you."

"You should not wait three weeks," said Little Wolf.

"I don't intend to," Slade replied. "I'm authorized to take you with me now, today, if you're agreeable."

"And be responsible for his return, of course," said Berringer. Clearly a man who liked to dot his i's and cross his t's.

Slade cocked an eyebrow at the agent. "With an understanding that the time left on his sentence is suspended, for his service to the court and people of the territory."

Berringer delayed replying for a long ten seconds, then he gave a jerky little nod and said, "Agreed, if he serves honorably. But if he attempts to flee—"

"It's not a jailbreak, Mr. Berringer," Slade said. "If Little Wolf agrees to help, he's taking on a dirty job that stands a chance of killing us."

"Of course," said Berringer. "I didn't mean—"

"All settled then," Slade interrupted him, then turned to Little Wolf. "If you agree, that is."

"We lose the light too soon today," said Little Wolf. "Come back for me tomorrow, at sunrise."

"No reason you should stay locked up tonight," Slade said and turned to Berringer. "Is there?"

"No, I suppose not," Berringer agreed. The small concession seemed to pain him, which was fine with Slade.

He hadn't thought about the time but saw the sense in waiting to begin their hunt tomorrow. As it was, they'd barely reach the spot where Strong Horse had been killed before the sun went down and left them camped out on the rez. Better to sleep indoors tonight, if possible, and get a fresh start in the morning.

He wasn't worried about making a mistake with Little Wolf. The Cherokee had earned his trust, and Slade hoped that the feeling might be mutual, though he supposed that no one from the tribe had any real reason to trust a white man.

Still, he'd thought there was a bond of sorts between them last time, when they shared their brush with death. Whether it carried over to the present was a question to be answered on the road.

Leaving the stockade, Berringer said, "I hope you'll dine with me this evening, Marshal."

Slade shot Little Wolf a sidelong glance and caught his shrug. "Sounds good," Slade told the agent. "We'd be glad to."

Having trapped himself, the agent made a little huffing noise, then answered, "Excellent. The more, the merrier."

As Slade recalled from his last visit, Berringer's rambling combination home and office—formerly his predecessor's—was at least double the size of any other dwelling on the reservation. Whether that antagonized the Cherokees was anybody's guess. Slade didn't plan on asking, and the BIA man seemed oblivious to any possible offense.

Inside the house, a pair of servants waited. They were Cherokees, of course, a man and woman, dressed in outfits that reminded Slade of something that a butler and housemaid might wear in a mansion back east. Slade didn't know if the getups were Berringer's notion or something left over from the old regime, and he wasn't about to ask.

Last time around, Slade hadn't been inside the reservation agent's home, much less invited to a meal, so it was new to him. The dining room was spacious, with a table long enough to seat a dozen people, but from Little Wolf's approach to it, Slade understood that Cherokees weren't often entertained within its walls. More likely guests included officers from Fort Supply or visitors from Washington, on rare occasions when they made it that far west.

After consulting with his butler, Berringer informed them, "Supper will be ready in a half hour or so. Marshal, would you care for a whiskey while we wait?"

Noting that Little Wolf was not included in the offer, Slade replied, "No, thanks. I'm steering clear of it until the doctor says I'm ready for it."

"Doctor? You've been ill?" asked Berringer.

"Lead poisoning, you might say. I was shot a couple times, last week."

"Last week?" Berringer fairly gaped at Slade. "But here you are, ready for man hunting."

"Some things can't wait," Slade said.

"If you don't mind my asking, was your injury related to the present matter?" Berringer inquired.

"I hope so," Slade replied. "But I won't know for sure until we find the men responsible."

Berringer poured himself what looked to be a double shot of whiskey as he mused, "Last week . . . last week . . . You're not referring to the raid I heard about? A ranch outside of Enid, if I have it right?"

"The very same," said Slade.

"Oh, my. I understand someone was killed?"

"Four men," Slade said. "Well, two that mattered."

"And a woman, I believe," said Berringer.

"She's still alive," Slade said. "So far, at least."

"A tragedy, by all accounts. And you suspect the same men killed our hunter? And the settlers, afterward?"

"I wouldn't put it past them," Slade replied. "But as I say, there's nothing certain yet. We're not exactly short of bad men in the panhandle."

Berringer flicked a glance at Little Wolf, who was examining a portrait on the wall, and said, "That's sadly true. I wish you luck, in any case."

"We'll need it, I suppose," said Slade.

"But nine or ten of them," said Berringer, sipping his drink. "Do you suppose it's wise to tackle them alone?"

"With two of us, we cut the odds in half," Slade said. "Besides, the judge's other deputies were out ahead of me, already searching high and low."

"You have an edge now, I suppose," the agent said. "Assuming that the latest murders were committed by the same gang."

"That's my thinking," Slade agreed. "But if I have an edge, it's Little Wolf."

"For tracking them," said Berringer.

"And fighting, if it comes to that," Slade said. "Of course, they may repent and voluntarily surrender."

"But you doubt it."

"Isn't something that I'd count on," Slade agreed.

Berringer sipped again and frowned. "You think that it's a good idea? Encouraging a Cherokee to hunt white men?"

"White outlaws," Slade reminded him. "And at the federal court's request. I'd say it was a public service."

"Well, of course. But what if . . . I mean, if there's killing to be done . . ."

"I'd have to quote the Bible," Slade replied. "Better to give than to receive."

"I understand," said Berringer. "But it's disturbing, as a racial precedent."

"Too late," Slade said. "You weren't around, the last time that I worked with Little Wolf. I guess the fellow you replaced forgot to mention how he helped me stop a family of murderers from killing homesteaders and headed off a war at the same time."

"I don't recall that story, no," said Berringer.

"You want to hear it, I can tell you over supper," Slade said. "But it might ruin your appetite."

"Perhaps another time," the agent said, looking a trifle pale.

"Suits me," Slade said. "Let's say he has my confidence, and let it go at that."

Berringer's butler chose that moment to appear, jingling a little silver bell as he announced, "Supper is served!"

6

Sleep had become Slade's enemy since Faith was shot, harassing him with cold-sweat nightmares that evaporated when he jerked awake, leaving him haunted by a sense of loss. He spent the restless night in one of Berringer's guest rooms, after confirming that there was a decent place for Little Wolf to sleep without returning to the camp's stockade, but Slade was up and ready to be gone before the household woke, with gray dawn barely breaking in the east.

And he found Little Wolf already waiting for him, with a tobiano mare patterned in black and white. The Cherokee disdained a saddle, satisfied to use a woven blanket in its place, and likewise had no saddlebags. A belt around his waist was balanced by a long sheathed knife on one side and a plump leather pouch on the other. A larger bag was slung across his shoulder, resting on his left hip, and he kept a rifle in his hands.

It looked to be the same Sharps carbine that had saved Slade's life when Kate Bender was bent on carving him like Sunday's roast, but since the guns were mass-produced over a period of thirty years, he couldn't rightly say. It was a single-shot weapon, but in an expert's hands could still fire eight to ten rounds per minute, and one hit with a .52-caliber slug was normally all it took to settle an argument.

"You want to have some breakfast first?" asked Slade.

"Had it while you were sleeping," Little Wolf replied, patting his stomach.

"Figure you came out ahead, then," Slade said, as he hauled himself into his saddle, face averted to conceal a grimace from the latent pain.

"Your wounds still pain you," Little Wolf observed.

"Healing," said Slade. "The men we're looking for—the ones I *think* we're after—thought they finished me a while ago."

"So, this is personal."

"In part," Slade said. "But I intend to bring them back alive and see them hang if they'll allow it."

"A divided mind is dangerous," said Little Wolf.

"I'm focused," Slade assured him. "If I have to do some killing, though, I'll need your word in court that it was justified."

It was the first time Slade had seen the warrior smile. Instead of answering directly, Little Wolf said, "I was told where Strong Horse died. We go now and should have full light when we arrive."

The other Cherokees were up and getting ready for another day as Slade and Little Wolf rode past their humble dwellings, off to the southwest. Slade wondered when Frank Berringer would make it to the breakfast table, waited on by servants while he ate and planned another day of overseeing captive people trapped on land that was as foreign to them as an island in the South Seas would've been to Slade.

Some people loved to lord it over others, couldn't bear a day in which they weren't directing people where to go and what to do. In Slade's experience, some of the worst were prison guards—whoever planned a life of supervising people locked in cages, anyway?—and certain gospel ministers were close behind the jailers. Toss in the majority of bureaucrats, and what you had was an establishment devoted to directing other peoples' lives.

I'm part of that, Slade thought and didn't like it much. One consolation was that his end of the deal involved restraining people—mostly men—who had already crossed the line by violating someone else's rights. He wasn't like a city cop who spent his days enforcing petty regulations that pertained to business, traffic on the street, and such. Without Slade, people died.

In fact, he thought, *they die, regardless.*

Little Wolf had been locked up when Strong Horse died, but he led Slade directly to the spot, based on directions he'd received. Slade wasn't sure what he'd expected, going on five days after the murder, but they found grass tinted rusty brown from dried blood, and the faint traces of tracks horses had left around the site. Examining the partial hoofprints, Little Wolf could tell which ones were shod and which were reservation horses, but he finally reported nothing that would lead them to identify a certain animal. Details were insufficient to say whether any of the shoes had borne peculiar markings, twisted nails, or something similar.

"They rode away southwest," he finally announced.

"And took the dead man's horse?" Slade asked.

A nod from Little Wolf. "Maybe to sell," he said, "or they want extra horses for a long ride coming up."

"We'd best be moving, then," Slade said.

"We won't catch them today," said Little Wolf, "unless they double back. How stupid are these white men?"

"I don't know yet, but they're careless," Slade replied.

"Because they let you live."

"Their first mistake," Slade said.

"Some of my people blame Sparrow," said Little Wolf,

as they rode on. "They think he should have followed these white men, instead of taking Strong Horse home."

"You feel that way?" asked Slade.

"I think that Sparrow would be dead," the Cherokee replied, "and more days would be lost seeking the killers' trail."

"Makes sense to me. Besides, your agent wouldn't like it if he'd tracked them off the rez."

A snort from Little Wolf, at that. He said, "Frank Berringer tries to forgive us."

"Oh? For what?"

"For being savages," said Little Wolf. "I think we cause him pain."

"Maybe he needs to find another line of work," said Slade.

"It is not work for him," said Little Wolf. "It is a mission."

"Well, we've got a mission of our own right now," Slade said. "And Berringer's no part of it."

Burch Thornton watched a wheel of vultures circling overhead a quarter mile off to the south and told himself it didn't mean a thing. He'd never put an ounce of faith in portents, and he saw no reason to start now.

Wade Hampton, riding next to Thornton, saw the scavengers and spat a stream of brown tobacco juice. "Found somethin' dead," he offered. "Wanna go and see?"

"No, thanks," said Thornton, turning from the birds to watch the other riders, straggling out before him.

He and Wade were bringing up the rear, no special reason, though in Thornton's case he didn't feel like being chummy with the rest of Sabiano's crew right now. A couple of them had been looking sideways at him since they'd left the pillaged homestead, and he didn't want to give them any further cause for agitation.

"Ain't your fault, you know," said Hampton.

"What's that?" Thornton asked.

"The little girl," Wade clarified.

"I didn't say a word," Thornton replied.

"No, but your puking said a lot."

Thornton felt color rising in his cheeks. Lowered his voice to say, "Jesus! Who does that?"

"Some a these boys," Hampton answered, "as you noticed. Me, I've got no taste for it, but that don't mean I gotta lose my breakfast, neither."

"With the woman, that was one thing," Thornton said.

"O' course. You did your part an' all. Nobody's faultin' you on that."

"But with a kid like that . . ."

"Don't waste your time tryin' to figure out why people do the shit they do," Hampton advised. "You think too much, it might start feelin' like you need to do somethin' about it, yeah? Where are you, then?"

"Nowhere," said Thornton.

"That's *exactly* fuckin' right. Because these boys"—he nodded toward the riders ranged in front of them—"don't hold with bein' judged. They take it hard, you understand?"

"I hear you," Thornton answered.

"Hell, a man gets used to anything, you give him time enough," said Hampton. "Sabiano, now, I'd say he's seen and done it all."

"I get that feeling," Thornton said.

"Which is exactly why you picked him, right?" Wade asked.

"What do you mean?"

"To settle scores, back there at Enid. Made that bitch who fired you sorry, didn't he?"

"I guess."

In fact, most of the raid on Faith Connover's ranch had been a blur to Thornton. Thinking back to it, he had a hard time sorting out the images that filled his mind. Gunsmoke and people running, shooting, falling. Weems and Braden spilling from their saddles, Gene with one foot still lodged in its stirrup as his horse dragged him away to God knows where. A bullet sizzling past Thornton's face, so close that he could feel its breeze before he turned and fled.

If pressed, he couldn't have explained what he expected from the raid. Some kind of satisfaction, obviously, with an opportunity to make Miss High and Mighty crawl before him, but it seemed to fall apart after they'd shot her sentries on the open range, before reaching the house. From there, it was an exercise in chaos, hardly real to him at all.

But he'd be hunted for it, Thornton knew, if anyone had seen his face. Faith's hired men knew him, and they wouldn't hesitate to name him for the hanging judge in Enid. Christ, for all he knew there was a murder warrant out on him right now. And if they linked him to the reservation killing, or the homestead slaughter two days back . . .

So what? a voice inside his head demanded. *They can only hang you once.*

And once was too damned often, right.

Thornton wished he was headed south, to Mexico, instead of wandering around the territory, eating Sabiano's dust. His problem, now, was getting shut of his companions without prompting them to murder him. Ideally, he could slip away and let the law chase Sabiano's gang until they all died bloody or were stretching rope, with Thornton lost in the confusion, hopefully forgotten.

Failing that, he hoped to run as fast and far as possible, beyond the reach of U.S. marshals. Maybe settle down some-where, under another name—or, if that didn't take, at least pursue his aimless drifting with a bit more caution, steering clear of trouble that would land him in a cell or on the gallows. People did it every day, he reasoned. What was one more, in the scheme of things?

But if the law caught him with Sabiano's raiders, they would have his ass on toast. The others wouldn't hesitate to sell him down the river, given half a chance, and choking on a rope wasn't the way he hoped to die. Nor being shot, for that matter, but if he had to make the choice . . .

He took a last look at the circling buzzards to his left and muttered, "Not today."

"Say what?" asked Hampton.

"Nothing," Thornton said. "Just talking to myself."

"First sign of goin' crazy," Wade replied.

And Thornton thought, *I wouldn't be surprised.*

The Crawford homestead was deserted but for half a dozen buzzards picking over something in a fenced corral beside the barn. Slade couldn't make out what it was, at first, but when they'd closed the gap to fifty yards he recognized the ripe remains of a dead horse.

First thought, the raiders tried to steal it as they had Strong Horse's pony on the reservation, but they couldn't manage it and shot the animal instead. It told him something more about the people he was hunting, that they didn't care for leaving anything behind.

Especially not witnesses.

Judge Dennison hadn't provided many details for the Crawford family massacre. Slade didn't need them. He had seen this kind of thing before and knew that female victims generally suffered most, unless they struggled to the death. Slade understood there'd been a wife and daughter here and didn't like to think beyond that point.

Four crosses on the east side of the house marked mounds of earth where neighbors had interred the bodies. There was evidence of chickens in the yard, but they and any other livestock that survived the raid had probably been carried off to benefit some other family. There was no harm in that, as far as Slade could see. He hadn't ridden all this way in search of chicken thieves.

The question now: had this crime and the reservation murder been committed by Burch Thornton and the other scum who'd struck Faith's ranch?

A trail led nearly arrow-straight between the Crawford spread and where Strong Horse was murdered on the rez, but linking two crimes didn't necessarily connect them to a third. There was no trail from Faith's spread to the reservation—or, if there had been, it was a convoluted path the other deputies had missed, and too much time had passed for Little Wolf to find it now.

Slade stretched his legs, avoiding the corral, and left inspection of the Crawford house to Little Wolf. The Cherokee still wore his normal poker face as he emerged and said, "The farmers died inside."

Slade had already calculated that, noting the bullet scars that still looked fairly fresh on walls and window shutters. Someone had employed an ax to breach the door, which had to happen once the Crawfords had run out of ammunition or the menfolk had been taken out of action, leaving Mrs. Crawford and her daughter cowed.

Four crosses meant that no one but the family was buried, and he couldn't see the gang hauling their dead away for any kind of sentimental reason. They'd left two behind at Faith's and didn't seem to worry that they'd be identified. That told him none of them had fallen here, and Slade regretted it. He might have learned something from corpses, but the gang had ridden out as strong as it came in.

"Anything catch your eye in there?" Slade asked his tracker.

"Much blood," said Little Wolf, "with footprints."

"Can you clear it up, how many men we're looking for?"

"Still nine," said Little Wolf. "But only four left tracks inside. One has a boot heel with a missing piece."

He knelt to sketch it in the dooryard's dust, but Slade said, "That's all right. I'll see it for myself."

The house had probably been pleasant once. Now it was rank inside, smelling of death and worse, littered with shards of broken furniture and smeared with blood where bodies had been dragged across the floor.

And bloody footprints, yes.

Slade found the ones that Little Wolf had noted, with a notched left heel. It didn't look like something done deliberately, or maybe even noticed by the man who wore the boots. But with a bit of luck, it just might hang him.

Slade remained inside the house for several minutes more, crouching to see the other rusty-colored footprints clearly, making sure there were no other useful markings to identify the men who'd turned a home into a slaughter pen. Still nothing that could tell him whether these men were the same ones who had raided Faith's place on his wedding day.

Slade reckoned he would have to ask them, when they met.

If any of them lived that long.

"Riders," Little Wolf announced.

Slade joined him on the porch and saw them, counted seven riding hard in the direction of the Crawford place, still roughly half a mile away. It made no sense, the killers coming back, but Slade had seen a lot of people do a lot of stupid things. If he got lucky, maybe they could end it here.

And if he didn't . . .

Mindful that he had no friends in the neighborhood, except for Little Wolf, Slade crossed to where his roan stood and retrieved his rifle from its saddle scabbard. It already had a cartridge in the chamber, so he simply had to cock the hammer with his thumb. Beside him, Little Wolf did likewise with his Sharps carbine.

Seven riders, which left two men unaccounted for.

Slade stepped away from Little Wolf, dividing the potential targets, as the riders stormed into the Crawfords' yard and reined up in a swirl of dust.

"The hell are you?" one of them near the middle of the pack demanded. He had dark hair underneath a flat-brimmed hat and looked a trifle wild-eyed from his gallop toward the house.

"He's law, Matt," said another of the riders, to Slade's left.

"Well, *he* ain't," Matt replied, glaring at Little Wolf.

"Stand easy," Slade advised the new arrivals. "He's with me, and we're here on official business. I'll require your names before you say another word."

Slade put the eye on the apparent spokesman for the group and waited until he identified himself as Matt Devine. It went on down the line from there, with Skeeter Hollis, Wendell Soames, Mike Patton, Ellis Tate, Ben Thompson, and Blue Jesperson.

"Your parents named you Blue?" asked Slade.

The young man blushed beneath his sunburn, while the rider next to him—Mike Patton—said, "It's short for Bloomfield."

"I believe I'd stick with Blue," Slade said. "Now, state your business."

"Same as yours, I figure," Matt Devine replied. "We're trackin' kidnappers."

Slade said, "Nobody was kidnapped here, that I'm aware of."

"He means from the Dalton place," Blue Jesperson explained. "'Bout fifteen miles behind us, to the north."

Slade glanced at Little Wolf and found him frowning, thinking through it. "When was this?" he asked nobody in particular.

"Last night, sometime," said Skeeter Hollis. "We just got the word this morning. Billy Dalton—he's their youngest—made a break for it on foot and got to Matt's place during breakfast."

"Saying what, exactly?" Slade inquired.

Devine took up the narrative, saying, "A bunch of riders hit his family's spread last night. Billy lit out in the confusion. Hates himself for it today, I guess, but what the hell. He's only six years old."

"Let's hear the rest," Slade said, already dreading it.

"We got together, ten or twelve of us, and rode on over there," Devine went on. "Too late to help. Looked like they finished up the other Daltons pretty quick. Shot Harry and his wife, along with Tad, their elder boy. Marlene's the one they carried off."

"A daughter?" Slade suggested.

"Turned sixteen last month," Ben Thompson said.

"What makes you think they came this way?" asked Slade.

"They left a trail," Matt said.

"Thing is, we lost it," Skeeter Hollis interjected. "I been sayin' that, the past five miles."

"Then we saw you," said Ellis Tate, "and figured . . . well . . ."

"You bein' here," Matt said, "I guess we ain't too damn far off."

"You're three days late for this one," Slade replied. "We'll need to go back for a look at where you lost the trail."

"The hell with that!" said Matt Devine. "We've wasted too much time already, jawing over it."

"You'll waste a damn sight more riding to Texas, if they headed east or west," Slade said. "But suit yourself. I only need one of you."

"I can show you where it was," said Hollis.

"Jesus, Skeeter!" Matt protested.

"Save it," Hollis warned him. "We already rode five miles out of our way because you wouldn't listen."

Slade ignored the squabble, moving past the line of horsemen to his roan, with Little Wolf behind him. Both of them were mounted when he interrupted Matt and Skeeter's bickering.

"You mentioned ten or twelve of you," Slade said. "What happened to the rest?"

"Went home," Blue Jesperson replied. "They thought the shooters might come sniffing for another place to loot, I guess."

"This boy who got away," Slade said. "How many raiders did he see?"

Matt answered that one, reasserting his authority. "He wasn't sure. Said four or five was in the house, maybe some more outside. He's just a kid and he was runnin', in the dark and all."

"Nobody down except the Daltons, when you reached their place this morning?" Slade asked no one in particular.

"Just them," said Ellis Tate. "Looked like the shooters took 'em by surprise and dropped the old man first."

That was the way to do it, coming at a homestead in the dark. Raiders would want an edge, to keep from getting shot up while their targets sat secure behind a barricade. A door unbolted or a window with its shutters open could be lethal.

"All right," Slade told Hollis. "Let's go find those tracks."

"Yes, sir."

"Hey, what about the rest of us?" Devine demanded.

"You can ride along, if you've a mind to," Slade replied. "But understand that I'm in charge, with Little Wolf. It's not a lynching party or a free-for-all."

"You're tellin' us we gotta follow orders from an Injun?" Matt protested.

"Nope. That's only if you come with us," Slade said. "*If you don't like it, choose another compass point and ride until your mounts give out for all I care.*"

"I still think they went south," Devine insisted.

"Adios, then," Slade replied and turned his mare away to follow Hollis and his buckskin gelding northward. Little Wolf rode to his left with the Sharps carbine still in hand.

They'd covered twenty yards or so when Slade heard Matt Devine say, "Shit! Okay, let's go."

Slade waited half a minute more before he glanced over his shoulder, found the other six trailing his three-man party back the way they'd come. It had to sting Matt's pride, but he would learn to live with it. Or not, whatever.

At the moment, Jack Slade didn't give a damn.

7

Slade didn't push it on his ride back to the point where Matt Devine and company had lost the raiders' trail. Skeeter Hollis likely would have galloped all the way and wound up with his horse exhausted after five miles, but they needed to spare their animals for the potential long haul ahead of them.

Slade calculated they could walk the five miles in an hour and a quarter, give or take, and cut that time in half by alternating with a trot. The Oklahoma sky was mostly clear, a few stray clouds, but none that threatened rain. The outlaws' tracks weren't going anywhere.

And while they followed Hollis northward, Slade had time to think.

It struck him as peculiar that the Thornton gang—the way he thought of it, for want of any other name—would stage so many raids in one vicinity within so short a time. Why would they draw attention to themselves in such dramatic fashion when they could have fled the territory and been off in Kansas now, or in Missouri, even down in Mexico. If they were short of money, they could always find it

on the road while putting miles behind them, getting clear
of one place where a sane man had to know that he was
being hunted.

Maybe it was simple, and they didn't care. Slade knew
some men like that—*had* known them; they were dead and
buried now—who didn't know their limits, thought they
were invincible. Or maybe they just got tired of living and
decided it was easier to hang around, let someone else
relieve them of their burden, when they didn't have the nerve
to end it for themselves.

One man or two, all right. But Slade had never heard tell
of a suicidal gang before. If they were cornered, maybe shoot
it out against the odds, but most outlaws would run after a
major raid, given the chance.

Unless they were insane.

He couldn't rule that out, given his own experiences with
the Bender clan and Connor MacGowan, the Jubilee ripper.
Some alienists claimed that any criminal activity was evidence of a disordered mind, but Slade had trouble buying
that. As far as he could tell, most crimes arose from greed,
anger, or lust—emotions that had dogged mankind since the
species crawled out of a cave or came down from the trees.

When they had put the Crawford place a mile or more
behind them, Slade told Little Wolf, keeping his voice
pitched low, "These may not be the men we're looking for."

"Riding the wrong way, at the wrong time," Little Wolf
observed.

"That's my thought, but it wouldn't be the first mistake
I ever made."

"But more important," said the Cherokee. "I think this
hunt is personal for you."

"Is it that obvious?" asked Slade.

"A white man would not notice," Little Wolf replied and
nearly smiled.

"It's just as well."

"The woman that you spoke of to White Uncle." Meaning Berringer and not quite sneering as he said it. "She was yours?"

Slade nodded. "She'd have been my wife," he said.

"And now? You said she is alive."

"Just barely," Slade replied. "Her doctor can't say how long she'll hang on or whether she'll be the same person that I knew, if she survives."

"A spirit that has seen the face of Death may change, it's true," said Little Wolf. "Some cannot bear to leave him. Others live, but crave Death's company until he comes for them again."

"That's reassuring," muttered Slade.

"But a few come back to life without regret," the tracker added. Trying to convince Slade or himself?

"I'll keep my fingers crossed," said Slade.

"How will you shoot?" asked Little Wolf.

"Figure of speech," Slade said and called to Hollis, riding thirty feet or so ahead of them, like he was leading a parade, "Yo, Skeeter! Are you sure you'll know the spot?"

"No worries, Marshal. I could find it in my sleep," the younger man replied.

"Just find it," Slade suggested. "Sleep comes later."

"Yes, sir."

Slade glanced back at the others, trailing them, and thought that he'd been lucky to find one among them with a level head. Whether they'd be of any use against the gunmen he was tracking was another question. By the time Slade had an answer, it would likely be too late to send the stragglers home.

Marlene Dalton supposed she was as good as dead. The idea didn't bother her as much as she'd have thought it would, after she'd seen her parents and her brother killed before her eyes. The gunshots that still echoed in her head weren't aimed at her, but they had killed a part of Marlene, just the same.

That hadn't been the worst of it, either. The sweaty, stinking pigs on top of her and turning her whichever way it suited them, until she'd wished that they would kill her and be done with it.

But no such luck.

Lately, while riding with her hands bound on a horse her kidnappers had stolen from her parents' farm, Marlene had started thinking that she ought to kill herself. Exactly how she'd do it was a puzzle that she hadn't solved but would keep turning over in her mind.

One thing that definitely *wouldn't* work was holding her breath till she died. Marlene had tried it once as a youngster, not to kill herself that time, but just to find out what would happen. After something like a minute she had burst out coughing while her brother laughed at her. He'd said that even people who could hold their breath until they blacked out wouldn't die, because your body took control as soon as you lost consciousness and made you breathe again, like it or not.

So, that was out.

She'd need some kind of weapon, but it didn't help that she was surrounded by men armed with pistols, rifles and knives. Marlene knew that she wasn't strong enough to overpower one of them, but maybe she could find a way when they were sleeping. Slip one of the six-guns gently from its holster, keeping it just long enough to put a bullet through her brain.

Or, if she got a gun, why not kill some of *them*, instead? She couldn't hope to get them all, but they would doubtless fire at her in self-defense, so it would be a double victory. Kill one or two of her abductors—maybe three, if she was quick enough—and let the others end her misery.

Her parents would have hated the idea, but what did they know, anyway? They couldn't even keep themselves alive, much less protect their children. Thinking that brought tears of guilt to Marlene's eyes, but it was true. Her father had been tall and strong, but when these monsters burst into his home, Marlene had seen the panic written on his face.

Papa had fought, of course, for all the good it did him. So had Tad, making a grab for Papa's rifle on the wall above the fireplace, but he hadn't reached it. Marlene knew she'd always remember the pain in his eyes as the bullets ripped through him, blood spraying and spilling before he collapsed to the floor.

One more reason to die. Let the hideous memories go.

Now that she had a plan of sorts, Marlene could wait and bide her time. Next time they stopped somewhere she might even try enticing one of them to take her, just to speed things up. The redhead with the birthmark on his left cheek couldn't keep his eyes away from her. She wouldn't have to offer much encouragement for him to have a go. He wore two pistols, which would double Marlene's chance of getting lucky when she grabbed for one.

The rest would be thunder and pain, but it wouldn't last long. The proof of that was lying in the slaughterhouse that used to be her home. And any form of death was preferable to the days or weeks of degradation that awaited Marlene in the company of her abductors. They would kill her when they tired of her, she understood, but why should she allow them any pleasure until then?

She thought of Billy, barely six years old, and wondered how he'd managed to escape last night. Irrationally, Marlene hated him for leaving her behind, then felt another stab of guilt at that, sharper than the regret at being angry with her parents or with Tad. She hoped that Billy lived, grew up, and hunted down the bastards who had massacred his family.

How long until they stopped to rest the horses or to torment her again?

For Marlene Dalton, death could not come soon enough.

"It's just another mile or so," said Skeeter Hollis. "Can't be any more'n that."

Slade hoped he had it right. A sense of wasted time oppressed him, every minute that elapsed reminding Slade that his quarry could still escape him. That he could spend the rest of his life hunting shadows and ghosts.

Now he was saddled with a half-baked posse that he didn't want or need. Okay, maybe they'd put him on the killers' trail by accident—but maybe not. If those who'd hit the Dalton homestead proved to be the raiders from his wedding day, so much the better. They could hang for all of it at once. But Slade wasn't convinced yet, and he wouldn't be until he had Burch Thornton in his hands.

Or in his gun sights.

It would help if he had ever seen the man, but it appeared their paths had never crossed during the short time Thornton worked for Faith. No mystery to that, but it was inconvenient now when Slade knew Thornton could walk past him on a street, unrecognized.

Still, there'd be time enough to think about that when he overtook the gang. Meanwhile, Slade worried more about his grudging helpers than the outlaws he was chasing. Kidnappers and bandits were predictable, up to a point. Slade's posse might not be.

Take Matt Devine, for instance. Slade didn't trust him entirely, thought he'd like to pick a fight with Little Wolf if he could get away with it. Unless he was a backshooter, Slade thought he'd lose that contest and would likely wind up dead, which would cause problems that Slade didn't need.

Another useless wrangle over race, distracting everyone concerned from finishing the job at hand.

The other stragglers would bear watching, too. Slade sensed that most of them followed Devine without investing much thought in the matter. That was fine, if they were headed off to a saloon some night, to raise a little hell, but when it came to man hunting, Slade wasn't leaving anything to a committee vote. The last thing that he needed was a pack of amateurs with lynching on their minds—or greenhorns who would freeze up at their first whiff of gun smoke.

Slade thought about the girl, Marlene. What she had suffered up to now, and what still lay in store for her unless he found her kidnappers and managed to extract her from their clutches. Slade only knew two reasons why a gang would snatch a young female, and one of them—the thought of selling her—couldn't be realized unless they carried her to Mexico. That left a short-term living nightmare for the sixteen-year-old farmer's daughter, lasting until they got tired of her or started worrying that she would slow them down.

In which case, Slade would likely find her body dropped along the trail. Assuming they could *find* the trail.

As if in answer to his gloomy thought, Hollis announced, "We're almost there."

Their young guide reined his buckskin to a walk, and Slade did likewise, Little Wolf easy beside him on his tobiano. Rapidly, the others overtook them, prompting Slade to frown.

"Hang back," he ordered, noting Matt Devine's pained look. "We need to see their tracks, not yours."

Five of them got it, while Devine came on glaring and huffy. Slade would have enjoyed belting him, but he needed a better excuse and it wasn't worth scheming to brawl with a youth barely out of his teens.

There were others more deserving of his anger, men who'd earned whatever might be coming to them, and then some. If Slade could only run them down . . .

"Right here," said Hollis, pointing to a patch of churned-up soil and grass.

From where he sat, Slade saw the line of tracks receding northward, toward the Dalton spread, beyond his line of sight. Where Hollis pointed, they had wheeled off to the west, as if on signal. Why? Where were they headed next?

Slade watched as Little Wolf dismounted, crouching to examine the hoofprints. He heard Devine say, "Here we go," and pinned the young smart aleck with a glare that could have driven nails. Devine shut up, at least for now, and turned his eyes away.

"Six horses," Little Wolf declared. "All shod."

Not even close, Slade thought and tried to mask his disappointment. Either half the men he wanted had split off from their companions or a different bunch was riding westward with a hostage from the Dalton farm. And either way, Slade had to follow them.

"All right," he said, resigned to it. "Let's go."

"You ever hear of anything like this before?" asked Matt Devine, keeping his voice around the level of a half whisper.

"Like what?" asked Wendell Soames, riding beside him on a rose gray stallion.

"Well, Billy, how about a U.S. marshal ridin' with a goddamn redskin. Have you ever heard of *that*?"

"Don't recollect I have," Soames granted, peering up the line at Marshal Slade, as if afraid the lawman might be listening.

"Hell, I'm not even sure it's legal," Matt pressed on. "The only Injuns in the territory are supposed to be on reservations, right? So, where'd this high-and-mighty fella get his hands on one to lead him all around? You ever think of that?"

"Guess not," said Soames.

"Damn right, guess not. For all we know, he might not even *be* a marshal."

"Matt, c'mon."

"I'm serious," Devine insisted.

"So, you think he stole a U.S. marshal's badge from somewhere, found hisself an Indian, and just decided to go chasin' outlaws for the hell of it?" asked Soames. "What kinda sense does that make?"

"How do we know that he's *chasin'* outlaws?" asked Devine. "We found 'em at that burned-out spread where folks was killed. Maybe they're part of it somehow."

"You lost me, there," Soames said.

"Part of the gang that took Marlene and did the rest of it," Devine responded with exaggerated patience, as if he was teaching long division to a simpleton.

"Okay. Why ain't he with 'em, then?" Soames challenged.

"Well, could be because they're smart," Devine replied. "What better way to stop a posse chasin' 'em than send one of their own out, make-believin' he's a lawman?"

"How's that help 'em?" Soames inquired.

"Lord, you're thick." Devine felt anger warm his cheeks. "The so-called marshal stops us lookin' for the men who took Marlene, all right? He leads us off to nowhere with his redskin—or they drag us right into an ambush."

Soames considered it, then shook his head. "I don't believe it."

"Fine. Don't take my word for it," Devine hissed back at Soames. "Nobody's askin' you to pick a side right now. Just keep your eyes open, all right? And keep your weapon handy if they jump us."

Swiveling his head, Soames scanned the open country-side around them and replied, "I don't see anyplace for 'em to hide."

"That's cute," Devine replied. "Why don't you ask Tad Dalton if they're tricky. Ask his parents. While you're at it, ask Marlene, we ever find her."

"There's a chance," Soames said. "At least they didn't kill her at the house."

"Mighta been better if they had," Devine replied.

"The hell does that mean?" Soames demanded, then he got it. "Oh. Well . . . I don't know."

"You think she'd wanna live after they've had her?" asked Devine. "What decent woman would? She's ruined now. Won't never find herself a husband."

"Me, I'd rather be alive," said Soames.

"Jesus." Matt Devine looked like a man who bore the whole weight of humanity upon his shoulders. "Why'n Hell I even bother is beyond me."

"You're gettin' all het up about the redskin," Soames advised him. "If he finds the pricks we're lookin' for, it's good enough for me."

"That's where we differ, Billy boy," Devine informed him. "When I do a thing, I like to do it right."

"We haven't gone wrong yet, that I can see," Soames said.

"Eyes open," said Devine. "That's all I ask."

"There any way to guess how long it's been since they rode through here?" Slade inquired of Little Wolf.

"Horse droppings," said the Cherokee. "Next time we find some, stop and feel them. Soft or dry? Smell them or taste, for freshness."

"Guess I'll pass on that," Slade said, "and take your word for it."

"Sometime this morning," Little Wolf suggested. "Maybe eight, ten hours."

"So, we're well behind them."

"Horses will need water, grass, and time to rest," said Little Wolf, "or we will find men walking."

"Still," Slade said, "with that lead . . ."

"And the woman helps us. She was taken for a reason, yes?" asked Little Wolf.

"I'm trying not to think about it," Slade replied.

"These men don't want a cook, I think," the Cherokee went on. "Not someone who will wash their clothes."

"I get the point," Slade said.

"But they must stop to take advantage," Little Wolf concluded.

"If they're smart at all," Slade said, "they won't be stopping while it's daylight."

"But tonight," said Little Wolf. "We may find them distracted."

Slade had no response to that. He didn't know the girl who'd been abducted and might never have a chance to meet her, but it made no difference. The crimes that bothered Slade the most were outrages directed against women, children—anyone, in fact, who qualified as weak and helpless.

Faith would scold him, Slade supposed, for putting women in the helpless category. Certainly her own example proved him wrong on that account. Not long ago, he'd seen her fight to protect her home from a gang of religious fanatics intent on murdering women and children —but where was she now? A victim and shell of herself, maybe lost to the world forever.

He changed the subject, telling Little Wolf, "When we catch up to them, we'll have to watch these yokels. That Devine could set them off in nothing flat."

"Why don't you send them home?" asked Little Wolf.

Slade had considered it, but now he said, "Their guns may come in handy, if they're manageable. Anyway, I figure that they'd just follow us anyway."

"You think Devine wanted the girl?" asked Little Wolf.

Slade shrugged. "Beats me. I couldn't say if he was more upset than any of the others. Could be out for an adventure more than anything."

"To prove himself," said Little Wolf.

"The manhood thing." Slade nodded. "That's another possibility."

"It makes him dangerous."

"I hear you," Slade replied. "I'll knock him galley west before I let him start a lynching party."

"These are not man hunters," Little Wolf observed.

"They're playing at it," Slade agreed and thought again that he should send them packing. But he had been straight with Little Wolf. There was no way to stop the farm boys following along behind them, hungry for revenge, glory, whatever motivated them. It seemed wiser, in the long run, keeping them close by, where Slade could try to exercise some measure of control.

And if they botched it, got themselves shot up, Slade wouldn't waste time punishing himself for their mistakes. His focus, for the moment, was on Marlene Dalton and her kidnappers. If they turned out to be the same men who'd shot Faith, so much the better. Slade could settle all of his outstanding debts at once.

But if, as he suspected, they were following a different pack of outlaw scum, then he was wasting further precious time, letting the men he really wanted stretch their lead and leave him far behind them.

Never mind.

Their first mistake had been attacking Faith. Their second—and perhaps their last—would be expecting Slade to let it go, give up on searching for them just because of a gulf of miles between themselves and him. If necessary, he would follow them to California, into Mexico, or all the way to South America. If one of them booked passage to a distant land, and Slade could manage to identify the ship, he would be sailing in pursuit. To Hell with jurisdiction and Judge Dennison.

He owed Faith that, at least.

If there was nothing else that he could do to help her, bring her back from the dark place where she had gone, at least he could devote his life to paying back the bastards who had sent her there.

And see them hanged, if possible. Or dead by any other means that came to hand.

Slade wasn't picky, just so long as each and every one of them was finally accounted for.

8

"We need ta stop soon," said the smelly oaf Marlene regarded as the leader of the gang. He had a short beard and his belly overhung the buckle of his gunbelt. "All of ya start lookin' for a place that's fit to camp."

Beside her, to her right, Birthmark was riding almost close enough to touch, eyes moving over her like slimy hands. Marlene could tell what he was thinking—anyone with eyes and half a brain would know—and she encouraged him by putting on a sort of smile. As stupid as he was, it got his hopes up.

Hopes and something else, she guessed.

Damned fool believing that a girl he'd raped and kidnapped would desire him as a lover. If she played her cards right, it could be his last mistake.

Marlene supposed they had an hour still to go, before the sun went down. Gray dusk would cover half that time, so she supposed they would be stopping sometime in the next half hour, if they found a spot with grass and water, maybe some cover from trees.

On her parents' farm there'd been a cool, clear spring.

One of the reasons her father had chosen the land when they first arrived in the Cherokee Outlet with Billy still a tadpole in Mama's belly. They'd been rewarded with good harvests, only brushed by one tornado in the past six years. It did a little damage to the barn and carried off one cow they never saw again, but Papa said they had been lucky.

All gone, now. A bitter waste.

The worst of it was knowing Papa had been wrong in what he told them each in turn when they were young. There *were* monsters that traveled in the dark.

She was among them now and made a silent study of her captors without seeming to examine them. The leader rode a bay gelding that fairly sagged beneath his weight. He was left-handed, wore an old pistol the length of Marlene's forearm, and carried a long knife resembling a cut-down cavalry saber.

Birthmark rode a sorrel mare. His pistols didn't match, one having wooden grips, the other with a handle carved from horn or bone. He was the only one with spurs, a tarnished pair that told you he was coming well before you saw him.

Number three, a maybe-Mexican, still hadn't spoken in Marlene's presence. The scar that ran halfway around his neck might be the reason for his silence, though she couldn't swear to it. He had a wet-dog smell about him, rode a salt-and-pepper gray, and wore his pistol situated for a cross-hand draw.

The fourth kidnapper didn't have much hair beneath his hat, although a gray fringe showed above his ears and straggled into mousy sideburns. He carried a small pistol tucked under his belt but favored rifles, packing two of them in saddle boots aboard his brindle stallion.

The last man, if you could call him that, was barely Tad's age, mounted on a rabicano with a white blaze. Like

Birthmark, he carried two guns—one tied down, the other in a holster slung across his chest, half underneath his left armpit.

The animals who had destroyed her life and any hope Marlene had ever had of growing up and being happy, with a family to call her own. She hadn't given that much thought before last night, but now it weighed on her with special sadness.

And it made her angry.

Mad enough to kill, in fact, if someone dropped his guard and gave her half a chance.

"Be gettin' dark inside the hour," Skeeter Hollis said, examining the sky.

"Looks like it," Slade agreed.

"We gonna keep on after nightfall?" Hollis asked.

"See how it goes," Slade said. "We might get lucky yet."

"Be some luck, that will," said Blue Jesperson. "They got a half day's lead on us, at least."

Slade didn't bother answering, bent his attention to the skyline where he hoped to see a clutch of tiny riders but was spotting none, so far.

"I figgered we'd be doin' better," Matt Devine chimed in. "What with your magic redskin readin' sign and all."

Slade stopped and swiveled in his saddle to confront Devine. "I warned you once about that mouth," he said. "Now, since your mama didn't raise you with a civil tongue, you've got two choices. Either bite it or turn that dun around and haul ass for home."

Devine's face turned beet red in something like a heartbeat. Slade saw him considering an answer, then deciding it would only make things worse. He didn't have the twitchy mannerism of a backshooter, but Slade decided he would still bear watching.

Just in case.

They rode on silently, without the weasel muttering Devine had kept up, off and on, since they had left the Crawford spread. Slade didn't fool himself into believing that he'd solved a problem, but at least he'd pushed it back a bit and gained some breathing room.

"You've made an enemy," said Little Wolf, a half mile later.

"Not the first," Slade told him. Thinking, *Likely not the last, either.* Which would depend on circumstance. How long he stayed alive, for one. Whether he kept his badge after he finished hunting down the killers he was seeking.

And if not, what would he do? Go back to drifting, playing poker for a living? Slade supposed it would depend on Faith. As long as she survived, with any hope at all of waking up again, he would feel bound to Enid. If she died, all ties were severed. Slade owed nothing to Judge Dennison or any other man.

Another forty minutes took the sun down in a blaze of crimson to the west, but Little Wolf rode on with Slade beside him. They could still make out the gang's rough trail by twilight, its westward direction arrow-straight, unwavering. There was a chance the riders might be slick enough to change their course once night fell, to throw off pursuit, but Slade wasn't about to bet on it.

"Much longer, and we'll be as good as blind," said Ellis Tate.

"Stop any time you're ready," Slade advised him.

"And what? Get left behind?" Tate challenged.

"Your call," Slade replied.

No one spoke up in Tate's defense, and he fell silent, keeping pace. Slade had his own doubts about riding on in darkness, wondering if they could hold true west by navigating from the stars, but Little Wolf seemed confident enough. Slade trusted him to know when they were done and asked no questions.

Another fifteen minutes passed, and Slade admitted to himself that he had lost the trail. He was considering a way to broach the subject tactfully when Little Wolf stopped short and pointed, his arm angled slightly to the left.

"See there," he said.

Slade squinted, craning forward in his saddle, making out a spark that flickered, then held steady more or less. Depending on the intervening distance, it could either be a campfire or a house in flames.

Slade bet on the campfire.

"Listen up," he told rest. "From here on, no one says a word."

Marlene was weary, aching from the long ride and the punishment she'd suffered. When the leader found a place that suited him and called a halt, she was relieved. Her nightmare would be over soon.

But while a part of her mind welcomed death as a release from shame and pain, another part still cringed in childish fear. Her parents had been moral people, not enthralled by any certain church, but still devoted to the concept of reward or punishment for earthly actions in an afterlife. Marlene supposed the violation forced upon her by her captors wouldn't count against her as a sin, but what she had in mind for them—and for herself—might be construed another way.

Would it be murder if she killed Birthmark or any of the others? If she provoked them into killing her, would she be damned for suicide?

And come to that, could Hell be any worse that what her life had finally become?

Marlene decided she would rather risk eternity with fire and brimstone than permit the scum who'd killed her parents and her brother one more hour of pleasure, mauling her. Maybe they'd all wind up in Hell together, and she could persuade the Devil that the bastards needed his particular attention while they roasted on a spit.

Dismounting with a stifled groan, she thought again of little Billy, wondered if he'd gotten lost in darkness after he'd escaped. Come morning, she supposed he would have found the Thompson farm, or maybe gone the other way to Jespersons'. In either case, somebody would have come to tend her family and see them buried decently.

But would they look for her?

She guessed they might, but didn't know how far the neighbors would pursue a gang of killers. They'd be frightened, for themselves and any family they left behind unguarded, while they rode off searching for Marlene. Most likely, if they couldn't overtake the gunmen in a short time—which they obviously had not—they would go home and send a rider off to fetch lawmen.

From Enid, that would be, although the little town of Jasperville was closer, and it had a constable of sorts. Marlene had glimpsed him when her family went shopping for supplies. He wore a badge, but she had never seen a pistol on his hip and couldn't picture him confronting one serious outlaw, much less five.

Stick to the plan, she told herself. *There's no help coming, and it's too late anyway.*

How could she live with what she'd suffered—and with Billy in the bargain, now that they'd be on their own? She might be fit to raise her brother, barely, but they couldn't run a farm alone, and there was no money for hiring hands. Not that she'd ever trust another stranger in her life.

Another fear that haunted her involved the possibility that if she lived, she might be burdened with a child from one of those who'd raped her. Mama had explained the way it worked when Marlene turned eleven, though she had already seen some of the animals around the farm engaged in mating. She could think of nothing worse than to be saddled with an infant she despised for all it represented, worried every day throughout her life that it would grow to be a monster like its father.

Not that she would know which one to blame.

Better for all concerned, she thought, to end it here, tonight. It should be easy, she imagined.

All she had to do was get her hands on someone's gun.

It was a slow approach, and cautious. Having warned the possemen about unnecessary noise, Slade couldn't keep their horses quiet, but the animals were calm and rarely huffed or snorted as they moved through darkness at a walking pace. Slade kept the firelight fixed in sight and watched it grow by slow degrees as they advanced.

Progressing, Slade discovered that the fire was something like a mile away when Little Crow first spotted it. A little earlier, before the sun had fully set, they would have missed it. Maybe ridden past the spot, or blundered close enough to spook the campers with their noise and start a shooting match before they were prepared.

Slade put no stock in Faith or Providence, whatever people chose to call it, but he'd earned his living as a gambler long enough to know that luck existed. Mostly, he believed that people made their own—that good luck came primarily from skill, knowledge, talent, and preparation, while bad luck came most often to the negligent, dim-witted, and distracted. Even so, there had been times when Lady Luck stepped in to save his ass, with cards or in a fight, and Slade did not discount fortuitous coincidence.

When they had closed to half a mile, Slade called the posse to a halt and faced the seven farmers who'd attached themselves to him and Little Wolf. Despite the distance still remaining to be covered, Slade spoke softly and invited no replies.

"The only thing we know so far," he said, "is that we've got somebody camped ahead of us. Might be the men we're looking for, or might not be. We can't take any chances, riding in and stirring up the pot, in case it's them and they've still got the girl alive."

Blue Jesperson began to ask, "You mean—?"

"No talk," Slade cautioned, cutting off the question all of them were thinking now. *Was* Marlene Dalton still alive? They hadn't found her body on the trail, had seen no buzzards circling in the sky, but that proved nothing.

"*If* she's still alive, and we go charging in there," Slade continued, "they'll do one of two things. Either kill her on the spot, first thing, or use her as a hostage. I don't like the choices, so we'll go in walking, slow and easy. Not a sound from anybody. If you step into a gopher hole and break an ankle, I don't want to hear a whimper. Anyone who can't follow instructions with his mouth shut, he can stay behind and hold the horses."

Matt Devine was glowering at Slade, while listening. Now he spoke up to say, "Just who in Hell do you think—"

"There's our volunteer," Slade said. "You'll wait here with the animals and keep them quiet, while the rest of us go in."

"Like Hell, I will!" Devine replied.

"Or we can truss you up and leave you," Slade informed him. "Either way, your call. But no more palaver."

Slade could feel Devine's glare burning into him, but the young man stayed quiet. "Right," Slade said. "The rest of you dismount and bring whatever guns you're taking. Nothing cocked, for now, in case you stumble."

"Marshal?" Skeeter Hollis actually raised his hand, as if he were in school.

"Last question," Slade advised.

"What if it ain't them, after all?"

"We'll see who's in the camp when we get there," Slade

answered. "If it's not the men we're after, then we come back here and reassess the situation. See if it's worth riding on tonight, or if we need to stop. Now, let's move out."

It seemed a long walk in the dark, though half a mile was half a mile, no matter how you sliced it. There was no moonlight to speak of, Slade watching for pitfalls and night-crawling rattlers, but he managed. Little Wolf was a silent shadow, away to his right, the others taking special care to walk without scuffing their feet.

They'd formed a kind of skirmish line, Slade's plan being to first survey the camp, then circle half of it with guns if they had found their quarry. He had men enough to ring the camp completely, but the risk in that was having untrained men shoot one another by mistake. Better to give their targets an escape route than to have his uninvited posse members slaughter one another. If it came to that, Slade thought that Little Wolf could locate stragglers in the dark, wherever they might try to hide.

A hundred yards out from the camp, Slade could see figures moving back and forth, between him and the fire. It made him want to hurry, when he thought about the girl, but haste produced mistakes that he could ill afford. A little closer, and he'd have the view he needed of the campers. Could decide if they were simple travelers or killers ready to hang at Judge Dennison's pleasure.

Forty yards, and Slade could count heads now. He saw five men in camp—and one young woman, barely dressed against the chill of night. A jug-eared fellow with a port-wine stain across the left side of his face was sitting with an arm around the woman's shoulders, squeezing her and saying something that provoked the rest to laughter. Warming up to entertain themselves, Slade thought, as he advanced under the cover of their noise.

His unintended followers would recognize her, Slade
supposed. On either side of him, their shadow shapes were
fanning out to their assigned positions. In another minute,
maybe two, they'd be in place and he could interrupt the
kidnappers before their victim had to suffer any more abuse.
Would they give up without a fight, or would it come to
killing?

Either way, it ended here.

Slade checked his flanks as best he could in darkness and
was about to hail the camp when someone in the night
shouted, "Marlene!" and charged into the firelight.

Matt Devine.

Slade cursed and raised his rifle, as the outlaws scrambled every which way, going for their guns. He called out,
"U.S. marshal! Raise your hands!" but might as well have
whispered in a hurricane. Someone kicked the fire into a
dying rain of sparks.

Slade saw the rest of it in jerky fragments, lit by muzzle
flashes. Marlene Dalton snatched a pistol from the jug-eared
gunman's holster as he pulled away from her and shot him
in the chest at point-blank range, setting his shirt on fire. As
he collapsed, she rose and turned in search of other targets,
fired a shot at Matt Devine, apparently not recognizing him,
and drilled him through one leg. Falling, Devine triggered
a shot that struck Marlene below one breast and dropped
her sprawling on her back.

That left four outlaws firing random shots into the night,
trying to target muzzle flashes from the weapons that surrounded them. Slade heard a bullet sizzle past his left ear,
there and gone, before he shot the man who'd fired it. Matt
Devine was lying low, whether in shock at what he'd done
or from his wound, Slade couldn't say. The kidnappers were
cut off from their horses, somewhere in the darkness to
Slade's right, as gunshots hammered them.

Slade heard one shot from Little Wolf's Sharps carbine,

taking down a runner on the far side of the smothered fire, and he was looking for another target when he realized that none were left standing. His possemen kept firing, though, their bullets raising puffs of dust or slapping into silent, unresisting flesh.

"Enough!" he bellowed to be heard. "Cease fire, god-damn it!"

Somehow, it got through to them. The shooting sputtered out, and Slade heard someone retching in the silence that descended afterward.

"Put down your guns," he ordered all of them. "I'm going in."

Slade moved across the killing ground, past Matt Devine, to reach the girl. She was already gone, eyes glazing over with the dusty look of death, no pulse discernible to Slade's touch at her throat or wrist.

Devine was still alive, against all odds, and Slade suppressed an urge to kick his teeth in as he passed a second time, circling the camp in search of a surviving gang member. He found one out of five still breathing, barely, and crouched down beside him, gathering the fabric of a stained shirt in his hands.

The dying gunman gaped at him and groaned. Slade shook him roughly, bending lower, hissing in his face. "Burch Thornton. Do you know him?"

"Mother?" wheezed the almost-corpse.

"I'll call her when you answer me," Slade said.

"Whozat?"

"I need to know if he was with you," Slade demanded. "Thornton. Were you with him at the Crawford place? At Connover's?"

The man blew crimson bubbles from his lips and slumped back to the ground, a deadweight in Slade's grip. Cursing again, Slade rose, found Little Wolf standing nearby, and called the others in. They gathered around Matt Devine, Slade standing over him, all of the young men looking wan and sickly.

"Your friend's hit in the leg," Slade said, in case they'd missed it. "Someone get a tourniquet on that, and bear in mind you'll have to loosen it from time to time, or risk gangrene. Disarm him while you're at it, too."

"How come?" Mike Patton asked.

"Because he killed the girl you all came out to rescue," Slade replied. "He's going back for trial on that."

"Jesus!" said Wendell Soames. "It was an accident!"

"That makes it manslaughter," Slade said, "and keeps him off the scaffold. He's looking at two to five years in the pen, if you don't let him bleed to death first."

Patton and Soames went to work on Devine, while the others hung back, keeping their distance as if they thought his trouble was contagious. Drawing lines for future reference.

"Skeeter," Slade said to Hollis, "go and find out if Devine was smart enough to leave the horses tied before he followed us. If you can find them, bring them back here."

Hollis bobbed his head and said, "Yes, sir," then slipped into the darkness.

"You three," Slade addressed the possemen remaining. "Gather up the guns from this lot. Get the bodies wrapped in blankets, tied off if there's rope enough. We'll need to pack them out, first thing tomorrow. What's the nearest town?"

"That's Jasperville," said Ellis Tate. "'Bout twenty miles southeast of here, I guess."

"They have a lawman there?" asked Slade.

"Town constable. He's got a cell or two."

"One's all we need," Slade said. "Make up the fire, for

light. You can decide among yourselves who takes first
watch."

"What are we watching for?" asked Jesperson.

Slade nodded toward the dark surrounding them and said,
"To keep coyotes off the dead."

9

Burch Thornton watched the sun come up after a sleepless night, bone-weary, stiff from lying on the hard ground, listening to every sound that emanated from the darkness. Time and time again during those hours, his thoughts had turned to getting out, whatever that meant.

Breaking free, at least. Slipping away from Sabiano and the rest at his first opportunity—but when would that be? If he hung around too long and let the lawmen overtake him, there would be no way to save himself. But even on his own escape might be a fantasy.

If anyone had seen his face during the Connover attack, the law would have his name by now. The warrants would be stamped and certified, the wanted posters coming close behind. Ducking a flyer might be possible, but with the U. S. marshals hunting him by name, spreading the word among themselves however that was done—by letter? telegraph?—where could he go to hide?

Thornton considered Mexico again, had hoped it might be Sabiano's thought as well, him being Mexican and all. Why linger in the Oklahoma Territory, waiting for a posse to show up? But riding south without the gang meant going it alone, and Thornton wasn't sure that he could handle that.

One man had done it. Perry Larson, lean and scar-faced, had run off the first night they had camped, after the raid at Connover's. Slipped past the posted guards somehow and took his horse from the remuda, must've walked it off while carrying his saddle. Not a sound, if that was even possible. Next morning, they woke and looked around to find him gone, like smoke from the dead campfire.

Where was he now? Most likely riding hell for leather toward a compass point where no one knew his name or ravaged face and wouldn't look askance at him. At least, until the next time that he stepped outside the law and got himself arrested, maybe killed.

Thornton had tried to put himself in Larson's place, wherever that was, riding off to who knows where without a worry in the world. But he kept coming back to recognition and the nagging certainty that one or more of Faith Connover's hired men must have seen him. Even in the midst of the excitement, dust, and gun smoke, he would be remembered.

Of the other guys in Sabiano's bunch, Thornton supposed that only Joe Weems shared that risk, because his brother had been killed at the Connover spread and would've been identified by now. The brothers ran—*had* run—together, that was known. The judge in Enid would assume that if Ike Weems went on a raid, his brother would be there, as well.

So, two of them were on the chopping block, but Thornton took no comfort from the shared calamity. He felt no kinship for Joe Weems and wouldn't have suggested that they run away together under any circumstances. Weems had never liked him much, would likely tip off Sabiano just to see what happened next. The end of Thornton, more than likely, if the Mexican was in one of his grumpy moods.

What Thornton needed was a town, someplace where he

could mingle with the citizens and lose himself, stay lost until the gang got bored and traveled on. But Sabiano wasn't taking any chances now, with settlements or constables. He liked the isolated homesteads better, where they could control the situation, leave no witnesses.

The others had begun to stir now, rolling out of blankets, cursing at and blaming one another for the near-dead fire. Wade Hampton tried to get it going, used some kindling that was damp with dew and nearly smoked them out.

Another night gone, when he could've tried to slip away. And another long day stretched in front of Thornton, going . . . where? Was this the day when something would go wrong and he would pay the price for it?

His head ached, and he needed coffee. Needed *something*, anyway. A new life, possibly, but he knew one thing beyond any question.

It was too damned late for that.

Slade had his posse saddling up at sunrise, hoisting blanket-swaddled corpses onto horses, tied off to the saddle horns. He had no way of knowing if he'd matched the riders to their proper mounts, but none of them complained and there was no resistance from the animals.

The same could not be said for Matt Devine. He'd been in misery all night, one or another of his friends attending to him, loosening his tourniquet every couple of hours until the fresh blood flow alarmed them. Devine hadn't slept, though he might have passed out around midnight, still moaning and groaning from pain. He was weakening now, barely able to help when his pals put him up on his dun, while withholding the reins.

"I can ride," he insisted. "I ain't a damn cripple."

"That's fine," Slade replied. "But you're riding with us,

into Jasperville, not taking off on your own. You'll be tethered to me till we get there and tuck you in jail."

"If I ain't dead by then," said Devine.

"It's a risk, wound like yours," Slade replied. "I won't lie."

"And you plan on locking me up for a dumb accident," Devine said.

"Make that killing a girl who'd already been kidnapped and raped," Slade replied.

"*She* shot *me*," Devine answered.

"So, plead self-defense at your trial. See how that suits a jury," Slade said.

"I just might do that," said Devine, seeming blind to the looks his companions were giving him.

"Your call," said Slade. "If we don't get a move on, you're likely to bleed out or hop into court on one leg."

They set off to the southwest, then, Slade leading Devine's horse by its reins, with Little Wolf across from him to keep the wounded rider boxed. Slade didn't think Devine had strength enough to make a break for it, guessed he would likely take a header from the saddle if he tried, but why tempt fate?

The boy had acted on a foolish impulse, maybe thought that he was getting back at Slade for shaming him; now he would have to pay the tab for his mistake. Instead of being thankful that he wouldn't hang, might only serve a year or two for snuffing out a young girl's life, Devine chose to adopt a victim's role.

Good luck with that, Slade thought, imagining Judge Dennison's reaction to a plea of self-defense, then put it out of his mind.

Instead, he thought about the time they'd lost chasing a false trail, nowhere close to locating the men who'd claimed at least three lives so far—and likely seven, with the Crawford raid. Nine horses at the homestead, unaccounted for, and while there was an outside chance the dead kidnappers could have staged that raid, then lost four men somewhere along the way, Slade wasn't buying it.

The men he sought—Burch Thornton, Joe Weems, and the rest—were still at large, likely preparing to commit another savage crime as soon as they encountered someone weak enough to victimize.

And Slade, meanwhile, was on his way to drop a whining idjit off in Jasperville, a half day's ride out of his way. Hell, by the time he finished taking statements from the other members of the posse, for Judge Dennison, he'd have to spend the night in town and start fresh in the morning. Ride back to the Crawford place and see if Little Wolf could find the first gang's trail again.

At least it didn't look like rain was in the offing, so the trail should still be visible. Slade hated losing precious time, but there was nothing he could do about it now. Devine had made his choice, and he must be delivered to what passed for local law and detained until Slade or another marshal could retrieve him for his trial.

The whole thing struck Slade as a waste. Nine people dead, counting the kidnappers, and now Devine was on his way to prison for surrendering to stupid pride. Slade didn't sympathize but knew there had been times in bygone years when he'd made reckless calls and could have gone the same way. Maybe worse.

All that behind him now, unless he snapped on meeting Thornton and the others who had turned his wedding day into a massacre. In that case, he supposed, all bets were off.

Would it be worth throwing his life away?

If Faith was lost to him, Slade thought it might.

It just might be, at that.

Devine complained so much during the ride to Jasperville that Slade threatened to gag him at one point. That worked

for several miles, until Slade realized that griping was the
only thing keeping the wounded rider conscious. Twelve or
thirteen miles into their trek, Mike Patton shouted, "There
he goes!" and Slade turned just in time to keep Devine from
sliding off his horse, headfirst into the dirt.

They stopped then and revived Devine enough to manage
sitting upright in his saddle while Slade tied his wrists to
the horn. That meant he had to slump a bit, and Slade supposed he'd have a stiff back when they reached their destination sometime after ten o'clock, but it was better than
allowing him to fall and snap his neck.

He didn't want the arrogant young fool to miss a day of
prison, as abbreviated as his final sentence might turn out
to be.

Two hours later, Jasperville appeared before them as a
smudge on the horizon. It could easily have been mistaken
for a grove of trees at that distance, but Slade held to his
course and was rewarded after thirty plodding minutes with
a stark outline of roofs against the sky. He'd never seen the
town before, wasn't expecting much, and the reality of Jasperville did not surprise him.

End to end, the town was one block long. Its main—and
only—street displayed the basics of a frontier settlement: a
dry-goods store, a produce market, a hotel with a restaurant,
a blacksmith's shop and livery combined, a barber's shop
with public bath, a gunsmith, lawyer's office, leather works,
an undertaker's parlor, whitewashed church, red school-
house, and a pair of undersized saloons facing each other
at the far end of the row.

Slade found the office labeled CONSTABLE stuck in
between the gunsmith and the lawyer, which made sense to
him. He led the straggling posse over there, dismounted by
a hitching rail with water trough below it, and was tying off
his reins when Jasperville's lawman emerged.

The constable was middle-aged, whatever that meant on

the prairie. Say later forties, at a guess. He stood five foot
nine or ten beneath a Stetson Boss of the Plains, overweight
for his size, in surprisingly small hand-tooled boots. He
wore a round badge stamped from brass but didn't bother
with a gun.

The constable looked first at Little Wolf, frowning, then
saw Slade's badge and made an attitude adjustment. "Can I
help you, Marshal?" he inquired.

"Name's Slade. Jack Slade. And you are . . . ?"

"Corey York, town constable of Jasperville."

Their handshake was perfunctory, York obviously more
concerned with what an Indian was doing out on Main Street
with a Sharps carbine. It took another beat for him to register
the bundled bodies tied across six horses.

"What's all this about?" York asked.

"The Dalton family," Slade said. "You heard about what
happened to them, I suppose?"

"Damn right," York said. "We've got the young one,
Billy, staying here in town with Bob and Ethel Guidrey till
we work out what to do with him."

"We brought his sister back," Slade said, "together with
the men that took her. I expect your undertaker will be busy
for a spell."

"The girl, too? Jumping Jesus! This has been a blight on
the community from start to finish. But what's this?" York
now seemed to notice Matt Devine for the first time, wrists
bound, the bloody binding on his leg. He moved to stand
beside Devine, peered up at him, and asked, "What happened to you, son?"

"You know him?" Slade inquired.

"O' course," York said. "His parents have a spread, out
west of town. They're in on market days and sometimes in
between. I see Matt on his own from time to time, at one of
the saloons."

"Well, now you see him as a prisoner," Slade said. "He

needs a doctor, and he's yours to keep until a deputy comes by for him, from Enid."

"Prisoner? What charge, exactly?" York demanded.

"He's the one who killed the Dalton girl," Slade said.

"Say *what*?"

Half swooning from his saddle, Matt Devine croaked out, "An accident."

"The charge is manslaughter," Slade told the constable. "We'll let a judge and jury settle it."

"Good God Awmighty! What am I supposed to tell his parents?" York inquired.

"Whatever suits you," Slade replied. "Just keep him under lock and key till you're relieved of him."

"Hey, Marshal," Skeeter Hollis said, addressing Slade. "Some of us need to get back home, you know? Tell folks we ain't been kilt and all."

"Nobody leaves until I have those written statements," Slade replied. Turning to York, he asked, "How are you fixed for writing implements?"

York looked confused at first, then said, "I've got some paper and a couple pencils in the office."

"Good enough," Slade said. Then, to his possemen, "A couple of you take your friend inside and get him settled in the lockup. Skeeter, can you find the doctor?"

"Yes, sir," Hollis answered.

"Go and fetch him, then," Slade ordered. "By the time you're back, the constable will have you all set up with pencils, paper, and a place to write."

"What are we s'posed to say?" asked Ellis Tate.

"Exactly what you saw and did last night," Slade said. "No more, no less. You'll all be under oath, so tell it plain and simple for Judge Dennison."

They didn't like it, but he got no argument from any of them. Hollis wheeled his buckskin to the left and galloped off to find the sawbones, while the others made an awkward job of helping Matt Devine dismount, then lugging him inside. Slade followed, Little Wolf immediately on his heels. As they approached the threshold, York held up one meaty hand and said, "He needs to stay out here."

Slade glanced from Little Wolf back to the constable and asked, "Why's that?"

York hesitated, looking dour, then said, "Um . . . well, you know."

"No, I don't," Slade said.

Another moment stretched between them, then the constable said, "Hell, forget it. Everybody in."

Slade nodded, told him, "After you," and followed York into an office that was crowded now, ten people in a room no more than ten by twelve, a desk and chair in one corner, a gun rack on the wall.

The cells were farther back, beyond another door. Two cages, roughly six by eight, each with a cot and chamber pot, no windows on the outside world. Both cells were empty, doors ajar. Thompson and Soames, half carrying Devine, went to the left and placed him on the cot in there, then hurried out, as if afraid they might be locked up with their wounded pal.

Back in the office, York produced two pencils and a sheaf of foolscap paper, laying them out on his desk. Blue Jesperson and Ellis Tate began writing their statements, glancing back at Slade from time to time, as if expecting him to coach them. When he offered no advice, Tate asked him, "You'll be reading these?"

"Before you go," Slade said. "So keep it straight."

"I didn't see what happened to Marlene, exactly," Tate replied.

"Then write down what you did see," Slade instructed. "Don't try sugarcoating it or filling in with your imagination."

"No, sir."

While they wrote, the others waiting, York drew Slade aside and said, "Mind if I ask you something? Not to give offense, you understand."

"Folks say that when they plan to be offensive," Slade observed.

"It's just . . . I never seen a U.S. marshal riding with an Indian before."

"He's tracking for me," Slade explained. "We're looking for a gang's killed seven people that I'm sure of, one of them a Cherokee."

York blinked at that. "Besides the ones outside, you mean?" he asked.

"Another party altogether," Slade replied.

"Sweet Jesus. What's the territory coming to?"

"I wonder that, myself," Slade said.

"About them others you brought in," York said. "We need to bury 'em, I guess."

"I'd think so," Slade agreed.

"You wouldn't know their names, by any chance?" asked York.

"Sorry. We didn't get around to introductions," Slade replied.

"Okay. I'll try to match 'em up with posters from my file, for what it's worth. Not likely anyone'll want to leave 'em flowers, I suppose."

"I'd bet against it," Slade agreed.

York glanced back toward the holding cells and shook his head. "Hell of a thing, with Matt back there. Ride out to help someone and wind up doing time."

"It makes a case for self-control," Slade said. "Word to the wise."

"Too late, I'd say."

Slade frowned and said, "It always is."

•   •   •

When Slade had gathered and reviewed the statements from his possemen, he let them go and waited for the town's doctor— a young medic named Mandeville—to finish up with Matt Devine. Emerging from the cell after a long half hour with his patient, Dr. Mandeville addressed the two lawmen and Little Wolf as if they were the kind of folks he spoke to every day.

"He'll live," the medic said, "provided that infection doesn't take him. I've cleaned out the wound—you likely heard him howling—and it's stitched. I'll come back while he's here and change the dressing once a day. Beyond that . . . well, he's lost a lot of blood and needs some time to build up his supply."

"I'll put that in my message to Judge Dennison," Slade said. Turning to York, he said, "I'll need a rider who can carry it to Enid. He'll be paid and get meal out of it, while he's there."

"No problem," York replied. "I'll see to it."

"The judge may send another deputy before I'm free to get around this way again," Slade said. "Maybe the prison wagon. Any way it goes, they'll have accommodations waiting for him at the other end."

"Another cell," said York.

"Until his trial, at least," Slade said.

"Seems like a shame," the constable remarked.

"There's shame enough to go around." Taking his leave with Little Wolf, Slade said, "We'll drop our horses at the livery, then go to the hotel. Be out first thing tomorrow and away."

York frowned at that. "You plan on staying overnight at the hotel?" he asked. "The two of you?"

"They didn't look that busy, riding past," Slade said.

"Um. Well."

Slade guessed what York was working up the nerve to say and cut him short. "You need to ask me anything, before we go, that's where we'll be," he said.

"Uh-huh." The constable was busy staring at his fancy boots.

Outside, as they untied their horses for the short walk to the stable, Little Wolf said, "You like making trouble, eh?"

"I don't know what you mean," Slade lied.

Little Wolf obliged him with an explanation. "Bet your life this hotel don't take red men."

"Maybe they're enlightened," Slade suggested.

For a second, he thought Little Wolf might laugh out loud, but finally Slade had to settle for a thin-lipped smile.

"Enlightened," said the Cherokee. "Another word for white."

"We'll see."

The blacksmith looked askance at Little Wolf, which came as no surprise, but he agreed to stable both their horses overnight for fifty cents apiece. Slade took his saddlebags and both long guns before he left the livery for the hotel. It felt a bit like marching off to war.

Along the way, Slade caught a few townspeople staring at them, taking in the spectacle of white and red together on Main Street, a lawman and an Indian who might have been a renegade, for all they knew. He guessed there would be talk of it for weeks to come in Jasperville, together with the Dalton slaughter and its bloody aftermath, including Matt Devine's arrest. The town was likely starved for news of any interest on normal days, and suddenly it had a glut of death and scandal to digest.

Slade left them to it and walked into the hotel, holding the door for Little Wolf. The clerk who greeted them was tall and rail thin, balding as if he'd outgrown his scalp. He wore a bowtie with his white shirt, and a pair of pince-nez spectacles that magnified his eyes to owlish size.

Or maybe that was shock at seeing Little Wolf, before he glimpsed Slade's badge.

"Good afternoon, Marshal," he said, his voice and spine both stiff.

"Good day to you," Slade said. "We need two rooms, before we get something to eat."

"Two rooms?" The concept seemed to leave the clerk flummoxed.

"One each," Slade said.

"Er, I'm afraid . . . that is to say . . . the hotel only welcomes white guests, Marshal."

"We're not looking for a welcome," Slade replied. "Just rooms to sleep in."

"As I say, the owners—"

"Let me have a word with them," Slade said.

"That won't be possible. They live in Kansas City," said the clerk.

"No reason they should ever hear about this, then," said Slade. "Unless Judge Dennison was forced to send a wire from Enid, to chastise them for obstructing federal investigators."

"You . . . I mean, the *two* of you?"

"That's right," he said. "We're on the track of murderers, and circumstance has caught us here. You understand that any effort to impede us is a crime, itself?"

Slade knew he was pushing it, but what the Hell?

"Well . . . I don't know." The clerk was waffling now.

"I *do* know," Slade assured him. "Think of it this way: you have a chance to rent two rooms tonight, when no one's lining up to ask for them, or you can spend it in the constable's spare cell."

The clerk swallowed a lump of something, plastered on

a smile that made him look like death warmed over, and replied, "Two rooms it is. Yes, sir."

"And meals, once we unload our gear." Slade turned to Little Wolf and asked, "Is steak all right with you?"

10

Burch Thornton was surprised when Sabiano changed his mind and said they would be heading south, to Mexico. It was the first smart thing he'd heard their leader say since they'd left two men dead at Faith Connover's ranch twelve days ago.

Reading my mind, he thought, and hoped it wasn't too damned late to shake the dust of Oklahoma Territory off his boots. Rising at dawn and holding breakfast to a minimum of beans and coffee, they still had five hundred miles or more to ride before they reached the Rio Grande. Call it two days, if they rode hard enough to kill the horses, stealing more along the way, but who could count on finding fresh mounts when the old ones dropped?

More likely, if they rode ten hours a day, switching between a walk and trot with stops to rest, they'd reach the Tex-Mex border in about five days—or more, if Sabiano got sidetracked by raiding homesteads for supplies, or for the Hell of it.

Thornton supposed it was better than nothing, but still wished he'd taken off on his own, days ago. He could be in

Old Mexico now, maybe drinking mescal in some little cantina, while a pretty little *puta* lied to him about how handsome he was. Not a bad life, as long as it lasted, and he could drift back to the border when money ran short, look for work or a clean way to steal some. Do that off and on for years, if he was lucky, and no one the wiser on either side of the border.

Riding south with Sabiano's gang increased the risk to Thornton—which, admittedly, was the only thing he really cared about. Lawmen were looking for the gang already, maybe not by name, but with a fair idea of eight or nine men traveling together. Crossing into Texas wouldn't shake off U.S. marshals, who could trail him anywhere they felt like, short of Mexico or Canada. Whoever saw them on the road was likely to remember them, unless they were eliminated, but a trail of stiffs would only help man hunters follow them.

No good way out.

It still made better sense for Burch to leave the gang and blaze his own trail southward, but he thought about the long ride, getting hungry on the road and maybe meeting Texas Rangers who'd been warned to keep an eye out for him, just in case. Safety in numbers was the rule, unless the numbers let you down or drew attention from the very folks you wanted to avoid.

Damned if I do, he thought, *and damned if I don't.*

The good news was, he'd never paid much heed to the idea of being damned—or saved, for that matter. The preachers yammered on about it, and he couldn't say for sure if they were right or wrong, but Thornton lived his life according to the big What If.

What if he never took another drink or had another woman, then he died and found out there was nothing on the Other Side? What if he never stole another dime from anyone—or maybe even paid back what he'd taken in the past—and then discovered there was no eternal punishment for sin, no sweet reward for following the straight and narrow path?

What if, in short, he wasted all his time on Earth, the only life he'd ever have, obeying rules laid down by crazy zealots who were dead set against anybody having any fun?

Screw that.

Thornton would take his chances with the sinners—which, in this case, meant with Sabiano's gang. A five- or six-day ride to Mexico would give him ample opportunity to sneak away if it appeared that staying with the gang might be more dangerous than leaving it.

For now, at least, it was enough just to be headed south. Leaving the Oklahoma Territory and its hanging judge behind. If he was lucky, maybe they could shake the marshals after all and find a clear path to the border.

And if not . . . well, Thornton told himself he wasn't frightened of a fight.

But even as the thought took shape, he knew it was a goddamned lie.

From Jasperville, it was a long three-hour ride back to the Crawford spread. Slade wasn't looking forward to revisiting the site of so much misery, but having seen it once already, it held no surprises for him. This time, he determined, nothing would distract him from pursuing the elusive *other* gang.

The men responsible for murdering four homesteaders, for killing Strong Horse on the reservation, and—he hoped—for leaving Faith and him to die on their appointed wedding day.

The tracks were where he'd left them, somewhat faded now from their exposure to a prairie wind that never died entirely. Even so, his guide seemed confident as they set off westward, following the trail.

"Some lead they've got," Slade said, unhappy with the

day and night they'd wasted chasing other bad men, and its grim result. Then yet another day, delivering the bodies and their prisoner.

"Still running," Little Wolf replied. And asked, "You follow them, no matter where they go?"

"That's my intention," Slade agreed.

"Because it's personal."

"It factors in," Slade said. "I won't deny that."

"Would you do the same, if they had only killed Strong Horse?"

"I like to think so," Slade replied. "On top of which, I owe you one."

"You are a strange white man," said Little Wolf.

"I've heard it said," Slade granted. "Never understood the whole thing about color to begin with. Anyone I've ever met bleeds red, as far as I could tell."

"Strange," Little Wolf repeated, then lapsed into silence with his full attention on the trail.

An hour past midday, they found a campsite where the gang had stopped, after the Crawford raid. How long ago? Slade counted backward, figuring it would've been his fifth night in the hospital. He was six days behind them, knew they could be well across the line in Mexico by now and feeling safe from any lawful extradition.

Not that it would keep them safe from Slade.

The only saving grace, he calculated, would be if they'd dawdled in the territory for some reason, drifting, seeking other victims they could rob and murder. Slade felt like a ghoul, hoping they'd been distracted from escaping to the detriment of other innocents, and turned his mind back to the task of following his quarry.

There was nothing at the campsite but the old, cold ashes of a fire, and marks discernible to Little Wolf where horses had been tied up overnight. Apparently, their tracks were concentrated and the Cherokee could tell where they had grazed in darkness, while their riders slept around the fire. Nearby, a stream had furnished water for the campers and their animals.

"Tracks here," said Little Wolf, scouting the camp's perimeter.

Slade knelt beside him, squinting at the marks he would've overlooked if doing it alone. "That's going north," he said, surprised.

"And coming back," said Little Wolf, drawing attention to another trail that doubled back from northward. "Two men went that way, and then returned."

"Scouting," Slade said.

"Or hunting," Little Wolf suggested. "Who can say?"

Hunting for human targets, Slade supposed. A pair of scouts dispatched to scour the countryside, report back to the others on whatever they might find. Or maybe looking out for lawmen on their trail.

"The rest stayed here?" he asked.

"Two nights, at least," said Little Wolf. He sniffed the breeze and pointed to the east, where it was coming from. "They dug a pit for squatting, over there."

Slade couldn't smell it, didn't want to, but he felt a surge of hope. If Thornton and his friends had lingered two or three nights at the same spot, either lying low or hoping for an easy mark to come along, it nullified that portion of their lead. Reduced the time he'd have to spend pursuing them, if Little Wolf could find the trail they'd taken when they finally departed from the camp.

It gave him hope, an unaccustomed feeling since the morning he'd awakened in the hospital at Enid, to discover that he'd live and Faith might not.

"So, can you work out where they went from here?" Slade asked his guide.

Little Wolf stood before another line of tracks worn in the prairie grass. "This way," he said. "Southwest."

•   •   •

Sometime after noon, Thornton could only guess within an hour, Sabiano called a halt as they were passing by a low hill crowned with trees. They looked like sawtooth oaks, but Thornton wasn't interested enough to verify it.

"I been thinking," Sabiano said. "We ought to leave a guard behind, to see if anybody follows us."

The first thought up in Thornton's mind: *Jesus, not me! Pick someone else.*

"You reckon someone's trailin' us?" Wade Hampton asked.

"You may be sure of it," the Mexican replied. "How far behind, I cannot say."

"We should be makin' tracks, then," Charley Fox chimed in. "Not waitin' here to find out who shows up."

The smile on Sabiano's face reminded Thornton of a Gila monster's, smug and satisfied. "You're right," he said. "We will ride on. My thanks to you and Wade for volunteering to remain behind and watch."

"The hell you say!" Hampton replied.

"One night," said Sabiano, as if Wade had never spoken. "In the morning, if you see no posse, follow us."

"They haven't found us yet," Fox said, "and *now* we have to wait around for them?"

"I have a feeling," Sabiano said. "I've learned to trust it."

"It's your feeling," Hampton answered. "Why don't *you* stay here and wait?"

"Because I give the orders," Sabiano said, "and you do as you're told. Ho-kay?"

Fox shifted in his saddle, looking nervous now. He scanned the other faces, looking for a friend, then asked, "Why us, I'd like to know?"

"It must be someone," Sabiano answered. "Why not you?"

"Because it ain't fair," Fox replied. "We oughta vote."

"I vote already," Sabiano said. "For you and Wade."

"The hell are we supposed to do if someone *does* come by?" asked Hampton. "Two of us against this posse you're imagining."

"If I imagine it, there is no danger," Sabiano said.

"And no damn reason we should stay behind," said Hampton.

Still smiling, Sabiano said, "You wish to challenge me? Maybe you lead the outfit, eh?"

Wade blinked at that. "I didn't say—"

"You only have to kill me, first," said Sabiano, right hand resting on the curved butt of his pistol.

"Nobody said that!" Charley blurted out.

"Because you stay here, either way," the Mexican assured them. "Watching for our enemies or feeding worms."

"Hey, now," said Fox. "No call for anybody gettin' killed. We'll stay the night and watch out, like you say. Right, Wade?"

Hampton hung on a moment longer, then said, "Sure. Why not?"

"*Gracias*, amigos," Sabiano fairly sneered. "We see you both mañana, when you catch up."

Thornton avoided looking at the two men who were chosen to remain behind, half giddy with relief that he had not been picked as one of them. What were the odds that they'd remain on duty, once the gang was out of sight?

He didn't know and didn't care.

What mattered now was that the group was headed south, and there'd be two fewer pairs of eyes to catch him sneaking off, if he decided it was best to try his luck alone. Nothing but good news, this time, and it made a welcome change.

Still, damn near anything could happen on their way to Mexico. They had to eat, which meant obtaining food somewhere, and *that* meant raiding in their leader's mind. He

never paid for anything that could be stolen, never hesitated
when he saw a so-called easy job.

That would mean trouble, and as far as Thornton knew,
there was no dearth of lawmen in the Lone Star State. Or
hanging trees, for that matter. The judge in Enid might've
wired the Texas Rangers to be watching out for Sabiano and
his crew, if they had been identified. That could mean
bounty hunters, too, if word got out and there was a reward
offered.

More worries smothering his moment of relief, leaving
Thornton to wonder if his life would be this way until its
bitter end. Jumping at shadows, watching for the one that
had a badge and warrant, or an itchy trigger finger.

It beat the other option, though, he thought.

At least a worried man knew he was still alive.

Slade caught another break, four hours after taking up the
trail from where his quarry had apparently spent two or three
days at their ease, lolling around like they were on vacation,
sending parties out to scout the territory while the rest
remained at ease. It was another camp, twenty-odd miles from
the preceding one—and once again, Slade's guide detected
evidence of riders spending more than one night on the spot.

Elated and confused at the same time, Slade asked the
question that was troubling him. "What are they thinking?
Seven killings that we know of and they drag their heels
like no one's even looking for them."

"Nobody's found them," Little Wolf reminded him.

"You're right. Damn it! Instead of running, they sit still
and let the hunt just pass them by," Slade said.

It showed more brains than he had given Thornton and
the others credit for. Maybe they knew Judge Dennison had
only half a dozen full-time deputies to cover all the territory
under his domain. Each marshal rode circuit over something

close to twelve thousand square miles. About the size of Maryland, that was. Taken in those terms, Slade supposed it was a miracle that any fugitives were ever found, at all.

His momentary anger past, Slade said, "Okay. Where did they go from here?"

"Sent riders out in all directions, like before," said Little Wolf. "But when they left together, all went south."

"They're tired of Oklahoma," Slade surmised. "Looking for something new."

"Or old," the Cherokee suggested.

"Right," Slade said. Old Mexico.

They would be safe there, legally, from extradition to the States. The government led by Porfirio Díaz since 1884, with no end yet in sight, maintained an ironclad policy of shielding fugitives from trial in other countries. If they watched their step in Mexico and, some said, greased the wheels of so-called justice with *mordida,* the traditional payoffs to Mexican authorities, they should be free and clear.

Texas Rangers sometimes crossed the Rio Grande without authority, Slade knew, and Mexicans sometimes returned the favor, as when they'd ambushed Old Man Clanton's rustling gang at Guadalupe Canyon, Arizona, back in 'eighty-one. Such incidents produced saber-rattling in Washington and Mexico City, but the border still leaked like a sieve.

Slade hoped he wouldn't have to cross it to complete his task, but if it came to that . . . why not? In his mind, there should be no sanctuary for a murderer.

If necessary, he would chase Burch Thornton and his cronies through the gates of Hell.

"He's got a goddamn nerve," said Charley Fox, aiming a brown stream of tobacco juice into the weeds.

Wade Hampton didn't have to ask which "he" Fox had in mind. Charley had been cursing Sabiano since the gang rode out of earshot, hours earlier, and showed no sign of letting up on it. Of course, he'd stopped miles short of challenging the Mexican when they were all together, but he talked a good fight now.

"Hey, you don't want to wait," said Hampton, not for the first time, "we can take off."

"And go where?" Charley asked him.

"Mexico," Hampton replied.

"Where *he's* going," said Fox.

"You ever been to Mexico?" asked Hampton, wondering if Fox had slipped a cog or two upstairs. "It's big. No reason we should ever see him, if we hang around down there a hunnerd years."

"You kiddin' me?" Fox asked. "Bastard would track us down in nothin' flat."

"How do you figure that?" Hampton inquired. "First, if we don't join up with him again, he'll never know if we stayed here or not. Second, he obviously doesn't give a damn about us, or he wouldn't leave us here."

"He'll know," Fox said.

"And third," Hampton pressed on, "how would he ever find us down in Mexico, for Christ's sake? What, you think he's gonna spend the next ten years ridin' around from town to town, lookin' for *us*?"

"He might," said Fox.

"You're loco, Charley."

"Yeah? So, why'n't you pull on him?" Fox asked.

"Because I didn't feel like dyin'," Hampton answered. "Sabiano's fast, okay? Faster than you'n me together. That don't mean he can see the whole damn world from where he stands."

"Hell, I know that," said Fox. "But he's a *Mexican*."

"So, what? You think they all know one another?" Hampton snorted. "God, that's dumb."

"I ain't dumb!" Charley snapped at him.

"Stop actin' like it, then," said Hampton. "Sabiano's just a man, all right? He puts his pants on one leg at a time, like anybody else."

"Don't be so sure," Fox said.

"You seen him jump into 'em from a standing start?"

"Forget about his goddamn pants. I just don't want to run afoul of him and wind up gettin' kilt," Fox said.

"It comes to that," Hampton replied, "I think the two of us could take him, if we play it right."

"One of them special rifles," Fox suggested, "that can shoot afar off."

"Well, we don't have none of those," Hampton reminded him.

"I know it."

"But he only wears one pistol," Hampton added.

"It's been all he needs, as far as I recall," Fox said.

"You ever seen him shoot against two men at once?"

"Those guys in Abilene," said Fox.

"But they were drunk and standin' right together," Hampton said. "My point is that he can't shoot two directions at the same time."

"Uh-huh. So, we split up, you're sayin'."

"That's the ticket," Hampton granted. "If we's far enough apart—"

"Then *maybe* only one of us gets kilt," said Fox, completing Hampton's thought. "I'm guessin' you don't wanna volunteer for that part, do you, Wade?"

"I grant you it's a gamble, but I'm talkin' hyperthetical," said Hampton. "It'd only come to that if we run into him, which I think is about as likely as a burro singin' 'Dixie.' *If* we meet him, *and* he wants to fight us, *then* we try what I'm suggestin'. Come to that, what have we got to lose?"

"Just ever'thing," said Fox. "To Hell with it. You still got any whiskey left?"

"I might," Fox said, knowing he did, in fact, have close

to half a bottle of Old Grand-Dad in his saddlebag. "Just let me look and see."

He fetched the bottle back and took a sip himself, before he passed it on to Fox. No point in losing out, if Charley started sucking down the liquor double-quick, to drown his nerves.

"Go easy on it," Hampton urged. "No tellin' when we'll have a chance to get some more."

"Don't be a skinflint," Fox replied. "Ain't like you paid for it."

Fox had him, there. Hampton had swiped the bottle from a place they'd visited before Burch Thornton wheedled Sabiano into going on a raid against the spread where he'd been fired for one thing or another. Stupid idea that turned out to be, though Hampton guessed that they'd be hunted just the same for something else, the way they carried on.

Not that the law had caught a whiff of them, so far as he could tell. Give Sabiano credit for the fact that they were still alive and free, even if he and Fox were left behind to buy time for the rest.

"How's this?" asked Fox, after another gulp of whiskey. "We stay here till sundown, like he told us, then ride south instead of waitin' for the morning. Find a place to camp ourselves, and take our own time ridin' south tomorrow?"

"Sounds all right," said Hampton, "if we don't run into Sabiano and the others in the dark."

"They'll have a fire, won't they?" asked Fox.

"Guess so," Hampton agreed.

"Then, we can spot 'em way off. No nasty surprises."

"That ain't bad," Hampton acknowledged. "Count me in."

"Awright, then. It's a plan."

Hampton looked north, a habit he'd developed since they'd been assigned to watch the trail, but this time he saw more than just a blank horizon in the distance.

"Shit!"

"What is it?" Fox demanded.

"Riders," Hampton told him. "Comin' this way."

Fox lowered the bottle, squinting till he spotted them. "You don't suppose . . . ?"

"I don't suppose a damned thing," Hampton said. "Gimme that bottle back and grab your Winchester."

11

Jack Slade eyed the western sky with trepidation, knowing they would lose daylight within another hour, at most. They'd made good progress, gaining ground on Thornton and his cohorts, but that only amplified Slade's disappointment as the day wound down and they were forced to seek another campsite.

He and Little Wolf likely could cover five or six more miles before full darkness overtook them, but by pushing it that far they ran the risk of a dry camp without forage for their animals.

Seeming to read his mind, the Cherokee pointed ahead and to their left, toward a hill with trees on top of it, and said, "We should camp there."

Slade knew that he was right but had to ask, "You think so? If we ride a little farther—"

"Trees mean water, shelter," Little Wolf declared. "High ground means farther looking, now and after dark."

That was a point. He'd thought about the gang stopping to camp again, maybe taking their time, and knew they'd have a fire to cook whatever food they carried with them.

On the open plains, if it was large enough and they were just a little careless, Slade or Little Wolf might spot it from a distance.

With a light to guide by, they could creep in through the darkness, as they had with Marlene Dalton's kidnappers. There were no hostages to hamper them this time, however. Clean shots all around, assuming Thornton's friends preferred to shoot it out. Catching the gang asleep would be a bonus, any way Slade looked at it.

Or, if the fire was too far distant, they could trek on through the night and try to reach it as the outlaws woke. Slade didn't mind tiring the horses, knew they'd have to hold an easy walking pace once it was dark, regardless. He could go thirsty himself, letting his roan drink up the water that was left in his canteen, if it meant catching Thornton and the others sleepy-eyed and clumsy.

They would resist, of course. Eight or nine men against himself and Little Wolf—who wouldn't? They were proven killers, had to know that they were marked for hanging if they rode his dust to Enid and a trial before Judge Dennison. What would they have to lose by putting up resistance?

Slade was counting on it.

All he needed, once the smoke cleared, was a statement from his guide that they'd used only necessary force. Judge Dennison might doubt him, might even relieve Slade of his badge, but he could never prove a murder charge without a witness for the other side. And if it meant returning to his old life, gambling for his keep, what did it matter?

Without Faith . . .

Of course, there was another way the confrontation might turn out. Two against eight or nine was lousy odds. There was a fair chance he'd be killed, and Little Wolf along with him, although the Cherokee had proved himself a natural survivor. In the last analysis, Slade wasn't all that sure it mattered whether he survived or not. What was the point of

riding back to Enid with a string of prisoners in tow, to learn
that Faith had died while he was gone? Or that her eyes
would never open on the world again, and she would stay
as he had left her, dreaming God knew what in darkness?

"So?" asked Little Wolf.

"You're right," Slade said. "I doubt we'll find a better
place before we lose the light."

"Jesus, they're turnin' this way!" Charley said.

Watching the riders over rifle sights, Hampton confirmed
the observation. He asked Fox, "You think they seen our
tracks turn off?"

"Don't make no sense," Charley replied. "Why not go on
after the others, if they're readin' sign?"

"In their place, I'd think two was easier than six," said
Hampton.

"Big mistake," Fox said. Despite their situation, though,
he sounded something less than confident.

"It's gettin' on toward night," said Hampton. "Maybe
they're just—"

"Damn! Is that'n on the left an Injun?" Charley asked.

"Hell if I know," Hampton replied. "He ain't wearin' a
hat, but—"

"Get an Injun on your trail, he won't give up unless you
kill 'im," Charley said.

"Suits me," said Hampton, as he cocked the hammer on
his Winchester model 1876. He stole the gun from a
sodbuster outside El Paso. Guy didn't need it anymore, after
Hampton—

"It *is* an Injun!" Charley blurted out. "You see 'im?"

"Maybe. Makes no difference," said Hampton. "Red or
white, they're both as good as dead."

But still, he had to wonder why a red man would be trailing them. Unless . . .

The reservation! Damn it all to Hell!

An image of a bloody scalping knife flashed into Hampton's mind and made his stomach churn.

"Goddamn it, Wade," said Fox. "They seen our tracks as plain as day."

"Don't wet yourself," Hampton advised. "Tracks tell 'em someone passed this way. Last thing they'll ever know."

"We shoulda left as soon as Sabiano and the rest—"

"You wanna run, get started," Hampton said. "Go on and draw their fire while I take care of 'em."

"Hey, now—"

"Whatever you decide, *shut up* and let me concentrate!"

Fox muttered something else, but Hampton didn't catch it. He was focused on the two horsemen approaching their position, still more than a hundred yards away. A rifle slug would kill at that range, Hampton knew, but whether he could put it in the bull's-eye was another question altogether.

Frankly, he had doubts.

At fifty yards, now, where a man took proper form and you could make out features on his face, that was a different story. Hampton was fairly certain of a hit at fifty yards, and if you hit a man with the Winchester '76 he'd know it. The .50-95 Express would put him down, and no mistake.

One clean shot's all I need, he thought.

At his elbow, Charley Fox kept talking to himself, a steady stream of whispering that Hampton couldn't translate, loud enough to fray his nerves without communicating anything.

"For Christ's sake, Charley, will you just—"

Fox fired, whether by accident or simply running out of patience, Hampton couldn't tell. He obviously jerked the trigger, missed both riders altogether, though their horses flinched and shied from the gunshot.

Instead of cursing, Hampton squeezed his rifle's trigger,

knew before the butt recoiled against his shoulder that the shot was wasted. He'd been aiming for the maybe Indian and likely didn't come within a yard of him. The first of eleven rounds gone, and the target was breaking away to his right, Hampton's left, speeding up from a trot to a gallop in no time at all.

There was no point in cursing Charley for his foolishness. What mattered now was sticking with the rider, dropping him—or, anyway, his animal—before he circled out of range.

"Goin' around behind us!" Charley shouted, as if Hampton wasn't lying right beside his dumb ass on the hilltop. Firing two more rapid shots with no result except the ringing noise they made in Hampton's ears.

"I missed him, Wade!" Fox whined.

And Hampton, thinking, *Tell me something that I* don't *know,* answering back, "Get after him, you dunderhead, before he comes around and shoots you in the ass!"

The first shot passed between Jack Slade and Little Wolf with room to spare on either side, long gone before Slade heard the rifle's crack and felt his mare react. He saw the puff of smoke beneath the hilltop oaks and broke off to his left, the only way to go with Little Wolf beside him on the right.

Divide the targets, hoping for the best.

More shots, as they rode off in opposite directions, but it didn't pay to think about them. Slade's roan hit her stride within a few yards, while he hunched over the saddle horn to minimize his profile. There were definitely two guns firing now, a big-bore and a smaller weapon, but a bullet's size was less important than its placement.

If the shooters couldn't hit him, he was good. If one of them turned out to be a trick-shot artist, good with moving

targets, he would likely knock Slade from his saddle well
before Slade stretched the range.

Where was he going, anyway?

There was no decent cover anywhere within Slade's line
of sight, except the hilltop that the snipers had staked out.
Smart thinking on their part—or someone else's, if the pair
of them were left behind to guard the trail, while others
slipped away.

Was Thornton one of them?

Slade wouldn't know him if they passed each other on
the street, but he and Little Wolf were under fire from *someone* in the gang they had been tracking. Simple travelers
might warn strangers away, but it required a hard sort to
start shooting from a distance without any sort of call.

No chance of taking them alive, unless they both ran out
of ammunition, and the rate of firing from the hilltop didn't
indicate that either man was overly concerned about a short-
age. If they kept it up and put enough slugs in the air, one
of them might get lucky with an accidental hit. Slade heard
the bullets sizzle past him, braced himself for impact, but
it didn't come.

A little farther and the shooter tracking him would have
to change positions, find another angle through the trees
that occupied the hilltop. Any break at all was welcome,
and if Slade could take advantage of it, time his movements
properly, it could be all the edge he needed.

Or he might just die in the attempt.

Same chance he'd taken in a dozen other fights, when
standing still and fighting face-to-face wasn't an option.
Another thirty, forty yards around the north side of the hill,
and he'd be covered long enough to try the move he had in
mind.

Somewhere behind him, Slade heard Little Wolf's
Sharps carbine slam a shot in the direction of their enemies.

How likely was it that he'd score a hit while galloping full tilt and under fire? Slade didn't have a clue but wished him luck.

And suddenly, there was a break in firing from the hill, toward Slade. Whether the enemy had lost his line of sight or simply needed to reload, Slade took advantage of the lull and swung his marc in toward the tree-topped rise. It might turn out to be a trick, the worst mistake he'd ever made, but Slade would never find out if he didn't try.

He was committed now and riding like his life depended on it.

Which, in fact, it did.

Wade Hampton fired a third shot at the rider racing to his left and missed again, cursing a blue streak as he pumped the lever action on his Winchester and tried to lead the moving target for a hit. If he could just . . .

His rifle's barrel slapped against the rough trunk of the sawtooth oak that sheltered him, made Hampton jerk the trigger in surprise, and there went number four, another total waste.

"Goddamn it all to Hell!" he raged, half rising from the ground where he'd been lying prone and scrambling to the far side of the oak, seeking a better shot.

And there were more trees in the way, of course. He ducked around them, stumbling where their roots rose from eroded soil like thick, dark snakes, and nearly fell flat on his face. Hampton could hear his own pulse in his ears, a drumbeat loud and fast enough to make him feel as if his skull was going to explode.

It was his own fault, Hampton realized. The whole damned thing. He should have waited, let the targets close to forty yards, or even thirty, where it would've been almost impossible to miss. They'd both be lying dead right now, instead of galloping around the hill to find a sneaky angle of attack.

And who in Hell *were* they?

An Indian, and—what? Wade thought he'd seen the glint of fading sunlight on a badge the other rider wore, but it could just as easily have been a button or some kind of optical illusion. What if these two hombres weren't pursuing Sabiano's gang at all?

Just wonderful, thought Hampton. *Start a fight for nothin', and I end up gettin' kilt.*

But he was still alive and kicking, still had seven .50-95 Express rounds in his Winchester, a bandolier with thirty more across his chest, before he had to pull his Schofield .45 and go to work with that. Hell, if he couldn't drop one man with all that firepower, Hampton wasn't convinced that he deserved to live.

Which didn't mean that he was lying down and giving up.

Oh, no. Not even close.

Mistake or not, he meant to walk away from this melee in one piece. Maybe even laugh about it later, when he'd had enough to drink.

But at the moment, all that mattered was a clean shot at his enemy. And Hampton wouldn't get one stumbling around like he was drunk or addlepated. Do it right, the best way he knew how, and go help Fox deal with his Indian.

Hampton regained his footing, made it through the trees—and gaped in dull surprise to see his adversary's roan running across the flat ground down below him with an empty saddle. Had he hit the rider after all, not realizing it? First thing, he had to double back and locate where he'd fallen. Find out if he'd need another shot to finish it.

Retreating, Hampton found a break between the trees and cleared it, dropping to a half crouch with his Winchester in front of him, ready for anything.

Except the shot that struck the tree trunk to his left, spraying his face with jagged shards of bark. His left eye burned as if someone had slipped a red-hot coal beneath its lid, then he was sprawling over backward, cursing, triggering a wild shot toward the sky.

Little Wolf fired one round from his carbine to distract the sniper who was trying clumsily to kill him, knowing that the shot would miss. He judged the man to be a coward, hiding in the shadows, hoping for an easy kill. Such men were easily intimidated, even when they seemed to have the upper hand.

Reloading was a problem, since he carried extra ammunition in a buckskin pouch, slapping against his hip, and Little Wolf already had his hands full with his carbine and the tobiano's reins. It hardly mattered, though, as long as he could dodge the next few shots and find a safe place to dismount, then close and meet his enemy on foot.

The blast of his .52-caliber weapon had the desired effect, forcing his would-be killer down and back, seeking more cover from the hilltop oaks. It was the best that Little Wolf could hope for, in the circumstances, and he took advantage of it, hissing to his horse and kicking lightly with his heels, urging the animal to greater speed.

Another crack sounded behind him, as the rifleman regained sufficient nerve to fire again, but that shot missed him by at least six feet. A pitiful attempt. The smile on Little Wolf's lean face was wicked, predatory, as his tobiano carried him around the east side of the tree-crowned hill, while veering closer to its base.

He chose the moment, unencumbered by a saddle and its stirrups as he leaped free and hit the ground running, trusting the horse to return when he called. *If* he called. There was no guarantee he'd survive, but contempt for the cowardly white man inspired Little Wolf in his sprint toward the hilltop.

Free-handed now, he reloaded the carbine by pulling its trigger guard down and then forward, to open the breech. Removing the spent brass, he fed a fresh cartridge into the weapon and snapped the breech shut without breaking his stride.

And he had nearly reached the hill before another shot rang out, raising a puff of dust a foot or so behind him. Motivated by the near miss, Little Wolf propelled himself upslope with longer strides, angling his carbine toward the spot where gun smoke hung between the trees.

No target yet, but he was getting closer. When the sniper showed himself again . . .

More firing from the far side of the hill, where Slade was after his man, but there was no time to think about the law-man now. Distraction of his enemy was good, but Little Wolf could not afford to let his own mind wander, if he meant to live and fight another day.

Two gunmen on the hill, if they were even from the same gang he and Slade were tracking, meant at least six more still riding southward, confident that they could get away with killing Strong Horse and the whites they'd murdered since the reservation raid. If Little Wolf lived through the next few minutes, he would do his level best to prove them wrong.

When he had almost reached the trees, the sniper rose to take another shot. Little Wolf dropped to one knee where he was, the Sharps already at his shoulder as he squeezed its trigger and rode the heavy recoil, squinting through its smoke.

He saw the heavy bullet strike his target, crimson mist enveloping the gunman as he fell. No hurry now, as Little Wolf reloaded, rose, and went to stand over the dying man.

His adversary was beyond pain now. Too bad.

He would return and claim the gunman's weapons later.
Now, he had to find Jack Slade.

Slade stumbled on his dismount, took a spill, and later calculated that it may have saved his life. Facedown on grass,
he heard a bullet whistle through the air three feet or so
above him, right around groin-level if he had been standing
when it passed.

Dumb luck, but Slade would take what he could get.

In answer to that shot, he triggered two rounds from the
rifle he'd grabbed as he jumped from his roan. He saw the
bullets strike one of the big sawtooth oaks, spraying rough
shards of bark, his human target rolling back and out of sight
behind the tree.

Slade used the time to rise and rush the hilltop, levering
another round into the rifle's chamber as he ran. It might
have been the time to give a shout, identify himself, but
since the shooter hadn't been concerned with who he tried
to kill, Slade didn't care to give away his edge. There was
already risk enough, he thought, of being followed by the
sound his running footsteps made or by his heavy breathing
as he ran.

Almost before that thought took shape, Slade's enemy
reared up before him, leveling a rifle from the hip. Slade
shot him on the run, seeing the bullet strike a little high and
wide of center, but it did the job and put the target down. A
moment later, Slade stood over him, kicking the sniper's
Winchester away, plucking the six-gun from his holster, and
discarding it. A long knife followed, from the left side of
his belt, leaving the wounded man unarmed.

Slade knelt beside him, watched the gunman's eyes swim
into focus from their first glimpse of oblivion, and asked
him, "What's your name?"

"Whyn't you go to Hell?" the sniper rasped.

"You're dying," Slade advised him. "Nothing to be done about it, now. The only choice that's left to you is how you finish up."

The prostrate man considered it, then said, "Hampton. Wade Hampton."

"Pleased to meet you, Wade."

"The Mex was right, I guess," said Hampton.

"Oh? What Mex is that?"

The downed man made a sound that could've passed for strangled laughter or a ragged cough, leaving his lips bloodstained.

"You don't know Sabiano? Jesus, that's a corker."

"What about Burch Thornton?" Slade demanded. "Was he riding with you?"

"Thornton, yeah. That little shit. All his fault."

"What is?" Slade inquired

"Talked Sabiano into helping him settle a score."

"Is he still riding with you?"

"Left us here to watch," the shooter said, his mind starting to drift. "Damnation."

"Doesn't seem entirely fair," Slade said. "Where were they headed? I can tell them you're displeased."

"South," said Hampton, gurgling deep inside his throat. "The Mex is goin' home."

"And Thornton with him?"

"All of 'em together."

"Any place particular?" asked Slade.

"Just south. Old Mexico."

"I'll give them your regards," Slade said, but he was talking to himself.

He heard a soft footfall, turning as Little Wolf approached. Slade rose to face him, said, "He talked enough for me to know we're on the right track. Somebody named Sabiano's taking the remainder of them down to Mexico."

"We follow them?" asked Little Wolf.

Slade nodded. "That's the plan."

"Camp here," the Cherokee suggested. "Leave at first light, with the extra guns and horses."

"Suits me," Slade said. "But first, let's drag this fellow and his buddy off the hill. No telling what might come around to visit them, tonight."

12

Burch Thornton thought that Texas looked and smelled a lot like Oklahoma. Pretty much the same landscape, so far. Same hot sun beating down on him as Sabiano's outfit moseyed south, the Mex taking his time.

Still, it was progress. Thornton understood the logic of proceeding at a normal pace instead of killing off the horses in a headlong gallop toward the Rio Grande. Aside from winding up on foot, he knew they'd draw attention from the sodbusters and any lawmen in the general vicinity, which was the last thing any of them needed at the moment.

Good news: they were out of Oklahoma Territory, headed in the right direction, and he hoped that any U.S. marshals fielded by Judge Dennison, from Enid, would be busy looking for them somewhere in the panhandle. Lord knew they'd left enough dead bodies to distract the judge's deputies.

But if man hunters cut their trail . . .

Bad news. The federals weren't bound by any certain jurisdiction, Thornton understood. If motivated, they could track you anywhere in the United States, push local lawmen to the side and do whatever struck their fancy, more or less.

Did any marshals in the territory care enough to take the hunt that far?

Maybe.

Of course, Thornton had known about Faith Connover's engagement to Jack Slade, one of the deputies in Enid, and he guessed it must've been their wedding that the raid had interrupted. Not his plan, but ruining her special day had been a kind of consolation prize, for missing what he'd really had in mind.

Slade, now, might be one who would track him until Hell froze over, if Judge Dennison couldn't restrain him—or he didn't care to. Thornton hadn't seen the judge among the wedding celebrants, but Christ, what if he was? Between them, Dennison and Slade could write his death warrant.

Unless he made it safely into Mexico.

One thing Burch Thornton knew about the laws of the United States: they ended at the border. No one could pursue him, once he'd ridden, walked, or crawled across the line into Old Mexico.

At least, not legally.

If Slade had made it personal, all bets were off. He had a scary reputation, but a lot of that could be the kind of talk you heard around saloons, with nothing to it. Anyway, while Thornton only knew a couple of the border towns in Mexico from personal experience, he had a mental image of a country half the size of the U.S., stretching away to South America if he went all the way.

And why stop there? Hell, he could keep on riding south until he came around the far side of the world, presumably, or hit an ocean were he had to board a ship. Slade wouldn't chase him *that* far.

No one would.

He thought of Fox and Hampton, covering the trail, and wondered how long they'd remained in place once Sabiano and the others had retreated out of sight. Suppose they stood watch through the night, as ordered, but nobody came along. Were Wade and Charley following the gang right now, still honor bound to Sabiano when the Mex had likely put them out of mind completely?

He'd have to wait and see.

Meanwhile, Thornton took off his hat and sleeved a gleam of perspiration from his forehead. He was tired of riding, but he knew they couldn't rest until they'd crossed the line.

And maybe it was just as well.

In Mexico, he'd definitely split with Sabiano, even if he had to creep off in the middle of a moonless night to manage it. Get lost among the people down there and the other gringo drifters. Hone his skill with Spanish until he could pass—and then, what?

Live his life, what else?

And hope he didn't have to spend it all looking over his shoulder, jumping at shadows.

But even that beat being dead.

Slade couldn't say exactly when they'd crossed from Oklahoma Territory into Texas, but he guessed it must have been around four hours after breaking camp. If they'd been farther east, he would've known because they'd have had to cross the Red River, but coming from the panhandle, they'd reach that later, followed by the Brazos and the Colorado on their way to Mexico.

Landmarks, if they were forced to go that far.

He'd listened to coyotes working on the two dead outlaws overnight, during his turn on watch, but didn't let it faze him. Dead was dead, and Slade reserved his sympathy for innocents.

Assuming anybody qualified in that regard.

The trail they followed had veered off a bit to the

southwest, but that made perfect sense. It was the shortest way to reach the Rio Grande, where the river curved northward between Del Rio and Boquillas. Thornton's crew—or Sabiano's, as he now considered it—would likely steer away from Langtry, where Roy Bean dispensed a rough-and-ready kind of justice as it suited him, but there were ample opportunities for river crossings up and down the line.

They were making decent time, but it still wasn't good enough to satisfy Slade. Calculating that five hundred miles of open territory lay between them and the border, it could be eight to ten days before they reached the Rio Grande, depending on their circumstances. Maybe half that, if they decided it was safe to push their horses during thirteen-hour days.

And all for nothing if they lost the trail somewhere along the way.

Slade trusted Little Wolf, had every confidence in his ability to track the gang, but he was only human. The terrain or weather might defeat them, or the gang might fall apart and leave trails leading off in all directions, forcing Slade to choose a path and sacrifice his chance of catching all of them together.

Unacceptable.

But he would have to play the cards as they were dealt to him.

In a perfect world, he would've found them all on day one and returned them to Judge Dennison for trial. No, scratch that. In a *truly* perfect world, he'd be a married man who'd never heard Burch Thornton's name, or Sabiano's, letting a late breakfast settle, trying to convince Faith they could use a bit more time in bed.

So much for perfect worlds. Instead, an arid stretch of Texas lay before him, with a line of tracks that seemed uncomfortably faint this morning. It would only take a cloudburst or a sandstorm to erase them, and his long ride would've been for nothing. Thornton and the rest would pass beyond his reach, maybe forever.

But it wouldn't stop him looking for them. Since they'd robbed him of the life he'd planned, what other use did Slade have for his time? If Little Wolf got tired of it and left him, he could keep on just the same. Sooner or later, Slade would find them all.

If he survived that long.

And if he didn't . . . well, maybe he'd find a way to stalk them from the grave.

It was 11:35, by Slade's watch, when he saw a plume of smoke on the horizon, off to the southeast of Sabiano's trail. He guessed that it was ten or fifteen miles away, at least, and could be anything. A farmer burning off a stubble field, for instance, or a wildfire on the open plain.

No reason it should be a homestead. None at all.

The track they were pursuing didn't deviate. In fact, its course was leading them away from where the fire was, nothing to suggest that Sabiano's gang had struck again, so far away and in the opposite direction.

Little Wolf sat watching him, as Slade decided. "No point going off that way," Slade said, "unless you think we're on the wrong trail, where we are."

"Same trail," the Cherokee assured him. "There has been no other."

The fire was someone else's problem. He would leave it to the Texas Rangers, local lawmen, or the marshals working for the federal court in Austin. Slade had business of his own to deal with, and he didn't feel like taking time away from it for someone else's. Knowing Texans, they wouldn't appreciate his meddling, anyway.

Skirting Paloduro, trailing Sabiano as the gang gave it a wide berth, Slade and Little Wolf reached the Red River's

Prairie Dog Town Fork a little past noon. It was a sandy-
braided stream, no trouble crossing it on horseback if they took
their time and gave the animals a chance to feel the current,
working with it, resting briefly on the southern bank and only
doubling back a hundred yards or so to find the outlaws' trail.

Not bad.

If they pushed onward until dusk, they should be somewhere east of Lubbock when they stopped to set up camp,
a good day's progress overall. Slade hadn't seen his other
targets yet, but he was on the right track and convinced that
he could overtake them, given time.

His wounds no longer bothered him, to speak of. Twinges
when he mounted or dismounted, maybe turning this or that
way in his bedroll, but they hadn't hampered him with
Sabiano's watchdogs, yesterday. Slade viewed the ambush
as a test, and he had passed it.

Now, Slade figured he was ready for the main event.

An hour past the river, long since dry beneath the Texas
sun, Slade heard his guide say, "Riders coming." Looking
up, he followed Little Wolf's gaze to the east.

The dust was coming their way, didn't seem to change at
all in size or shape, which told Slade they were standing
more or less directly in the path of the approaching horsemen. They were still a couple of miles away, but riding hard,
the way it looked. With nothing that resembled decent cover
anywhere close by, Slade weighed his options.

"We could kill the horses trying to outrun them," he told
Little Wolf, thinking aloud. "And why should we be running, anyway?"

"Texas," the Cherokee replied, as if that answered
everything.

"You've got a point," Slade said. "My badge should carry
some weight, even if they're on the prod."

"You hope to reason with them," Little Wolf responded,
sounding skeptical.

"It's worth a try," Slade said. "But just in case."

He drew the lever-action shotgun from its saddle boot, choosing the twelve gauge over his rifle for work at close quarters. One buckshot round in the chamber and five more in the tubular magazine meant Slade could fill the air with forty-two double-ought pellets within a matter of seconds, each one the size of a .33-caliber bullet. The twenty-inch barrel would give a fair spread beyond ten feet or so, and he still had the Colt for backup, if it came down to that.

Resting the Winchester across his lap, Slade watched the dust cloud drawing closer, rolling like a freak sandstorm across the open plain.

The riders reached them five minutes later, slowing into the last quarter mile and reining to a halt when they were still some thirty feet from where Slade sat with Little Wolf, astride their animals. Slade counted seven men before their dust caught up with them and started settling. Two of them were wearing Texas Ranger badges, dull rings with a star cut in the center, while the rest wore scowls as symbols of presumed authority.

One of the sweaty civilians, farthest to the left from where Slade sat, spoke up to say, "A white man with a red-skin. You don't see that ever'day."

"Look closer, Deacon," said the older of the rangers. "White-un's got a badge."

"A by-God U.S. marshal," said the second ranger. He was five years younger than the other, give or take, but had a world of mileage on his long, thin face.

"The redskin ain't his prisoner," said Deacon. He was short and heavyset, with a mustache displaying what he'd had for breakfast. "Otherwise, he wouldn't have that Sharps."

"You fellows want to speak with us, or sit and talk about us?" Slade inquired. "If it's the latter, we'll be on our way."

"You got a name?" the older ranger asked.

"Sure do," Slade said, and left it there.

The ranger bit back what he meant to say and took a breath to calm himself. "Do you mind sharing it?" he asked.

"You first," Slade said. "The only name I've heard so far is Deacon, and he doesn't look like anyone who'd represent a church."

"Hey, now!" Deacon leaned forward in his saddle, putting on his best mean face. "You want to watch that mouth."

"Do I?" Slade asked. He let the shotgun's muzzle drift toward Deacon, sorry that he couldn't spare the blowhard's Appaloosa from the spray of buckshot, if he had to fire.

"Hold on!" the older ranger interjected. "Let's cool down a minute, here. My name's Elijah Pool. As you can see"—he raised a hand to tap the tin star on his shirt—"I'm with the Texas Rangers. This," he added, nodding to his left, "is Ranger Brett Favor."

Slade scanned the other faces in the line and asked, "The rest?"

"Our posse," Pool replied. "We're tracking a Comanche raiding party, hit a couple homesteads east of here, the past two days."

"We haven't seen them," Slade replied, then introduced himself. "Jack Slade. I'm down from Oklahoma with my guide, chasing a gang of renegades headed for Mexico."

"Your *guide*?" another of the posse members echoed. "You kiddin' me?"

"It never crossed my mind," Slade answered.

"So, these renegades of yorn," the second ranger said. "They anybody we might know of?"

"I've got four names for the seven of them," Slade replied. "Burch Thornton, Tommy Garrity, Joe Weems, and one with half a name. A Mexican called Sabiano."

"I know Sabiano," Pool informed him. "Heard about 'im,

anyhow. Mean hombre, way the stories tell it. Kill you soon as look at you."

"He's killed a few, up our way," Slade conceded.

"And the two of you are goin' after seven?" Favor asked, sounding amused.

"We started after nine," Slade said. "It's seven now."

"You'n the Injun," said another of the posse members.

"We're running just a bit behind," Slade told him. "Had to stop and kill another bunch of five, along the way. It slowed us down a little."

The whole line shifted restlessly, a few of them exchanging nervous looks. "Well, we won't keep you from it, then," said Ranger Pool. "If you should see those Indians we're lookin' for . . ."

"We'll keep our eyes peeled," Slade replied. "Good hunting to you."

"And to you," Pool said. Then, to his men, "Come on. We're burnin' daylight."

Slade and Little Wolf sat watching as the posse rode away westward, then resumed their journey south.

Another camp, but this time they were only staying overnight, so Thornton didn't mind. They had to stop sometime, couldn't just keep on riding through the dark and risk laming their horses. Still, he felt a sense of urgency, wished they were closer to the Rio Grande or well across it, into Mexico.

There'd been no sign of Fox or Hampton all day long, and Sabiano didn't seem to miss them. Whether he assumed they had run off or maybe stumbled into trouble, he said nothing on the subject. Didn't seem to spare the missing men a solitary thought.

Good news for Thornton, when he finally decided it was time to quit the gang. He wouldn't go while they were still in Texas, but their first night on the far side of the border, when they'd reached the town that Sabiano talked about. What was its name?

Something with water in it. Agua Verde? Agua Fria? Never mind.

By any name, it would provide enough distraction for the others that they wouldn't give a second thought to Thornton. Likely wouldn't even miss him the next morning, when they were all crapulous and laid up with their *putas*. He could have a good head start, and if they never got around to looking for him after all, so much the better.

If a man couldn't get lost in Mexico, he wasn't really trying.

Sabiano had him fetching firewood, which was good. It gave Thornton a chance to think about a life in Mexico, and how he might support himself. He wasn't much on working, never had been, but he'd find something to do. And if it started going stale on him, well, there was nothing to prevent him heading west into the territories. Try his luck where no one knew him, in New Mexico or Arizona, maybe ride on through the both of them to California and take a gander at the ocean.

Sure. Why not?

One skill he'd mastered was the art of putting problems out of mind. As long as Thornton knew no one was searching for him, that his wanted posters hadn't circulated too far outside Oklahoma Territory, he could let himself relax. And if, by chance, he ran into a U.S. marshal somewhere down the road, he'd see what happened next.

Backshooting was a thought that came to mind.

It made Burch Thornton smile.

"So, how close are we, do you think?" Slade asked across the campfire.

"Two, maybe three days," said Little Wolf. "Unless they stop again."

"They'll beat us to the border, then."

The Cherokee considered it and nodded. "I think, yes."

"Have to decide whether you want to cross it with me, then," said Slade.

Little Wolf shrugged. "It makes no difference. Once off the reservation, it is all the same."

"The Mexicans won't think so," Slade replied. "Their Federales, or whoever. Once we cross the line, my badge means nothing. Truth be told, it could cause us more problems than it solves."

"So, take it off," said Little Wolf.

"I made a promise to the judge," Slade said. *And one to Faith,* he thought but kept it to himself.

"To bring them back alive," said Little Wolf.

"If possible."

"With seven men, I don't think so," the Cherokee replied.

Slade couldn't argue with his logic, so he said, "Then, if you're coming with me, try to stay alive, all right? I'll need your word that anything we do is self-defense."

"Your judge will trust an Indian?" asked Little Wolf.

"He's funny, that way," Slade replied. "It's like he's color-blind, at least where doling out the law's concerned."

"Then, if I meet him, I will know two strange white men."

"It might catch on someday," Slade said. "You likely shouldn't hold your breath, though."

Little Wolf said, "Once a month they bring a preacher to the reservation. He reads from your Bible in an angry voice and tells us that in Heaven we will all be white and happy."

"That's a new one," Slade admitted. "Never heard it when my folks were dragging me to church."

Before he'd run away from home, that was, to strike off on his own and live in sin. Slade thought about the minister he'd met in Jubilee, not long ago, teaching his flock to blame the Jews for any troubles they encountered in their lives. That one went up in smoke, together with his church, but there were plenty more to fill his place.

Some people said it took all kinds to make the world go 'round, but Slade thought crackpots must be breeding faster than the normal folk.

Speaking of which, Slade had misgivings about passing into Mexico with Little Wolf. Until a few years earlier, the Mexican government had paid a bounty for the scalps of murdered Indians, put off the trade at last when operators like the Glanton gang padded their tab by scalping Mexicans and turning in their hair under the guise of genuine Apache scalps. But even without bounties on the table, centuries of racial warfare left a legacy of hatred that was handed down like something in the blood.

They wouldn't just be tracking Sabiano's gang, once he and Little Wolf crossed into Mexico. Their manhunt would be strictly illegitimate, Slade's badge worth no more than a button on his shirt. He couldn't legally arrest his quarry on the wrong side of the border, would be judged a kidnapper if caught removing them—and might be charged with murder if he had to kill in self-defense.

How did they execute their murderers in Mexico? Porfirio Díaz was basically a dictator, his iron will barely masked by vague illusions of democracy, while he rode roughshod over critics. Slade supposed a military firing squad would be the due, if he was jailed for killing Sabiano and his cohorts when he finally caught up to them.

It was a risk that he accepted willingly.

He owed that much to Faith, at least. Even if he could never look into her eyes again.

13

The passing days and nights all ran together for Burch Thornton. Four days riding south through Texas since they'd crossed the Oklahoma line, and while the landscape changed a bit from flat-out desert to a plain of stunted trees and thickets, he lost track of time and place. They camped each night at sundown, rose at dawn, and aimed their horses southward.

It was dry and hot and dull—the last part a relief, at least, compared to dodging posses all the way. Thornton supposed it was a lucky break, and if their food was running low from lack of homesteads robbed along the way, at least they hadn't left a trail of bodies to attract a bunch of Lone Star lawmen.

On the afternoon they reached the Rio Grande, Thornton didn't realize it right away. He saw a river in their way, of course, but they'd already forded half a dozen on the long ride south, and this one didn't look like anything a fellow would write home about. Less than a hundred yards across from where he sat, and shallow-looking, with a bed of sand and mossy stones.

It only hit him when he noticed Sabiano sitting on his

grullo gelding, smiling at the flat, dry land across the river. Thornton didn't know why he was so damned happy, until Sabiano said, *"Mexico lindo. Mi hogar."*

Thornton knew enough Spanish to translate it: *Beautiful Mexico. My home.*

The truth be told, it wasn't all that beautiful to Thornton— just another dried-out chunk of Texas, if somebody asked for his honest opinion—but there *was* a certain beauty to the knowledge that they would be leaving the United States at any moment now.

Halfway across the river, he supposed the border lay. Thornton couldn't pick out the spot precisely, and he knew that crossing over wouldn't transform him into a Mexican. But if his luck held, it would make him safe.

Assuming any marshals who might still be following the gang abided by the law.

"Tonight, we sleep in Agua Verde," Sabiano told them. "Or, with all the *putas* there, maybe no sleep."

Laughing at his own joke, their leader spurred his horse into the water, followed seconds later by Miguel Fortunato, then Tommy Garrity. Thornton gave his own piebald mare a nudge, holding the reins ready to steer around the worst patches of slimy stones that might cause it to stumble, spilling him.

It would be bitter irony to come this far, then wind up walking if his animal went lame. His target was the village Sabiano had been talking up for days on end, inflated by imagination to a paradise where liquor flowed like water and the women had never learned to say "no." Most likely, it would be another clutch of run-down houses and cantinas, serving up mescal and blowsy whores, but Thornton's only interest in the nightlife lay in the extent to which it might distract his comrades.

One night running wild with alcohol and *putas* was enough for Thornton. Let the others have their fun, while he slipped out of town and made his getaway. While they were sleeping in and nursing headaches, he'd be well away on day one of a brand-new life.

Whatever that meant.

And, by God, he *did* feel something like a little tingle, right around midstream, as he forded the Rio Grande. It might've been Ned Worley splashing Thornton as he galloped past, or maybe not. In any case, next thing he knew, his mare was drying off in Mexico, while Thornton breathed free air.

I made it, didn't I? he thought, silent congratulations to himself. *I made it after all.*

"Texas is getting old," Slade said.

He didn't like complaining, guessed that Little Wolf could do just fine without it, but the words slipped out while he was studying the landscape, wishing it would change. Some parts of Texas, as he knew from personal experience, were green and lovely. There were mountains, too, although he was relieved that none lay in his present path. The state was huge, with a remarkable variety to its appearance. It was just his luck that they were following a course where everything looked more or less the same.

Two days since they had met the ranger posse, and in all that time they hadn't passed a farm or seen another traveler along their route. The weather was cooperating, nothing in the way of rain, flash floods, or major wind that would erase the tracks of Slade's intended quarry. They'd found campsites where the hunted men had spent their nights, leaving ashes behind, but they never quite seemed to gain ground.

At first, Slade thought the outcropping of rock ahead might be a strange mirage, but as they closed the distance he discovered it was real. At some point in the distant past, a slab of granite had been thrust up through the soil and fractured somehow, into chunks the size of stagecoaches and buckboards, jumbled all together in a heap, with one great blade of stone extending toward the sky like an accusing finger. Weeds and wildflowers had sprouted in the cracks, and Slade imagined rattlers denning in the crevices between and underneath the massive stones.

He was content to ride around it, leaving them alone if they returned the favor, and drew his roan off toward the left side of the pile when Little Wolf spoke up.

"Riders."

Slade stopped and asked him, "What, again?"

Another dust cloud in the distance, headed their way, coming from the east this time. Three miles away and then some, Slade supposed. It seemed to be a larger cloud than had been raised by Ranger Pool and his companions, when they'd turned up two days earlier.

More riders, then.

Not Sabiano and his people, unless they had ridden farther south, then circled to the east and doubled back for reasons Slade couldn't pretend to understand. It made no sense, so he dismissed the notion.

Someone else.

"We should take cover," Little Wolf advised.

"Sounds reasonable," Slade replied and thought about the snakes again, as he was following the warrior and his tobiano, toward the granite pile.

He couldn't judge the riders from a distance, had no way of knowing if the dust was raised by outlaws, cowboys moving livestock, or a train of wagons bearing cargo westward to Fort Stockton or El Paso. If the new arrivals were hostile, Slade could take comfort in a ready-made fortress of stone. Or, seen another way, he might just be surrounded and cut off.

Still, it was better than a running battle on the open plain, against a larger, stronger force.

Once they were past the nearest jutting walls of stone, Slade found a clearing large enough for half a dozen horses, where the grass had grown knee-high. There were no snakes in evidence, no buzzing of their rattles in the shadows, but he watched his step as he dismounted and withdrew his long guns from their scabbards, climbing to a higher vantage point.

And Little Wolf was there before him, peering eastward toward the dust cloud that seemed so much closer now. Slade's eyes were sharp enough to pick out mounted riders, no sign of them pushing cattle or escorting wagons, but for any further details at that distance, he relied on Little Wolf.

"Comanches," said his guide. "I think, the ones the rangers talked about."

"Well, shit," Slade answered.

He could think of nothing else to say.

The town of Agua Verde lay twenty-five miles due south of the point where Sabiano's crew had crossed the Rio Grande. It was an easy ride, through mostly open country, but impatience made the trip seem longer than it was. Burch Thornton craved a quick shot of tequila, maybe two or three, before he started scouting his escape route.

Having crossed the border, now they had to watch for Federales and for members of the *Guardia Rural,* beefed up by President Díaz in recent years to deal with local problems when the army was not readily available. Most of the Rurales were little more than bandits with official sanction, paid nine pesos per week—less than a dollar, overall—and left to scrounge for a living as best they could when not punishing peasants for various crimes.

Small wonder that the country simmered with an undercurrent of rebellion, starting at the grass roots with the poorest of the poor, but when had it been any different below the border? In his twenty-seven years, two-thirds of them spent drifting far and wide, Thornton had learned that things were more or less the same, no matter where he went. The rich got richer, and the poor sought ways to grab a few crumbs for themselves.

What else should he be wary of in Mexcio, once he was on his own?

Apaches, sure. Geronimo's surrender, seven years ago, had ended most of their disturbance in the States, but farther south some of the tribes still raised their share of Hell from time to time. Lone travelers were easy prey, and if they vanished in the wilderness, who'd either know or care?

Same thing with bandits on the prowl, but Mexico wasn't unique in that respect. For all the talk Burch Thornton heard about a so-called civilized society, he hadn't seen much evidence that it existed west of Kansas City. Granted, he hadn't been to Denver or Los Angeles, but if their atmosphere was anything like that in Oklahoma City, they were still far short of qualifying as refined.

No matter.

Thornton didn't fit with high society, never would, and he didn't aspire to. Experience had taught him it was better when the filthy rich ignored him. Why distract them from their chore of counting money, when it only worked against him in the end?

If he went back to stealing—which was likely, given his aversion to hard work and taking orders—Thornton knew he could survive by filching from the working class or small-town merchants, without bothering the upper crust. He was a gnat, and gnats were generally left alone unless they bothered someone big enough to swat them dead if irritated by his buzzing in their ear.

Word to the wise: an outlaw who intends to reach a ripe old age must know his place. And for the time being, at least, Burch Thornton's place was Mexico.

• • •

Little Wolf had left the reservation with sixty cartridges for his Sharps carbine. He had used three so far: one wasted in the battle for the hilltop, to distract his enemy, and two clean kills. He knew he must be careful now, to save enough for when he found the gunmen who had murdered Strong Horse.

It did not trouble Little Wolf that he might die here, in a fortress made of jumbled boulders, facing off against Comanches who were more like him than Jack Slade ever could be. Conflict between native tribes and nations was an old, old story, used at times by white men to divide and conquer. Still, he knew that the Comanches would not hesitate to kill and rob him, right along with Slade, if he gave them a chance.

It was the way of things, had always been, and likely always would be.

There was still a chance the raiders might ride past and fail to notice them—but then, what? Every step he took with Slade from that point forward might lead them into an ambush when they least expected it. Better to pick the killing ground themselves, where they had an advantage and the enemy had none.

Except their numbers, guns, and skill.

From half a mile, he counted thirteen mounted braves. The number had no bad-luck connotation for Comanches, or for any other native tribe. Such petty superstition was a white man's handicap. The number simply meant more shooting. Fewer cartridges to spare when they were done.

If they were still alive.

"Nine rifles," Little Wolf told Slade. "Four carry bows and arrows."

"You can see all that from here?" Slade asked.

"Can't you?"

"Sorry I asked," the lawman said. "You want to take a chance they'll miss us?"

"Fight them now or maybe have them hunt us later, when we have no cover."

"Right," Slade said. "You're right. You want to start the party, then? Or is it down to me?"

There would be no negotiation with the renegades. Already, they had fled their reservation, shed the blood of whites, and were running from the law that meant to kill them, either with a bullet or a hangman's rope. They literally had nothing to lose, no reason in the world to stop and chat with Little Wolf, much less a U.S. marshal.

"I will do it," Little Wolf replied.

"Okay," Slade said, cocking his rifle. "Ready when you are."

Little Wolf devised a plan. It was cold-blooded, but there was no place for guilt or squeamishness in battles to the death. Survivors did what was required of them, and losers died.

The targets were a hundred yards away when Little Wolf chose one among them as his first kill, sighting down the carbine's twenty-two-inch barrel. He felt every ounce of the weapon's eight pounds in his grasp, the smooth stock warm against his cheek.

Ready, and . . . *now!*

The carbine kicked against is shoulder, muzzle rising slightly, but the heavy bullet was well on its way by then, hurtling toward impact at eighteen hundred feet per second. It struck with the force of a hammer blow, punching a hole in the chest of the rider he'd chosen and rolling the already-dead man backward, off his pinto's rump.

Another second, while the twelve survivors registered the shot—and then, all Hell broke loose.

• • •

Thornton's first sight of Agua Verde didn't disappoint him. He'd expected nothing special, and the town was all of that. Its layout was the same as every other small town he had ever seen in Mexico, drifting along the border, with the centerpiece an old adobe church facing a dusty plaza, four cantinas situated catty-cornered on the square, with other small shops filling in the gaps. He saw a blacksmith's and a shoemaker, dry goods, an undertaker's setup with a coffin standing out in front, some other things that didn't interest him.

With four taverns to choose from, Sabiano picked the farthest on their left, leading their small parade across the square with locals eyeing them suspiciously. Why not, considering the way they looked and all the weapons they were carrying? Thornton supposed that Agua Verde didn't see much in the way of traveling philanthropists

In passing, he observed that none of the cantinas on the square displayed a name. He recognized them from their bat-wing doors and general appearance, guessing that the locals made their way from one bar to another as they pleased, or settled on a favorite and stuck with it. No fancy advertisements here.

Considering the hamlet's run-down look and sleepy atmosphere, they would've been a waste of paint.

En route to the cantina, Sabiano and the others stopped to let their horses drink from a round fountain in the middle of the plaza. None of the observers called out to object, so Thornton nosed his mare into the circle, waiting while she drank her fill. From there, it was a short ride to the chosen tavern, with its hitching posts out front.

Inside, the place was dark and smoky, barely lit by lanterns on the walls and fat white candles on a pair of chandeliers made from old wagon wheels. The bar was on their left as they went in, a fat man polishing it lazily. Thornton counted a dozen small, round tables, wondering if that was optimism or the place was thronged at night with drinkers who hid out somewhere during the day.

Maybe he'd find out later. Maybe not.

"*Hola*, amigos," said the bartender. "You bring new friends to see us, Señor Sabiano."

Sabiano smiled and said, "Paco, you still remember me."

"*Claro!*" the bartender replied, as if offended by the notion that he might forget a favored customer. "You always drink mescal."

"And so I will, tonight. Your best bottle for me. These others buy their own."

"*Sí, sí. Con mucho gusto!*"

He produced a bottle and a glass, was turning to accept another drink order when Sabiano asked him, "What of Angelina? Do you think she will remember me?"

"*Desde luego,* Señor Sabiano. Shall I call her for you?"

"She's upstairs?" asked Sabiano. "The same room, perhaps?"

"The very same." A worried look now pinched the fat man's face. "But she is with a customer, señor. A short while longer, and—"

"I'll just surprise her, eh?" said Sabiano, turning from the bar with his bottle in hand, ignoring the shot glass, to make his way upstairs.

Thornton waited for his turn to order, but the flow of booze was interrupted by a squeal from somewhere on the second floor, followed by Spanish curses in a voice he didn't recognize. A moment later, Sabiano appeared at the head of the staircase, dragging a naked man by one ankle.

The naked man struggled, kicked at him, but didn't connect. Sabiano was all smiles when he reached down to punch the stranger's face, then grabbed him by his hair and pitched him headlong down the stairs.

"Nobody else disturbs us, eh?" he warned the room at large. "I may not be so nice, next time."

A second after Little Wolf took down the point rider for the Comanche raiding party, Slade squeezed off and dropped the horseman just behind him. He was off a little, thought his bullet must've drilled a lung when he was aiming for the heart, but it was close enough.

The rest of the formation broke apart in nothing flat, the warriors whooping as they veered in this or that direction, galloping off to encircle the rock pile. Slade tracked the last man breaking to his right and fired a snap shot, nearly missed, but was rewarded with a puff of crimson from the young Comanche's thigh.

Enough to slow him down, at least, and maybe finish him if Slade had nicked the artery. He wouldn't know until the smoke cleared, if he lived that long, and in the meantime there were other adversaries to concern him, each one of them angling for a clean kill-shot.

Slade kept his head down as he changed positions, circling to his right and following the group of riders who had broken off in that direction. Some of the Comanches were returning fire, with no clear targets, bullets whining off the granite boulders into space. Slade knew that even ricochets could kill, though, and he watched his step, hearing the Sharps speak once again behind him as he moved.

In their position, the Comanches had three choices: they could run away and cut their losses; they could ride around the rock pile, burning ammunition in the hope of getting lucky; or they could dismount and storm the fortress. Slade assumed that pride would keep them in the fight, and they were probably too smart to play the role of circling targets in a shooting gallery.

It came as no surprise, therefore, when Slade saw three

horses race past the east side of the rock pile without riders. He was ready for the sound of footsteps scrabbling over stone and lay up and waiting in the shadow of a boulder with the shotgun raised and steady, having switched off with his rifle.

And when they topped the nearest slab, framed in relief against the sky, he met them with three blasts in rapid-fire, clearing the field before they could react. A red haze lingered in the air when they were gone, then settled glistening on the granite where they'd stood a moment earlier.

Slade didn't need to check them, knew that even if they weren't killed outright, they were done. Between the buck-shot and the drop of twenty feet or more, it would require a miracle for any of them to survive.

Slade grabbed his rifle from the ground beside him as he changed positions yet again. No time to spend reloading, as he searched for targets, heard the Sharps crack twice in something close to record time, proof positive of Little Wolf's proficiency.

If both those shots were hits, it meant—how many adversaries still remaining? Five or six? Slade let it go at that, kept moving with the sound of gunfire ringing in his ears, passing their tethered horses in the middle of the makeshift fortress. Neither seemed especially perturbed or anxious to get out of there. They didn't rear or lunge at Slade as he ran past, and in another moment he was on the rocky rampart facing southward, where two more Comanches had dismounted and were closing in on foot.

Slade used his rifle this time, dropped one on the run, then ducked back as the other brave unleashed an arrow. It flew high and wide, hissing a yard above Slade's head, and he was back on point an instant later, while the lone brave tried to nock another arrow on his bow string.

It was nothing like an even contest, and Slade didn't care. He had no time to waste, no inclination to become a pincushion while playing fair. He shot the bowman without hesitation, watched him fall, and turned back toward the last place he'd seen Little Wolf, just as the Sharps spoke up again.

"They leave," said Little Wolf, as Slade approached him.

On the flats, already moving out of range, three riders hunched over their horses' necks, one of them holding bloody fingers clamped onto his thigh. Slade could have chased them with a bullet, but he followed Little Wolf's example. Let it go.

There'd been enough killing for one day as it was.

Tomorrow, he supposed, would take care of itself.

14

Burch Thornton woke in Agua Verde with a headache and a woman that he didn't recognize. The pair of them were naked underneath a tangled sheet, so he supposed they must've got acquainted overnight, but he remembered nothing of it.

Damned tequila.

After half an hour or so of drinking in the bar downstairs, he had decided it was best to keep on acting normal, their first night in town, and slip away sometime tomorrow or the next day. Sabiano had informed them that he meant to spend a week or so in Agua Verde, getting reacquainted with the whore he called his *novia*, before they hit the road again.

"Still safe in *Meheeko,*" he muttered to himself, as he slipped out of bed and grabbed for his pants. It was hot already, half past nine o'clock, according to the pocket watch he'd stolen years ago, somewhere in Kansas.

Lawrence? Wichita? What difference did it make?

Planning his day, Thornton decided he could either make a few new memories with the young woman in his bed or have some breakfast. Huevos rancheros, with chorizo on the side.

Maybe some coffee, if the bartender could make a cup that didn't taste like it was strained through someone's dirty sock.

Strangely, the thought of eating didn't rile his stomach now. Food first, Thornton decided. Then he'd give the little *puta* something to remember.

Jack Slade sat astride his roan, facing the Rio Grande, and stared off into Mexico. If he obeyed the letter of the law, he'd come as far as he could go in tracking Thornton, Sabiano, and the rest who'd tried to murder Faith. There was no law against civilians entering the country, but he'd have no more authority than any other traveler. Less than a simple citizen of Mexico, in fact.

"They crossed here," Little Wolf had told him, moments earlier. And kept on going southward, obviously, since the gang wasn't around to welcome them in person.

So, he had a choice to make.

On one hand, he could do the legal thing. Turn back, retrace his path to Enid, and report his failure to Judge Dennison. With Little Wolf, he'd clear the books on Fox and Hampton, but the other murderers could go their merry way in peace, secure until they broke some law in Mexico and maybe got the Federales on their trail.

Slade could do that. But could he live with it tomorrow, and for all the days that followed?

On the other hand, he could remove the badge that bound him to uphold the law and follow his gut instinct. Ironically, if he caught up with Thornton and the rest in Mexico, Judge Dennison had no authority to try Slade for whatever happened on the wrong side of the Rio Grande. The most that he could do was strip Slade of the badge that burdened him right now.

In that case, Slade would need some other way to make a living for himself in Enid, if he hung around waiting for Faith to wake, hoping she'd recognize his face.

And if he made the long ride back to find her dead?

Then nothing mattered anyway.

"So, are you coming with me?" Little Wolf inquired.

"I am," Slade said. He unpinned his badge and dropped it into his shirt pocket.

Crossing over seemed too easy. Slade felt like there should've been a drum roll or trumpet blast, but nothing signaled the decision he had made. Whatever happened next, at least he'd made a choice to *act*, instead of marking time and hoping things might work out for the best.

I've done it now, Slade thought, and found he didn't mind at all.

They spent five minutes on the south bank of the river, spotting places where the different members of the gang had come ashore, then gathered back together, pushing south. With what destination in mind?

"They should feel safe now," Slade said. "Safer, at least. My guess would be they're making for some town or other that this Sabiano knows about."

"And when we find them?" asked his guide.

"I told the judge I'd try to bring them back," Slade said.

"You're just another gringo, here," said Little Wolf. "And I made no such promise."

"Meaning I can't hold you to it," Slade replied, nodding. "I hear you. It's not likely that the seven of them will surrender to us, I suppose."

"It is a dream, I think," the Cherokee told Slade.

"Their call," Slade said. "I'll give them one chance, anyhow, then let the chips fall where they may."

"We kill them, then," said Little Wolf.

Slade frowned and said, "I wouldn't be surprised."

Joe Weems and Monty Stofer came downstairs together as the bartender was serving Thornton's breakfast. Both of them looked queasy, peering at his plate of food, but they sat down across from him and ordered coffee to get started.

"Christ, how can you eat that swill so early in the morning?" Stofer asked, making a sour face.

"It's good," said Thornton. "And it ain't that early. Almost ten o'clock."

"That's early, after all we drunk last night," Weems said. "You musta stuck to sarsaparilla."

"Maybe I just hold my liquor better'n the two of you," Thornton suggested.

"That wasn't all I seen you holdin'," Stofer said, trying a leer for size. "What happened to that little calico queen you was squirin' last night?"

"Looks like I wore her out," Thornton replied, around a mouthful of chorizo.

"The hell you say!"

"The hell I don't," said Thornton, trying hard to keep it casual. "Go back upstairs and have a look, you don't believe me. Room four, on your left."

The pair of them sat staring at him for a minute, before Weems said, "Hell, I never thought you had it in ya."

"Wasn't me I had it in," said Thornton.

"Live and learn," said Stofer.

Changing the subject, Thornton asked them, "What's the deal with Sabiano and his doxy?"

"You know the way he is," Stofer replied. "He drops in every year or so, expectin' her to be there waitin' for him like a wife or somethin'. Likely doesn't give a thought to her while he's up north and raisin' hell."

"Last ranch we hit," Weems said. "Sure didn't seem like he was thinkin' of her then."

"Maybe he was, but couldn't wait," Stofer suggested.

"That bronc buster he pitched downstairs is gonna have a sore head," Weems put in. "I wouldn't be surprised to see him come back, spoilin' for a fight."

"Some sport at least," Stofer replied. "I seen the under-taker's place when we was ridin' in."

"Not far to go, for one of them," Thornton observed.

"You think that other Mex can handle Sabiano?" Stofer asked, almost a challenge.

Thornton shrugged. "I never seen him draw," he said. "Fal-lin' downstairs without his pants don't say much, either way."

"You wanna put a bet on that?" asked Weems.

"A bet on what?" asked Thornton.

"On the fight!" said Stofer.

"What, you mean the one you're havin' in your head right now?" Thornton forked up the last bite of his huevos, chewed and swallowed it, then said, "The guy shows up lookin' for Sabiano, let me know. I'll stake my money where there's somethin' real to bet on."

"Hell, you know the boss could take him," Stofer said.

Smiling to keep them pacified, Thornton said, "Hey, I didn't say which way I'd bet, did I?"

He wouldn't mind if Sabiano took a stranger's bullet, though. If that should happen, Thornton knew damn well the other members of the gang would spare no time or energy pursuing him, when he lit out. He owed them noth-ing. All he meant to Stofer and the others was an extra mouth to feed, more competition for a bottle or a hooker.

Speaking of which . . .

"Well, now," he said at last, wiping his plate with the last half of a tortilla, rising as he stuffed it in his face, "You boys'll have to get along without me for a spell. I'm goin' back to bed."

The trail that Slade and Little Wolf were following had joined a road of sorts. Not much of one, granted, but it was still a track that had been worn by wagons over time, and other riders. It was angled from the northwest to southeast, from their perspective, and would likely lead them to El Paso if they turned right and pursued it far enough.

Dismounting from his tobiano, Little Wolf knelt down beside the road, scanning the tracks that ran in both directions. Slade ticked off four minutes in his mind before the Cherokee rose to his feet again and nodded to the left, southeastward.

"That way," he declared.

Slade could've asked if he was positive, but what would be the point? He'd trusted Little Wolf this far and had eliminated two of Sabiano's thugs as a result. Defiance of his guide at this point in the game would likely send him off on a wild goose chase to New Mexico.

"Okay," he said. "Let's go."

A half mile farther on, they passed a small sign reading AGUA VERDE, 5 MILLAS. Five miles to something that translated as "green water." Slade supposed it had to be a town, unless the Mexicans had signs to spare for advertising stagnant ponds.

"An hour, give or take," Slade said.

"You think we will be welcome?" Little Wolf inquired and almost smiled.

Slade shrugged and said, "I didn't come to make a lot of friends."

The Rio Grande lay twenty miles behind them, more or less. So far, they'd met no other travelers, which suited Slade just fine. A town meant people, though—in this case, Mexicans—and Little Wolf was kidding him about their possible reaction to a gringo and an Indian arriving in their midst, but Slade knew it could wind up being serious.

A town might also mean some kind of law enforcement, which would be a problem in itself. He didn't plan to broadcast his intentions on arrival, simply have a look around the place, as quietly as possible, and see if Sabiano's men were in the neighborhood. If that turned out to be the case . . . well, he would wait and see what happened next.

Burch Thornton was the first name on Slade's list, but he was bent on finishing the gang at any cost. If he could talk them into giving up and riding back with him to face Judge Dennison, so much the better, but Slade viewed that as an idle fantasy.

Why would a group of seven killers volunteer to hang?

It took more like an hour and a quarter, by Slade's watch, before they rode into the dusty village square of Agua Verde. It was sunbaked and deserted in the early afternoon, siesta time, giving the general impression of a ghost town.

While their horses guzzled water from the plaza's fountain, Slade surveyed the town. He counted four cantinas, spied the livery beside a blacksmith's shop, picked out the undertaker's setup and a church that cast its long shadow across the square. He'd have to name the other stores by what was showing in their windows, since translation of their signs eluded him. There was no sign of constables, Rurales, or the like.

"Not much to see," Slade said.

"With four saloons," said Little Wolf, "I think they like mescal."

"We'd better take care of the horses, first," Slade said, turning his roan in the direction of the stable.

A sleepy town. And yet, he had a sense of sharp eyes tracking them as they proceeded toward the livery. Slade couldn't tell if they were hostile eyes, but in a place like this, so far from home, he couldn't count on finding any allies.

They had to rouse the hostler, but he didn't seem to mind, after the first shock of awakening to find two strangers standing over him, both armed, and one of them an Indian.

He called himself Juanito, spoke some English, and agreed to board their horses for a modest daily fee after he satisfied himself that neither of them meant to rob or scalp him.

When their deal was set, Slade asked, "What kind of lodgings are available in town?"

Juanito thought about it for a moment, frowning, then said, "No hotel, señor. At the cantinas, there are rooms to sleep in with *las putas,* but I don't think . . . um . . ."

He glanced toward Little Wolf, then choked on whatever he meant to say. Slade got the point and knew it wasn't lost on his companion.

"What about the stable?" Slade inquired. "It looks like you've got room to spare."

In fact, he'd counted sixteen stalls, and only half of them were filled.

"Oh, *sí,*" Juanito said, recovering his smile. "But only straw for bedding here, señor."

"Beats sleeping in the dirt, the way we have been," Slade replied. He turned to Little Wolf and asked, "Suit you all right?"

"Best to keep the horses close," his guide replied.

"Okay, then. Can you watch out for our gear, while we go look around the town?" Slade asked Juanito.

"*Sí, efectivamente*, señor! No one steals from Juanito in Agua Verde."

Slade decided it was time to press his luck. "Speaking of horses, can you say if some of these were left within the past two days?"

Juanito looked embarrassed as he said, "Señor, my customers value their privacy, the same as you, eh?"

"Fair enough," Slade granted. "Is there anyplace where we can eat in town, with no trouble?"

"They will serve food to anyone at Bolivar's," Juanito said. "Tequila or mescal, I cannot say."

"Food's all we need," Slade said. "Which one is Bolivar's?"

Juanito led them to the stable's entrance, indicating the cantina at the northeast corner of the plaza. "Bolivar can speak *inglés*," he said, "but not so good as me."

"We'll take our chances," Slade replied.

Before they left Juanito with the horses, Slade picked out a place to stow his saddlebags and paused to choose which long gun he should carry with him on their rounds. With firepower in mind, he picked the rifle and trailed Little Wolf into the street.

Crossing the plaza didn't take long, but Slade felt a nervous twitch between his shoulder blades the whole time they were in the open, half expecting to be shot. Juanito's hedging made him think some of the horses at the livery were new arrivals, but that didn't mean that Sabiano's people had been riding them.

Coincidence?

The dark hole known as Bolivar's was nearly empty when they crossed the threshold, two men facing each other from opposite sides of the bar. The one who seemed to be in charge nodded a greeting, kept his face expressionless, and said, "*Hola*, hombres. You hungry? Thirsty?"

"Both," Slade answered. "What's to eat?"

"Carne asada *y frijoles*," said the bartender.

"Let's make it two of those," said Slade. "And beer?"

"*Dos* cervezas, *sí*. Sit anywhere you want."

Burch Thornton heard a strange voice speaking English as he made his way downstairs, the bartender responding in his own way, with the sullen tone he seemed to use for everyone but Sabiano de la Cruz. The other voice was gringo, Thornton knew that much before he could make out

what either man was saying, and it froze him halfway down
the creaky stairs.

He hadn't put his gunbelt on before he left his room, was
holding it coiled up in his right hand, and didn't want to
grapple with it now, in case the buckle made a clinking
sound that would betray him. Caught before he heard the
voice with one foot in the air, his other leg bent at the knee
and holding up his weight, Thornton lowered his dangling
boot as slowly as he could. The muscles in his off-leg quiv-
ered, threatening to tip him over for a headlong tumble down
the stairs, and Thornton couldn't brace himself against the
wall, because his near hand clutched the gunbelt.

Finally, he got it done, still standing awkwardly with his
feet on different steps, and reached out with his free hand
for the handrail on his left. Better. Once he had overcome
his fear of falling, Thornton could apply himself to
listening.

But damn it all, he wasn't close enough.

Descending any farther meant an added risk with every
step he took, but what were Thornton's other choices? Staying where he was, halfway between the tavern's first and
second floors, accomplished nothing beyond making him
feel stupid. On the other hand, he stood to make as much
noise on the staircase if he backtracked to his room—and
in the process, he would lose his chance to eavesdrop.

Mouthing silent curses, Thornton took another downward
step, placing his foot as near the wall as possible, where
squeaky stairs were less likely to make a noise. His creeping
progress thus required a clumsy, spraddle-legged way of
moving, since he had to keep *both* feet from resting on the
middle of a sagging tread. Only his tight grip on the handrail
kept Thornton from wobbling comically as he descended
two, three, four steps more.

Another four steps, and he could've seen the stranger
who was talking to the bartender, but that felt premature.

The last thing Thornton wanted was to show himself before he had at least some vague idea of who he might be facing, down below. He couldn't even draw his pistol as it was, one hand clutching the banister, the other carrying his gunbelt.

Still, it could be worse. The stranger could be on his way upstairs, or one of Thornton's cohorts might come blundering along behind him, telling him to get his lazy ass out of the way before he had a chance to hear—

"—Riders," the unfamiliar voice said. "Six or seven, maybe?"

Bolivar the barkeep took his time before responding, "No, señor. No ones like that."

"They would've come to town sometime within the past two days," the stranger said.

"I doan theenk so," said Bolivar.

"Well, if you see them—"

Thornton missed the rest of it, crab-walking back the way he'd come, praying he wouldn't slip and fall. The gringo in the tavern was a man hunter, no doubt about it in his mind. And instantly, his plans for slipping out of Agua Verde in the middle of the night were shot to Hell. Could it be Faith Connover's Marshal Slade come to avenge her? Had he followed them all the way to Mexico? The thought made Thornton shiver, but it was the only thing that made sense. Who else would be crazy enough to follow them across the border, outside any known jurisdiction.

He had to warn the others, for his own sake.

And he had to do it now.

15

The second cantina was smaller than Bolivar's, darker inside—which was hard to believe—and smokier still. The barkeep was thin, in contrast to his heavyweight competitor across the plaza, but he shared the former's ignorance of any strangers killing time in Agua Verde.

"*Ninguno*, señor," he'd insisted. "None but you and your amigo *indio*."

A mug of warm beer got them nowhere, but they still had two more taverns left to try. And after that? With no hotel in town, they didn't have a lot of options left. Slade couldn't picture going door to door, begging for information in his shaky Spanish.

What, then?

He could go back to the livery, put the squeeze on Juanito for more information—and what? Pummel the only halfway friendly face they'd seen in town, so far? They might have better luck just staking out the place, see who retrieved the other horses, but if none of them belonged to Sabiano's gang, Slade could waste precious days hanging around the stable.

"I thought we'd hit quicker than this," he said to Little

Wolf, eyeing the two cantinas that remained. "Which one you want to visit next?"

Before the Cherokee could answer him, a pistol shot rang out. Slade ducked instinctively into a crouch, raising his Winchester with no target in mind. The bullet struck the wall behind him, dusting his hat brim and shoulders with flakes of adobe.

"There!" said Little Wolf, angling the muzzle of his Sharps back toward the first cantina they'd gone into. Slade was moving when a muzzle flash winked at him from the shadows of an alley, over there, the second shot another miss.

He sent one back in answer, from his rifle, eardrums battered at the same time by a boom from Little Wolf's carbine. Return fire evidently made the hidden gunman change his mind, but instantly, a second gun went off, this one trying to nail them from the northeast side of Bolivar's.

Two shooters, then, at least. And Slade had barely formed that thought when number three cut loose from Bolivar's flat roof, two stories up. The third man had a rifle, lever action by the speed with which he fired three rounds into the plaza. Slade was out of range by then, already back inside the second bar, with Little Wolf beside him.

"Shooting from the first place we went into," he observed. "Tells me we didn't get the story straight from fat-boy Bolivar."

"He told them we were there," said Little Wolf.

"Somebody did. I doubt any vaqueros hereabouts would try to kill us for the hell of it." Slade faced the nervous-looking bartender and said, "Back door?" When that got no response, Slade translated as best he could. *"Puerta trasera?"*

"Sí, sí," said the barkeep, pointing to his left along a narrow hallway.

Seconds later, they were standing at the back door, Slade's hand on the doorknob. "No way of predicting what's outside," he said.

Little Wolf cocked his Sharps and said, "Do it."

If it was Sabiano's gang out there—and who else could it be?—they might have someone covering the tavern's rear exit. Had there been time to put a man in place while he and Little Wolf were questioning the bartender and getting nothing for their effort?

Maybe.

Either way, Slade knew that he was wasting time. He braced to take a bullet, hoped that he'd have time at least to drop the man who put him down, and shoved out through the door.

Nothing. No shots, no shouts of warning from a lookout. Cautiously, with Little Wolf behind him, Slade edged toward the building's nearest corner facing back toward Bolivar's cantina.

Easy. *Easy.*

He reached the corner, risked a peek around it, and nobody took his head off. Good luck, there, but glancing at the place for half a second didn't tell him anything. There might have been a man-shape crouching on the roof, probably *had* been, but the other shooters were invisible.

Three guns against them, so far, which left four gang members unaccounted for. Slade didn't mind bucking the odds—had ridden all this way to do precisely that, in fact— but he'd prefer to have at least some vague idea of where the other shooters were, before he showed himself.

Too bad there wasn't time to play a waiting game.

"Ready?" he asked and got a nod from Little Wolf.

Without another word, Slade lunged into the open, running hard toward Bolivar's.

Sabiano had been busy when Burch Thornton started rapping lightly on his door, hissing something at him in a whisper-voice that Sabiano didn't recognize, first thing. When he had pulled his pants on, opening the door with gun in hand, Thornton had come in looking panicky, ignoring Angelina in her naked glory on the bed before she pulled a sheet over herself.

Not normal.

Next had come the story of a gringo lawman down in the cantina, asking questions. Sabiano had supposed Thornton was simply drunk, at first, but he had listened, then got dressed reluctantly and called Miguel to join them when they went downstairs.

To find the stranger gone. But he had been there, Bolivar confirmed. Not one, but two of them. A gringo and an *indio*, the white man asking for Sabiano by name. Bolivar swore that he had told them nothing and had no idea where they were going next.

Routing the others from their beds had taken time, but Sabiano had been on the roof with Thornton when the pair he sought came out of Vergara's cantina and paused on the threshold. Sabiano's rifle had been at his shoulder, sights settling on the gringo, when Miguel and Ned Worley cut loose with their pistols below him and spoiled it. Sabiano's shots had missed both men, as they ducked back into Vergara's, out of sight.

"You didn't shoot," he snarled at Thornton.

"Christ, it all happened too fast!"

"Sometimes, I think you're useless," Sabiano told him.

"No, I—"

"Are you a *cobarde*?"

"What? A coward?" Thornton seemed to think about it for a heartbeat, letting anger rise within him, then spat back, "Hell, no!"

"I wonder," Sabiano sneered.

"Listen, I—shit! It's them! They're crossing over!"

Sabiano turned to find the gringo and his long-haired

indio halfway across the street that separated Vergara's cantina from Bolivar's. He raised his Winchester and fired, heard Thornton's Colt this time, and saw their bullets kick up spurts of dust behind the moving targets.

"*Mierda!*"

Sabiano pumped the rifle's lever-action, chambering a fifth cartridge while Thornton blazed away with his revolver, but the Indian triggered a shot that struck the near edge of the roof, flinging a storm of wooden splinters into Sabiano's face.

"*Hijo de puta!*"

Sabiano blinked his eyes clear, bent back to his rifle—but the men were gone. They'd crossed the street and vanished somewhere down below him, maybe looking for a way to enter Bolivar's unseen.

He clutched at Thornton's shirt and said, "Tell Garrity to get the horses! Do it now!"

The gringo bobbed his head and scrambled to obey the order, leaving Sabiano alone on the rooftop.

Anxiously looking for someone to kill.

Flattened against the rough adobe wall, feeling its sun warmth through his shirt, Little Wolf paused to reload his Sharps carbine. The single-shot weapon was slower than Slade's lever action, but it was reliable and had served Little Wolf well.

True, his last shot had missed, but it still did the job, spoiling the rooftop sniper's aim. The pistolero with him was a hasty shooter, wasting ammunition in a rush, instead of aiming for the kill.

That made four guns revealed, so far, though one of them—the second who had fired, from the northeast corner of the tavern—had retreated to some other vantage point while Little Wolf and Slade were out of sight. If he'd remained in place, they would have met him as they crossed the street, and someone would be dead by now.

So, it was now a game of hide-and-seek, with seven players on the other side. The numbers did not frighten Little Wolf, although he recognized the enemy's advantage. He had been outnumbered all his life, by whites who stole his people's land and lives, but he had never learned to knuckle under and submit.

He never would.

Strong Horse's murderers might kill him yet, but until they did . . .

"This way!" Slade whispered, edging farther down the wall as dusk fell over Agua Verde, casting long shadows into the plaza. Little Wolf followed the lawman, covering their back trail as a hedge against surprise from that direction.

Soon, they stood at Bolivar's back door. It was another danger point, perhaps with gunmen crouched inside and waiting for a target to appear. The only way to test it was to look and see what happened next.

"Ready?" asked Slade, still whispering.

Little Wolf nodded, tightened his grip on the carbine.

The back door opened outward, Slade retreating under cover of it, dropping to a crouch. When no gunshots exploded from the tavern, he ducked forward, led the way inside. A final backward glance showed no one creeping up behind them, and two strides took Little Wolf across the threshold.

"Better shut the door," Slade said.

It cost them daylight, but it was a good idea. Little Wolf closed the door and latched it, thus preventing anyone from coming in the back way after them. Whoever waited for them now, intent on murder, must be in the tavern or upstairs.

No further conversation was required as they edged forward, Slade in front, with Little Wolf leaving enough room in between them for maneuver as required. They would make easy targets in the hallway leading into the cantina, but an enemy would have to face them for a clear shot that might cost his life.

When they had nearly reached the barroom, Little Wolf heard voices raised—one angry, and the other fearful. From their tone, he knew the cringing one was Bolivar. The other, also speaking Spanish, could be anyone.

It made no difference. The whole gang was responsible for killing Strong Horse on the reservation. All of them owed Little Wolf a debt of blood.

Thornton found Tommy Garrity, no problem, waiting two doors down from Bolivar's cantina with his pistol drawn, a snarl etched on his face. He raised the Colt as Thornton came around the corner, cocking it, then eased the hammer down but kept the iron leveled.

"You wanna point that thing some other way?" Thornton suggested.

Tommy snorted, might've been his version of a laugh, and said, "I almost dropped you there, amigo."

"Real funny. Listen, I've got word from Sabiano."

"Lemme guess," said Garrity. "You missed 'em both?"

"So far," Thornton agreed.

"Well, I won't. When they come around that corner—"

"Never mind that," Thornton interrupted. "Sabiano says for you and me to fetch the horses."

"What?!"

"You heard me right," Thornton replied.

"We're running?" Garrity demanded. "From one lawman and an Injun?"

"I don't call the shots," said Thornton. "If you wanna beef about it, you'll find Sabiano up on top of the cantina. Me, I'm following my orders."

Tommy thought about it for a second, then cursed bitterly and put his gun away. "How come we gotta miss the party? Can you tell me that?"

"I didn't ask him," Thornton said. "But if you've got a mind to—"

"Yeah, yeah. See him on the roof. I heard you the first time. Let's git, then, if we're goin'."

Thornton set the pace, a brisk jog toward the livery where they had stashed the horses on arrival in the village. Garrity grumbled along beside him, mad about retreating, missing out on any chance to kill somebody, harping that it wasn't fair for lawmen from the States to show their ugly mugs in Mexico.

Hot air, but if it kept him moving, Thornton didn't care. He couldn't say, himself, why Sabiano had decided to pull out of Agua Verde rather than remaining, fighting to the last man if he had to, with the marshal and his redskin. Maybe it was just a reflex, running when the law showed up.

Of maybe he was thinking down the road.

A fight in Agua Verde, never mind who got the short end of the stick, would likely bring Rurales to the village. Maybe even Federales, once word got around, as it was bound to do. It wouldn't matter if they buried Slade and his companion, once the troops showed up.

Thornton knew Sabiano wasn't only wanted in the States. The government down here was just as apt to hang him—maybe shoot him down without the benefit of trial—as old Judge Dennison in Oklahoma Territory. Lounging with his *puta* might be fun, but Sabiano wasn't dumb enough to stick around and sacrifice himself for her.

The only person Sabiano loved that much was Sabiano.

They reached the stable, found Juanito wide awake for once and looking anxious at the sound of gunfire coming from the plaza. He was obviously scared, servile as ever, nodding like a puppet on a string when Thornton said they needed all the horses saddled up *muy pronto*.

Even with Juanito helping, all three of them hustling, it took time to saddle seven horses. They were barely getting to it when the shooting started up again, but muffled now, as if the guns had moved indoors.

Meaning that Jack Slade or the Indian, and maybe both of them, had gotten into Bolivar's.

"Goddamn it! We should be there with 'em," Garrity told Thornton.

"You go on, then," Thornton said. "I'll finish up what Sabiano wanted us to do."

"Suppose he needs our help."

"I told you, go," Thornton repeated. "It'll take me longer, but I'll get it done."

He wished that Garrity would go and give him room to mount his animal and ride out while the rest of them were busy.

"No, I guess you're right," said Garrity, taking another saddle from its place against the wall. "Let's finish up and get down there, before we miss the whole damn thing."

Joe Weems had been a little nervous when he heard about the Oklahoma lawman showing up to look for them. There was no way he could take all seven of them, but it had to make you stop and think. A man riding that far, with just an Indian for company, and all for what?

Weems got his answer when Burch Thornton told them who it was, the deputy whose wedding day they had disrupted for the Hell of it, a notion Thornton had come up with in the first place, talking Sabiano into it with promises of easy money to be had. In fact, they hadn't cleared a dime, and lost two men on top of it, his brother one of them.

Weems might've gone for Thornton after that, but Sabiano talked the rest of them around, explaining how you took your chances on the road and it was no one's fault.

But now, Weems had a chance to pay the marshal back.

Okay, it wasn't *his* fault Ike got killed, but *someone* had to pay for it. Why not a lawman dumb enough to cross the border looking for a fight?

Weems had a sawed-off shotgun cocked and ready when he heard a clatter on the stairs and Sabiano entered the cantina proper. He was smiling, sort of, but it had a nervous feel about it.

"Ándale!" he said. "We're clearing out. Come on!"

"Leaving? What for?" Weems challenged.

"I choose not to fight this battle here and now," the Mexican replied. *"El presidente* has too many of his damned *soldados* in the neighborhood. *Comprende?* I have someplace better, if they wish to follow us."

"I don't like running," Weems informed him, "when they're here in front of us, right now."

"Stay, then," said Sabiano. "Please yourself."

He turned his back without another word and passed through a side door, out into the night.

Weems watched the door swing shut, considered running after Sabiano while he had the chance, but stood his ground. Running had never suited him, although he'd done enough of it from posses and the shadow of a noose. Today, by God, he would be standing firm for Ike.

The shotgun was a double-barreled Greener, made in England, taken from a stagecoach guard who hadn't needed it after Weems had finished with him. What he liked best about it was the ejector mechanism, made to pop out empty cartridges each time the gun was opened, so the shooter didn't have to pull them out by hand, when he had better things to do.

Like fighting for his life.

Weems kept the Greener loaded with number three buck-shot, his personal favorite, with eighteen .25-caliber pellets packed into each shell. He hardly had to aim the weapon, but in this case, for the marshal's sake, Weems thought he would make an exception. He would—

Footsteps in the hallway, leading from the backdoor to the barroom. Hastily, Weems looked around for cover, chose the bar as his best bet, and stepped behind it.

"*Hola*, señor," said Bolivar, already squatting there.

"*Hola,* yourself," Weems said. And smiled.

Slade hesitated at the entrance to the main cantina, listening. There'd been a scuffling sound, like boots on floorboards, and perhaps a brief exchange of muffled voices, but he couldn't place the sounds precisely. Once across the threshold, they'd be in a shooting gallery with little cover and no time to think about a strategy.

The way to handle it was fast and low, counting on their opponents in the barroom to expect a walk-through at the doorway, or at least a cautious peek around the corner. Count on someone waiting with a weapon—make it *two* someones, if they were talking—and most likely they'd be aiming in the range between a normal-sized man's hips and shoulders. Going for a shot to put him down, so they could finish it at leisure, no great risk.

But if he hurried them along . . .

Slade tried explaining what he had in mind to Little Wolf with hand signs, got a frown and nod back in return. Clutching his Winchester, Slade took a deep breath, got a running start, and launched himself into the tavern. Landed belly-down and slid across the tile floor, waiting for a shot.

It came—a shotgun blast, in fact—but it was high, as Slade had hoped. Still sliding, as the spray of buckshot passed a yard or more above him, Slade twisted and swung

his rifle's muzzle toward the bar. A man he didn't recognize
was standing there, angling to make his second barrel count
for something, face set in a scowl.

Slade fired without a chance to aim and saw his bullet
strike the front edge of the bar, not close enough to wound
his target even if it splintered, but still near enough to spoil
the man's aim. The second shotgun charge cleared off a
table, spraying shattered glass and candle wax across the
room.

The shooter ducked as Little Wolf came through the
doorway with his Sharps and slammed a round into the
back-bar mirror, bringing down the bulk of it, while fragments clung to nails at either end. Some of the bottles ranged
behind the bar came down, as well, which wouldn't help the
shooter's footing when he made another play.

One man, so far, but Slade was sure he'd heard two voices
while he lingered in the corridor outside. Two men, at least
two guns. And yet . . .

"Hey, Marshal!" called a voice, its owner still concealed
behind the bar.

Slade tipped a table over, noisy, and he rolled behind it.
Not much cover, but it beat lying exposed. When no one
fired at him first thing, he answered, "What? You want to
talk, now?"

"All I wanna know is if you killed my brother," said the
gunman.

"Hard to answer that, when I don't know your name,"
Slade said.

"Because you've done so many, eh?" A throaty laugh,
and then: "My name's Joe Weems."

"In that case," Slade replied, "the answer's no. Somebody
else shot Ike, while he was busy terrorizing folks he never
met before. You'd know that, having been a part of it."

"Seemed like a way to pass the time," Joe Weems replied.

"So, now you plan on joining him, or what?" asked Slade.

"I plan on sending you to Hell," Weems said.

"You'd best get to it, then," Slade said. "I've got other men to deal with, and we're wasting time."

More scuffling, with a bleated protest, and the shooter rose again. This time, he held the bartender in front of him, left arm around his throat, right hand holding his shotgun braced across the captive's shoulder.

Slade didn't have a clear shot as the double barrel swiveled toward his table, left the first shot to Little Wolf, and heard the Sharps go off like cannon fire. It was a good hit, probably enough to drop the target, but he staggered backward, triggering both barrels of his shotgun toward the ceiling, while the barkeep squealed and dove for cover.

Slade fired, then, and nailed Weems to the wall, a blank look on his face as he died standing up, then slithered down and out of sight.

Slade was already up and moving when he heard the horses gallop past outside. Too late to target any of the riders cleanly as he reached the sidewalk, he tried a long shot anyway and missed.

"We follow them?" asked Little Wolf, standing beside him in the dark.

"It's why we came," Slade said.

16

Time to get out of town.

Slade hadn't seen anyone resembling a lawman since they'd entered Agua Verde, and no telegraph station, but that didn't mean there was no method of communication with the outside world. He had no way of knowing where the closest Fedcrales or Rurales might be stationed, and he didn't want to take a chance on meeting them right now, with one man dead and six more on the run.

Slade had no spare time for questions, or for sitting in a cell—much less for being hanged before his work was done. After, when he had found Burch Thornton and the rest, then he'd be willing to discuss the consequences. At the moment, no.

Juanito at the livery was glad to see them go. His living might depend on strangers, for the most part, but the class of visitors he'd gotten lately left a lot to be desired. Better to lose a bit of income, Slade supposed, than to be caught up in affairs that led to killing, when he had no stake in them.

Ten minutes after killing Weems, Slade had his roan mare saddled, Little Wolf already seated on his tobiano. Finding tracks at night was hopeless, but they knew the general direction Sabiano's gang had taken, southward, and he guessed they couldn't go far wrong by simply following.

But not fast enough to risk crippling the horses or to spring an ambush, if their enemies were confident enough to stop after a little while and try their luck again. Not reckless, but not dawdling, either. Slade hoped Sabiano didn't have the skill to navigate through darkness and didn't have another hideout close enough to reach by feel, without a moon to light his way. If that hope failed him, then they'd lost the gang already and might waste days trying to find their tracks again.

But if the fugitives got tired, or worried about getting lost, then he and Little Wolf still had a chance. If Sabiano camped tonight, with or without a fire, they had a chance of overtaking him.

Little Wolf hadn't failed Slade yet to pick up and follow a trail. He seemed justly proud of his abilities, and he was motivated by the murder of his friend. Pride and revenge might not be admirable qualities, but if they got the job done, Slade was fine with it.

Couldn't complain, in fact, because the same emotions motivated him. Coupled with hatred of the men who'd taken Faith away from him, who knew for how long.

Slade wondered if she had awakened yet or had gone to her reward, whatever that might be. If there was anything at all beyond the daily life that men and women led on Earth. For Faith's sake, if she passed, Slade hoped there was.

As for himself, it made no difference.

He'd made a vow to Faith and to himself. Slade wasn't turning back until the rest of Sabiano's gang had been run to ground. Dead at his feet, or riding with him back to Enid for a murder trial, he meant to see them all accounted for.

To come this far and be this close, then let them slip away would be intolerable. Slade had no idea how he would function, knowing that he'd never delivered justice to the gunmen who had wrecked his life.

If it was hopeless, why go on at all?

That kind of thinking got Slade nowhere, and he quickly stifled it. He would go on, no matter what, because he could. Because he had to.

Trailing grim Death to the end of the line.

Joaquín Morelos y Pavón stared at the gringo lying dead behind the bar, in Bolivar's cantina, calculating how soon he could slip away from town. Like everybody else in Agua Verde, he had been attracted by the gunfire. Now, he had been seen and could not simply disappear without inciting comment.

Something that he definitely did not need.

If someone saw him riding out of town, then the Rurales came, it would not take a genius to connect the two events. And once Morelos was identified as an informer . . . well, his life would not be worth a peso in the village where he had been born and raised.

These were bad times in Mexico, with the pervasive hatred of Porfirio Díaz among the campesinos who endured the taxes, rules, and regulations of a government in which they had no voice. Collaboration with the Federales and Rurales was a ticket to the grave in villages like Agua Verde, where disgust with military rule had reached the boiling point. Morelos smelled a revolution in the making, but he would not live to see it happen if his secret was revealed.

In Mexico today, each person chose the best way to survive. Joaquín Morelos y Pavón, once a respected carpenter, had found survival doubly difficult since amputation of his right arm following a snakebite four years earlier. Unable to pursue his trade, he lived from hand to mouth— *one* hand, a bitter little joke—and did the best he could to stay alive.

If that meant selling information to the damned Rurales

now and then, if it resulted in one of his neighbors being
jailed for smuggling or avoiding payment of his taxes, it was
just a part of life. Morelos might be damned after he died,
but in the meantime, he still had to eat.

The present matter, now, was different. A group of outlaws, most of them unwanted gringos, had turned Agua
Verde into their own private battleground. None of the locals
should be angry if Morelos sounded the alarm—in fact, they
should be grateful to him—but he knew the way their minds
worked. When they remembered other incidents, putting
the pieces into place, he would be branded as a traitor.

Caution, then, was paramount.

Leaving the cantina as more villagers arrived, Morelos
knew what he must do. He would go home and wait for
midnight, then slip off and ride his burro to Piedras Negras,
where a small detachment of Rurales had their headquarters.
He knew the way by heart, and while he would not reach
the other village until dawn, sleepless, it would be worth his
time and effort.

For Sabiano de la Cruz and half a dozen gringo murderers, Morelos would receive enough money to live another
month or two, at least. When he returned to Agua Verde in
the afternoon, alone, with the Rurales on their way to capture Sabiano and the rest, he'd have a story ready and
rehearsed, about job-hunting on the nearby farms.

Not perfect, but Morelos thought it would be good
enough. He would not brag about his newfound wealth, or
spend beyond his normal means. Frugality was part of life
in rural Mexico.

Who knew when he would have another chance like this?

Thornton was tired of riding, worried that his horse might
stumble at any time and snap a leg. When Sabiano called a

halt at last, two hours out of Agua Verde, the relief dulled
any apprehension that they might have been pursued.

Even an Indian would have to wait for daylight.

Wouldn't he?

Six of them left, their number cut in half since they had
ridden onto Faith Connover's land at Thornton's urging.
Once again, he thought of Perry Larson, wondered where
he'd got to, if he ever thought about the gang at all, these
days. But then, why would he when he'd made his break?

Thornton, meanwhile, had missed his chance.

"No fire," said Sabiano, as he stepped down from his
grullo. "Stofer and Miguel, take the first watch. Wake Garrity and Worley in two hours."

"'Fore you all slip off to dreamland," Worley interjected,
"how about you tell us where'n Hell we're goin' next?"

"You want a destination?" Sabiano answered. "I intend
to honor all of you by showing you my home. The place
where I was born."

"Where's that?" asked Garrity.

"I doubt you've heard of it," said Sabiano. "Santa Bárbara
de Esperanza. I can tell you that the name is longer than the
town's main street."

"Not much to do, I take it," Stofer said.

"Not much, it's true," their leader granted. "No reason
why anyone should seek us there. But if they do . . ."

He left it hanging, with the implication that whoever followed them would have good reason to regret it. Thornton
didn't put much stock in that, after the way they'd fled from
Agua Verde, but at least he had a destination now.

Thornton had jerky and some hardtack in his saddlebags,
didn't consider offering to share it as he got his piebald mare
unsaddled, found a grassy patch for her to graze on, hobbled
her, and made his bed nearby. Without some kind of light,
he couldn't check the ground for crawling things, but finally

decided he had less to fear from snakes or scorpions than
from the men he rode with.

Thornton didn't have a friend among them, in the true
sense of the word. When there was trouble, it was each man
for himself and always would be. Talk about the so-called
honor among thieves was simply that: a lot of empty talk.
Thornton didn't imagine he could trust a single member of
the gang to help him out of trouble if it didn't suit their needs.

They sure as Hell couldn't trust him.

It felt like failure, stopping for the night, but Slade knew
they'd come far enough without a light to guide them. Any
farther and they risked losing their quarry altogether, making all of it for nothing.

So far, Slade and Little Wolf had taken down three members of the gang. Slade had considered that the gang might
scatter, that some of them might elude him, but he couldn't
quit until he'd done his utmost to find all of those who'd
made his wedding day a bloodbath.

But if some eluded him, in fact, Slade pledged that there
were two who wouldn't get away. Burch Thornton, as he
understood it, was the root of the attack, its planner and its
driving force. Behind him—or above him, take your pick—
was Sabiano, leader of the gang, who'd gone along with
Thornton's scheme to raid a peaceful ranch and terrorize or
murder its inhabitants.

Slade didn't like to think about what Thornton and the
others had planned to do with Faith, but certain mental
images were hard to shake. With Thornton, in particular,
Slade thought they'd come in handy when he faced his man.

Stoking the rage.

In Sabiano's case, Slade still had no idea of his full name,
much less a viable description, but it wasn't vital at the

moment. If the manhunt went on long enough, he'd likely pick up details on his way. Not something Slade looked forward to, but he was in for the long haul.

They made no fire, ate corn dodgers for supper, and drank water from a stream that Little Wolf had sniffed out in the dark somehow. Their horses had enough grass for some frugal grazing overnight, and Slade scraped out a hollow for his bedroll in the sandy soil.

"You want the first watch or the second?" Slade asked Little Wolf.

The Cherokee responded with a question of his own. "You think the men come back?"

"Not likely," Slade admitted. "But we don't know who else may be wandering around out here. Apaches or banditos, maybe even Federales on the prod. I'd hate to come this far and wake up dead tomorrow."

"Wake up dead?" Slade couldn't see if Little Wolf was smiling, but he sounded like he was.

"If there's anything beyond, you know," Slade said. "Your Happy Hunting Ground, for instance."

"If there is, you go to peace and paradise," said Little Wolf. "If not, to nothing. Either way, why be afraid?"

"The missionaries who came out to see you on the rez most likely mentioned an alternative," Slade said. "A Not-So-Happy Hunting Ground."

"Your Hell."

"Not mine, specifically," Slade said. "But, yeah."

"I think a white man made it up to frighten children," Little Wolf replied.

Slade smiled into the darkness. Said, "I hope you're right."

"How do you picture it?" asked Little Wolf. "This Hell."

"Right now," Slade said, "I'd call it dying with a job of work unfinished."

"Man hunting," said Little Wolf.

"It's what I do," Slade said. "I'll take first watch."

The jerky he had eaten lit a fire in Thornton's gut and wouldn't let him sleep. Hard ground beneath his blanket made it worse, impossible to rest, even if sleep eluded him. His back ached by the time he gave it up and rolled a cigarette to pass the time.

It wasn't long before Tom Garrity came by to check on him, making his rounds. He hunkered down and asked, "Can't sleep?"

"Somethin' I ate," Thornton replied, keeping his voice down to avoid disturbing anybody else.

"Not nerves, then?" Garrity inquired.

"Why'n Hell should I be nervous?" Thornton challenged.

"Well . . . you know."

"I don't."

"The marshal," Garrity went on. "Supposed to be the one from Enid, way I heard it. He must be upset, the way you spoiled his party."

"*I* did? All of us was there," Thornton reminded him.

"Oh, sure. But it was *your* idea, right? I recall you sellin' it to Sabiano. Sellin' hard."

"Might wanna take it up with him," Thornton suggested.

"All I'm sayin' is, this marshal—what's his name?"

"Jack Slade."

"Okay. He's trailed us all this way, knowin' his badge is worthless on the Mex side of the river. So it's personal."

"I doubt he ever heard of me," said Thornton, lying to himself and Garrity together.

"That a fact? You don't think anybody might remember that his woman sent you packin', right before the shindig?"

Thornton didn't answer that. His cigarette had burned down almost to his fingertips. He flicked the glowing butt off into darkness.

"Thought it might explain your trouble sleepin'," Garrity suggested.

"I already tole you—"

"Yeah, somethin' you ate. Hey, since you're up, you wanna finish off my watch?"

"No, thanks. This jawin's made me sleepy, after all."

Garrity snorted, rising to his feet. "Good luck with that," he said. "You got about an hour left, before your turn on guard."

Thornton said nothing more, as Garrity moved off into the shadows. Shouting curses after him would only be a sign of weakness, make him look pathetic. All the worse, since everything that Garrity had said was true.

All the more important, now, for Thornton to get shed of Sabiano and the rest, as soon as possible.

But not yet. Not tonight.

He lay down, drew his blanket over him, and shut his eyes. If nothing else, he could pretend to sleep and thereby claim a minor victory. Thornton stopped short of snoring, shied away from overacting, trying to ignore the way the hard ground gouged his hip and shoulder. He'd be achy in the morning, but it hardly mattered.

Once they got to Santa Bárbara de Esperanza, he was cutting out. Let Sabiano and the others wonder what became of him, assuming any of them gave a tinker's damn.

Better for Thornton if they didn't. Let them focus on the marshal and his Indian while they were hiding out, instead of wondering where Thornton had run off to.

Something he would have to think about, himself. With all of Mexico in front of him, where would he go?

Away.

216 Lyle Brandt

And let the Devil—or the marshal—deal with those who stayed behind.

Joaquín Morelos y Pavón enjoyed riding at night. He knew the countryside and took his time, letting his burro find the path of least resistance through the scrubland without urging it to reckless speed. Unlike so many of his people, he was not a slave to superstition. He did not believe that ghosts or demons ruled the night, though some men he'd encountered in the dark were even worse.

Like Sabiano de la Cruz, for instance.

The Rurales would be glad to know that Sabiano had returned, and having missed their chance to corner him in Agua Verde, would pursue him southward. That should spare Morelos any awkward questions in his village, when he made it back. And if they came to see the dead gringo, what of it? Nobody in town paid much attention to Morelos, anyway, so why start now?

From time to time, he heard bats circling overhead, voicing their high-pitched hunting calls, but they did not disturb him. Even if they were *vampiros*, he was not concerned, because the flying leeches only fed on sleeping animals. As long as he kept moving, both Morelos and his aged burro would be safe.

He had prepared the story he would tell to the Rurales, blaming no one in his village for the welcome that the outlaws had received. With Sabiano's reputation, it was easy to believe that he had cowed the villagers—might even be the truth, if viewed a certain way. His treatment of the customer who'd paid for Angelina's time would serve as confirmation of a sort.

And the reward posted for Sabiano's capture was incentive in itself for the Rurales to pursue him. They could build a reputation on his capture—or his death, as seemed more likely—and put money in their pockets at the same time.

Morelos doubted whether Sabiano or the others would be caught alive. The simpler way, and less expensive for the state, would be to claim that they drew weapons when confronted by arresting officers. Their reputations would support it, and in fact, the tale would probably be true.

When they were dead, perhaps with Sabiano's head packed in salt and shipped off to Mexico City as proof, no further questions would be asked. *El presidente* did not quibble over minor subjects, such as life and death. His interests ran more toward maintenance of power and enrichment of himself.

As for Joaquín Morelos y Pavón, he would be satisfied with a more modest reward. Perhaps fifty pesos in gold.

It seemed a small price for a man's life, but the man meant nothing to Morelos. All of them together were banditos, murderers. Someone, somewhere, might mourn their passing, but it would not be in Agua Verde. Not unless the *puta* Angelina missed her Sabiano.

In a fleeting fantasy, Morelos saw himself consoling her, then shrugged it off. A one-armed former carpenter would always have to pay.

And in a few more hours, Morelos would be able to afford it.

Let his neighbors keep their so-called principles, protecting brutal *asesinos* who abused them, treated them like trash. Joaquín Morelos y Pavón might never be a rich man, but he knew that golden silence would not feed him, pay his rent, or put him into Angelina's bed.

A well-placed word could do all that.

And would, before the sun set on another day.

17

Slade and Little Wolf broke camp at first light, with nothing much to do except for rolling up their blankets and, in Slade's case, saddling his horse. By the time an orange glow lit the eastern sky, they'd put a mile or more behind them and were making decent time.

They'd found the Sabiano outfit's tracks again, by then—or, rather, Little Wolf had found them, with the skill that almost made Slade reconsider the existence of a sixth sense in selected human beings. Left to do it on his own, Slade thought he could've spent all day searching in vain, or maybe wound up in Sonora by mistake.

Slade didn't know if Sabiano had the wherewithal to lead his riders through the night toward whatever their destination proved to be, but he was hoping that the riders would have stopped to rest, wait out the hours of darkness, once they figured they were safe from hot pursuit. If Slade's luck held, Sabiano might not have a full nine-hour lead.

But either way, Slade knew he would press on.

In retrospect, Slade wished he'd taken time to find a map of Mexico before he started tracking Thornton and the rest, but there'd been no predicting where the hunt would lead him. Even with a map, of course, he wouldn't know what Sabiano had in mind when he left Agua Verde, where the outlaw might be headed next.

Was there some place significant to him, somewhere he longed to see again, before he made his stand? Or was he simply running, spooling out his time and hoping his pursuers would get tired and give up the chase?

That wouldn't happen, but the outlaw couldn't know that. Prior experience might have convinced him that a posse only worked so hard and rode only so far. But, on the other hand, if he knew Slade had trailed him all the way from Oklahoma Territory . . .

That was information Thornton might provide, if he knew Slade by sight, if he'd seen Slade and Little Wolf in Agua Verde. All Slade knew so far, for sure, was that someone had tipped the gang after he started asking questions. Whether he'd been recognized or not was anybody's guess.

But if he had—

"Big hats," said Little Wolf.

Slade followed the direction of his gaze and saw a group of riders in the distance, east of their position, riding southward. And if he could see them . . .

"Over here," he said and steered his mare into a stand of scrub for cover. Might have been too late, if any of the riders had already glanced in their direction, but Slade saw no sign of them diverting yet.

He got the spyglass from his saddlebag and tracked the horsemen. Little Wolf was right about their hats, each of them sporting a wide-brimmed *sombrero*. They also wore crossed bandoleers, bright with brass for their carbines, and every man wore at least one pistol strapped to his waist. The lead horseman and one other rider had sabers, to boot, as if they had prepared for a cavalry skirmish.

"Rurales," Slade said, passing over the 'scope to his guide.

"Hunting us," Little Wolf speculated.

"Could be," Slade agreed. "Or, they could be our new competiton. If someone sold out Sabiano, odds are there's a price on his head."

Still no sign those riders from the *Guardia Rural* had spotted them, and Slade began to breathe a little easier. He was resigned to further bloodshed, but he wanted it to be the right blood, spilled at his discretion.

"Shall we follow them?" asked Little Wolf.

Slade thought about it. Shook his head. "I'd rather follow up the tracks, if you're agreeable," he said. "That bunch may not know where they're going."

"And if they beat us to the others?" asked the Cherokee.

Slade thought about that, too, and told his first lie of the day.

"I came for justice," he told Little Wolf. "It doesn't matter much who serves it up."

Capitán Segundo Adolfo Domínguez Carbajal had served as a *teniente* in the Mexican army before he was promoted and seconded to the *Guardia Rural* in Chihuahua, eighteen months earlier. Since then, he had enjoyed a relatively easy life, with more authority than he had ever wielded in the military. Now, his word was law. He held the power of life or death.

Domínguez owed that power to *la ley de fuga,* the "law of flight" that permitted Rurales to shoot any suspect or prisoner who might attempt to escape. In practice, it amounted to a writ of summary execution, carried out at the whim of a unit's commander. In the year and a half since his change of careers, Domínguez had personally killed eleven—or was it twelve?—runners, while overseeing his squad's execution of twice that many.

These were bloody times in Mexico. And today, the *capitán segundo* thought, might be the worst yet.

Or the best, depending on your point of view.

It was Domínguez's good fortune that he'd been available to meet the one-armed man from Agua Verde and to hear his story about Sabiano de la Cruz. Wanted for half a dozen murders in Chihuahua, plus assorted rapes and robberies, the outlaw was worth three thousand pesos, dead or alive. Add on the possible rewards posted for his companions, all of them clearly banditos, and Domínguez could look forward to an unexpected payday.

All he had to do was find the gang, kill anyone associated with it, and put in his claim. Officials in Mexico City loved to hear that famous outlaws had been killed in flight or resisting arrest. It served a dual purpose, counteracting claims that *el presidente* was a criminal himself, while reminding campesinos everywhere that they were vulnerable if they dared to take a stand against authority.

Whatever served the president was good for *Capitán Segundo* Domínguez.

At least, it was today.

The time might come, Domínguez understood, when no amount of threatening or violence would quell unrest among the people. If and when that day arrived, he would be placed at risk, might have to flee for parts unknown and hope that no one recognized him as a former member of the *Guardia Rural*.

Or, by that time, he might be dead.

In Mexico today, few things were cheaper than a human life. Domínguez proved that very point himself, each time he passed a death sentence on yet another prisoner. Between banditos, rebels, and the normal daily hazards of his job, longevity was not the *capitán segundo*'s primary consideration.

He preferred to make the most of each day as it came, in knowledge that it might turn out to be his last.

But not this day.

Domínguez had reserved it in advance, for killing Sabiano de la Cruz and all the border scum who followed him.

Burch Thornton's backside ached, and he was tired of running. Not that he felt any urge to stop and face Jack Slade, much less his Indian. Far from it. But he'd eaten dust enough from Sabiano and the others to be sick of them and reinforce his plan to leave them all behind.

As soon as they reached Santa Bárbara de Esperanza—*if* they ever reached it—he would finalize the details of his scheme and put it into action. By the time Sabiano and the rest sat down to breakfast in his hometown, Thornton would be on his way to a new life, discarding every vestige of the person he had been.

It should be easy. What would any stranger know, except the name he gave when they were introduced, the history he made up for himself along the way? No new acquaintances would care enough to probe his background, and they'd have no means of doing so, even if they were so inclined. One thing about the West was that it let a man start over. If he didn't have a scar or birthmark that distinguished him, and if he kept his nose clean for a while, he could be anyone he chose to be.

Well, not a doctor or a lawyer. Obviously not a teacher, nor a master carpenter, though he could drive a nail all right. But something simple, like a cowboy or a handyman, maybe a store clerk if it came to that.

Why not?

Who would there be to point a finger at him, calling him a thief and killer, Peeping Tom and would-be rapist? Nobody at all.

Thornton would be reborn, not in the Jesus kind of way that preachers talked about, but as a point of fact. And if he happened to stray from the righteous path once again, at some point in the future . . . well, it would be somebody else, with a new name, whose face wound up on the posters.

"How much further?" Tommy Garrity asked Sabiano.

"Three, four hours," Sabiano answered, without looking at him. "If you're tired, amigo, stop and rest."

Garrity glared at Sabiano's back but kept his mouth shut. Thornton caught it, recognizing somebody who might be useful to him in a pinch. Better if he could simply slip away unnoticed, in the middle of the night, but if some mishap should expose him, it was good to know who else was chafing under Sabiano's thumb.

For all he knew, the rest of them might feel the same way, too, but Thornton didn't plan to take a poll. The less he said before he made his getaway, the better. He could act contented when he had to, even in the worst of circumstances, putting on a happy face to make it stick.

And if push came to shove, Thornton didn't mind backshooting, either. It beat the Hell out of facing Sabiano in a stand-up fight, where he was sure to come out second best.

Something to think about, for later, if his first plan went awry. Survivors always looked ahead, trying to cover all eventualities.

And come what may, Thornton intended to survive.

Little Wolf was not at ease in Mexico, although he managed to conceal it well enough. He knew that Mexican authorities had paid large bounties for the scalps of native tribesmen within living memory, and that Chihuahua's law permitting that inhuman trade had only been repealed within the last ten years or so. That kind of state-sanctioned brutality left a legacy of violence and hatred that would damage generations yet unborn.

Not that the Cherokee was worried about *his* scalp, in particular. He feared no man but recognized inherent danger in the atmosphere as he rode farther south with Slade, trailing the men who had murdered.

Truth be told, he hadn't been too fond of Strong Horse when the other brave was still alive. But the attack infuriated every Cherokee, while giving Little Wolf a ticket out of jail to hunt the murderers. Life on the reservation was already bad enough, but if his tribe was not secure even within the confines of the land allotted them by Washington, then what was left?

Another truth: there was a certain level of exhilaration found in hunting men that Little Wolf found lacking when he hunted other animals, for food. It was not simply knowing that a human was more dangerous, in many cases. Man hunting, as he had done with Slade, also permitted Little Wolf to vent some of the pent-up rage that was a part of every native tribesman's personality.

It had been sweet to kill the outlaws, even if they weren't the ones who murdered Strong Horse. Little Wolf believed that Slade felt the same way, after the injury that Sabiano's riders had inflicted on his woman and their friends. He understood that Slade had promised to take some of them alive, for trial in white man's court, but so far that plan was not working.

It was another of the many things that Little Wolf would never understand about white men. They killed one another in war over trifles, while slaughtering red men, women, and children for land or no reason at all, then made a great show of respecting their own kind who preyed upon them like coyotes on rabbits.

The Cherokee Nation had laws of its own, handed down from the days before white men encroached on their home in the East, but they were practical and functional. Persons accused of a crime were permitted to mount a defense, but failure to convince the tribal council of a subject's innocence led to a sentence of death or exile, depending upon the offense. Only the white man built grim prisons. Only white man made a game of justice with their lawyers dressed in finery.

Little Wolf would be glad when their long ride was over, their bloody work done. And what, then? He had promised to go back with Slade and confirm that the outlaws they'd killed were resisting arrest, but Little Wolf was having second thoughts. A white judge might not care for anything he had to say, and a return to Oklahoma meant returning to the reservation, under Agent Berringer.

What other options did he have?

He could remain in Mexico, but Little Wolf knew no one there, although he understood that there were Cherokees somewhere in Mexico. Sequoyah led them once, though he'd been dead for fifty years. It should be possible to find them, but they would be strangers to him, and he had no faith that Mexican authorities were any easier to deal with than the whites he knew at home.

Something to think about, as he led Slade along the trail blazed by their enemies. He did not have to make his choice today, but Little Wolf suspected that their quest was coming to an end.

When they were finished, and if both of them survived, he would consider how much he owed Slade and what his debt was to himself.

Slade saw the sign when it was still too small to read, but served at least as confirmation that the track they had been following all morning was in fact a road of sorts. As they drew closer, he made out pale letters, long since faded by relentless sunshine, but still legible.

It told him SANTA BÁRBARA DE ESPERANZA—5 MILES.

Slade translated as best he could. "Saint Barbara of hope. Sounds like a peaceful spot."

"You think so?" Little Wolf inquired.

"I wouldn't want to bet my life on it."

"It may not be their destination," said the Cherokee.

"We'll find out if they skirt around it," Slade replied. "If they go in, we do."

He was stating the obvious, but Little Wolf didn't object. He did say, "If they spend the night, they will be watching for us."

"Right," Slade said. "We can't just ride in, bold as brass."

They had not only Sabiano and his men to think about but the Rurales they'd seen earlier, if they were headed to the same place. Two groups of opponents for the price of one.

"If we surprise them," Little Wolf suggested, "we must wait for sundown."

Waste the afternoon, Slade would have said, but what was the alternative? If Santa Bárbara de Esperanza was a large town, they might manage slipping in by daylight, unobserved. A little burg, of Agua Verde's size or smaller, was another story. They'd be on display to anyone with eyes, a mile or more before they reached the settlement.

"We'll have to judge it when we get there," Slade decided. "Check the layout from a distance, with the telescope, and then decide what's best."

"The glass won't tell us if they've stopped to spend the night," said Little Wolf.

"No," Slade agreed. "It won't."

Which meant they might waste half a day, then infiltrate the town only to find that Sabiano and his men had passed on through, headed for God knew where. In which case, they would also waste another night, gain nothing from the time, and run a risk of losing Sabiano's tracks entirely.

On the other hand, if they found Thornton and the rest in Santa Bárbara de Esperanza, Slade would have to find some way of taking them without endangering civilians or alerting Mexican authorities. All wasted planning, if the gang put up a fight, but he had made a promise to Judge Dennison—to Faith—and would at least attempt to keep it.

"What if the big hats have taken them?" asked Little Wolf.

Damn it, another problem to consider. Slade didn't fancy his odds of staging a jailbreak to rescue the gang, then corral them and herd them all back to Judge Dennison's court. More than likely, he thought, the Rurales would shoot first and ask questions later—or not bother asking the questions at all.

Would Slade be satisfied if someone else killed Thornton and the rest? He thought about it and decided that he wasn't sure.

Better if he could get to them before the big hats had a chance. What happened after that depended on the outlaws.

And how well Slade could control his killing rage.

Another day, another goddamned dusty desert town.

Burch Thornton doffed his hat and drew a sleeve across his sweaty forehead, cursing as an errant salty drop slid into his left eye and stung him. Miserable desert heat had damn near wilted him, together with his piebald mare, and he had emptied his canteen two hours earlier.

If nothing else, they'd find some shade and something wet to drink in Sabiano's pitiful hometown.

Pitiful at a glance, because it was a smaller place than

Agua Verde, boasting only one cantina he could see, so far, and very little else. A grocery that had more flies than produce in its single dirty window, and a stable that announced its presence with a reek of old manure. The other shops were unidentifiable in passing, and the houses Thornton saw were hovels with adobe flaking off their walls.

Nothing to brag about, that he could see, much less to make a body homesick. What drew Sabiano back?

No one came out to greet them in the midday heat, which came as a relief to Thornton. He'd been worried that the town might have a lawman, but it seemed too small for that. If there were any resident Rurales, he supposed they must be taking a siesta. If they turned up later . . . well, if Thornton hadn't found a chance to slip away, he'd follow Sabiano's lead and see how that played out.

In his imagination, it went badly, drawing more attention to the gang and bringing more law down on top of them. Better by far if he could disappear before another round of fireworks started and he found retreat cut off, perhaps for good.

But not in daylight. He would have to wait until night fell on Santa Bárbara de Esperanza, then get the hell out while the getting was good.

He wasn't dreaming about new lives, now. Before he got to that stage, Thornton had to save the life he had. And with Jack Slade somewhere behind them, no doubt coming on with the determination of a bloodhound, that was likely to be difficult enough.

Thornton pulled up in front of the cantina, waited for the others to dismount, then stepped down from his mare and led it to a nearby water trough. He waited until the others were inside and out of sight before he found a place to tie his reins around the tavern's hitching rail and followed.

Just a few more hours, he told himself. *No problem.*

He could last that long and use the night for cover when he fled. Meanwhile, a drink of anything would cut the dust from Thornton's throat.

He might even enjoy it. Stranger things had happened.

But he wasn't taking any bets on that.

18

The telescope gave Slade a close-up view of Santa Bárbara de Esperanza, but the angle wasn't great. The place where they had gone to ground, the best cover available to them, was out of line with the main street. Adobe buildings blocked Slade's view of any traffic passing back and forth through town.

Assuming there *was* any traffic.

So far, the place looked like a virtual ghost town. In an hour's worth of watching, Slade had only seen only two signs of human life: an old man stepping out to pee behind one of the houses, and a boy who came out of another with a bucket, walking several paces off before he dumped its liquid contents on the ground.

He'd taken turns with Little Wolf, watching the little sunbaked town, but neither one of them had seen a man who might be one of Sabiano's riders. Which made sense, considering the hour and the fierce heat of the day that left Slade sweating in the sparse shade of the velvet mesquite trees that sheltered them. Slade figured anybody with an ounce of common sense would be indoors, which helped him not at all.

Despite the hard ground underneath him and the heat that made even his horse stand listlessly in a patch of insubstantial shadow, Slade could feel his mind drifting and losing focus, wandering toward sleep. To break the spell, he concentrated on a large red ant scurrying past him, likely scouting for a nearby colony. Slade crushed it with his thumb, then snatched his hand back quickly as the dying insect stung him.

Jesus!

Something to be learned there, maybe. Even when you thought an enemy was down and out—

"Riders," said Little Wolf.

He handed Slade the glass and pointed, but the rising dust gave them away. Rurales, probably the same ones they'd seen earlier, but how had Slade and Little Wolf arrived before them? He supposed they could've visited another village first, or checked some farms along the way.

For what?

Rurales made routine patrols, of course, but the timing was not lost on Slade. Smart money said the big hats were out looking for himself and Little Wolf, or else for Sabiano's gang.

Most likely both.

Little Wolf began to say, "If they are in the village . . ."

"Yeah," Slade said, cutting him off. "I know."

"I think there are too many of them."

"Definitely," Slade agreed, wishing his gut would listen to his brain.

There was no way that he and Little Wolf could take a dozen lawmen *and* the Sabiano gang. No way at all. It would be suicide to try.

But he supposed it wouldn't hurt to wait and watch, find out what happened next. If Sabiano's men were in the village, he at least could have whatever satisfaction might derive from seeing them arrested—or more likely, killed. Rurales weren't well known for bringing suspects in alive, particularly when the subjects were both armed and dangerous.

And now, the Hell of it was that he likely wouldn't see a thing. Their angle on the town was wrong. At best, they might hear gunshots while they sat and waited. If there was a gunfight, how would Slade know who had won?

By seeing who rode out of town when it was over.

The Rurales would, presumably, ride back the way they'd come, either alone or with corpse-laden horses in tow. Sabiano's men, if they emerged victorious, might run to any compass point, but there was no way he'd mistake them for the big hats, even at a distance.

Watch and wait, then, while he hoped . . . for what?

No answer came to mind. Slade lay and waited for the action to unfold.

Capitán Segundo Domínguez was glad to see the huddled shops and homes of Santa Bárbara de Esperanza, still a mile ahead but visible at last after the long ride from Piedras Negras. He was saddle sore and in a foul mood after wasting time at three small farms along the way, asking if anyone had seen suspicious riders passing by.

Now, he would search the town. Or to be strictly accurate, his men would search the town while Domínguez sampled the local cantina's supply of cerveza and liquor. There would be no charge for anything he drank, since no bartender in Chihuahua would be foolish enough to seek payment.

Pacifying the *Guardia Rural* was a cost of doing business in Mexico. Some officers might have demanded women with their beer and tequila, but Domínguez was seldom that greedy. Besides, any time he might spend with a *puta* would only put him that much farther behind his quarry.

Farther away from his rightful reward.

As they approached the village, Domínguez riding at the head of the column, he sketched a plan of action in his mind. First, find the cantina. Then, keeping one man with him for personal security, send off the rest in two-man teams to scour every house and store for any sign of people who did not belong.

Outlaws, gringos, an Indian. Domínguez would be pleased to deal with each of them in turn, or all at once.

His patrol entered Santa Bárbara de Esperanza with a clatter of hoofbeats, trailing dust that settled slowly as they circled once around the village square. Domínguez spotted the cantina—only one to choose from in a settlement this small—and rode directly for it, once their circuit of the plaza was completed. His men fell into line behind him, waiting for their leader to dismount before they followed suit.

Domínguez wasted no time issuing his orders. "*Subteniente* López will remain with me," he said. "The rest of you, form pairs and search the town. Bring any strangers here to us, for questioning."

López took charge from there, barking the names of those assigned to search together. "Cruz, go with Lavista. Franco with Acosta. Basañez and Montalbán. Almada with Muñiz. Fernández and Velasco. Start at the north end of town and go from there. *Rápidamente!*"

Domínguez waited long enough to see his men hop to it, then turned from the dusty square and entered the cantina, López on his heels. The place reminded him of every other small-town tavern he had visited since he was old enough to buy tequila for himself. It smelled of sweat, stale beer, tobacco, old adobe. Any nod toward cleanliness was marginal.

Domínguez felt at home.

The place had half a dozen customers, all seeking respite from the midday heat. Domínguez scanned their faces, settled on a pair of gringos seated at a table in the farthest corner from the door. They gave him furtive glances as he entered, one man whispering what could have been a warning to the other.

"This way," said Domínguez to his *subteniente*. "Ready with your pistol, eh?"

Burch Thornton heard the first shots from a privy at the rear of the cantina. He had finished buttoning his fly, was reaching for his gunbelt at the far end of the seat he'd occupied a moment earlier, and nearly dropped it down the hole as gunfire battered his eardrums.

Muttering a string of curses, Thornton pulled the belt around his waist, buckled it, and drew his Colt. It was the .41-caliber Thunderer model, supposedly favored by Billy the Kid and John Wesley Hardin. Thornton laid no claim to matching either one of them for speed or accuracy, but the weapon made a lot of noise, and if he managed a hit it would put down his man.

Clutching the pistol in his right hand, Thornton let his trembling left undo the latch that held the privy's door shut, eased it open just a crack, and squinted into bright sunlight. No threat was visible from where he stood, but even as that thought formed, more shots echoed through the open back door of the small cantina.

What to do?

He'd left Tom Garrity and Monty Stofer at a four-man table when he went outside to answer Nature's call. At least two other members of the gang, Worley and Fortunato, had been upstairs with their whores. Thornton had no idea where Sabiano was, maybe roaming around the little burg in search of long-lost family.

To Hell with him. Thornton was looking out for number one.

He cracked the privy door another foot and peered around it, making sure that there was no one crouched in ambush on the other side. When he had satisfied himself the coast was clear, Thornton stepped from the little sweatbox and considered what to do.

He could return to the cantina, ten or twelve long strides from where he stood, and find out what was happening inside there, but he'd run a risk of being sucked into the gunplay. Or, his other option, run back to the livery and vamoose out of town before trouble came looking for him. What he *couldn't* do was stand around outside the shitter, wasting precious time.

The livery won out. His saddlebags were there, and he'd left nothing in the tavern that he couldn't live without. The key word there was *living*, and the best way to improve his odds for that lay in getting out of Santa Bárbara de Esperanza while the rest of Sabiano's gang and their opponents kept each other busy.

By the time the smoke cleared, win or lose, the others wouldn't give a second thought to Thornton. When they recalled him later, if they did, he'd simply be a fading memory. They might wonder if he had gotten out alive, but wouldn't really care.

And if they lost, they'd all be sucking cactus from the bitter root end, anyway. No thoughts at all, of any kind.

Keeping his Colt in hand, eyes on the open back door of the tavern, Thornton started making tracks. The stable was located at the far south end of town, but "far" was relative. The town itself was only three blocks long.

If he could make it that far, saddle up his piebald mare, and make it out of town before someone from either side laid eyes on him, he had a chance.

If not . . . well, then, he had the Thunderer.

"Much shooting," Little Wolf observed. His tone was flat, completely neutral.

"If Sabiano's gang is in there, plus the twelve Rurales," Slade replied, "they have plenty of guns."

"You don't mind if the big hats die," his guide remarked. It didn't sound like a question to Slade.

"What, because they're police?" he inquired.

"If they are."

"That's a point," Slade acknowledged. Many of the articles he'd read in newspapers portrayed the *Guardia Rural* as a pack of legitimized bandits. But even if the ones engaged in battle at the moment weren't corrupt, what did it mean to Slade?

He couldn't think of anything.

"We can't help anyone by barging in," he said. "The Mexicans won't thank us for it, and it could distract them to the point of getting killed, so it's our fault. They damn sure wouldn't ask whose side we're on before they started shooting at us."

Little Wolf said nothing and kept his keen eyes focused on the desert town where gunfire echoed in the streets. Each time Slade thought it was subsiding, there would come another rattling surge of shots across the open ground that lay between him and the settlement of Santa Bárbara de Esperanza.

Not much hope, Slade thought. *And no saints, either.*

Maybe God would save the town, but Slade didn't expect it. If he had a hope for the engagement's outcome, it would be for innocent civilians to escape unharmed, while Sabiano and the rest were wounded and disarmed, unable to resist him as he led them back to Oklahoma Territory for their trial and hanging.

Which omitted the Rurales from his thinking altogether— or, was Slade prepared to wish them dead, after they'd beaten down the gang enough for him to do the mopping up? He didn't like to think of it that way, but maybe it was close.

The truth: he wouldn't know one of the big-hat riders from another if they passed him on the street. Slade didn't know them, didn't *want* to know them. And if they were killed today, he was fresh out of tears. Call it a late addition to the tab that Thornton, Sabiano, and the rest already owed.

The sun had shifted since they found their stand, and Slade took time to move his horse, letting it take advantage of what shade there was. He offered Little Wolf the telescope, before he made the move, but his companion silently declined, a head shake all the answer he could spare.

He's seen enough, Slade thought. *Well, so have I.*

That didn't mean he felt like riding in and adding two more guns to the inflammatory mix of outlaws, might-be lawmen, and the town's assorted occupants. For all he knew, some of the villagers—hell, *all* of them—might be on Sabiano's side. In which case, there was no way he and Little Wolf could take the gang or rescue the Rurales.

He'd stick with his original decision. Wait it out, see who emerged victorious, and go from there. If Thornton's buddies took the big hats down, it would be Slade's turn to go after them. Again. If they came out of Santa Bárbara de Esperanza draped across their saddles, it was finished.

But if they came out in irons . . .

"I guess we'll see," Slade whispered to his roan, while gunfire crackled in the clear, dry air.

Thornton had nearly reached the stable when a too-familiar voice reached out to stop him. "Where you running to, amigo?" Sabiano asked from somewhere to his left.

Thornton stopped short and spun to find the bandit leader watching him, hip cocked, Winchester cradled in his arms. He thought fast, let his startled look melt into gratitude, as he replied, "Looking for you. All Hell's broke loose. We need you."

"I have ears," said Sabiano. "It is the Rurales, *sí?*"

A jerky nod from Thornton answered him. Grunting, "Uh-huh."

"And you were looking for me . . . where, amigo?"

"Any-damn-where I could think of," Thornton said. "You weren't at the cantina with the rest of us."

"Tha's right," the Mexican agreed. "I wasn't."

Feeling sickly, Thornton pressed him, "So, you comin' back with me or not?"

More gunfire, coming from the general direction of the tavern. Thornton fought a suicidal urge to draw on Sabiano, try to take him down, and then keep running to the stable. Anything to save himself.

"To fight with the Rurales?" Sabiano thought about it for another moment, then said, "*Sí.* Why not. You lead the way, amigo."

Thornton swallowed hard, braced himself for a shot in the back as he turned and started back toward the cantina, moving closer to the storefronts and the little cover they provided. Sabiano didn't shoot him, though; just came along behind him at an easy pace, like they were headed for a picnic, rather than a massacre.

Funny, but not in any way intended to wring a laugh from Thornton. By all rights, he should have been inside the stable, saddling his horse right now. Instead, he'd wound up volunteering to be killed.

Thornton nearly jumped out of his skin as two Rurales suddenly appeared before him, jogging from an alley on his left, into the street. He might have chuckled at their huge sombreros, but the guns they carried stifled any such impulse. The pair of them were veering off toward the cantina, where the battle was in progress, when they saw Thornton and Sabiano on the far side of the street.

One of them shouted something that had "gringo" in it, but the rest was lost on Thornton as they swung around, raising their carbines. His pistol might have weighed a hundred pounds, the way it wobbled in his grip until he used both hands to lift it, thumbing back the hammer, grappling to acquire a target.

Sabiano shot the taller of the two Rurales with his Winchester before Thornton could aim. The loud report behind him made him jerk the Colt's trigger reflexively, the six-gun kicking in his grasp. Against all odds, his bullet struck the other Mexican, a lousy leg shot, but it dropped his man to one knee, while his carbine shot flew high and wide.

Thornton was aiming for a second shot when Sabiano finished it, the crack of his Winchester numbing Thornton's ears and sending the Rurale's big sombrero on a tumbling flight to nowhere, stained with blood.

"You see, it's easy," Sabiano told him. "Now, let's go and finish with the rest."

"Sounds like it's winding down," Slade said.

It had been twenty minutes, give or take, since the first gunshots, and there could be no doubt about it as the firing sputtered down to stray shots here and there. That didn't tell them who had won, or whether anyone was standing in the village. Shooters running out of targets, or the village running out of shooters. Take your pick.

Slade's problem was deciding when—or if—to move. It could be fatal if they blundered in on one side or the other, mopping up. Surprising winners in a gunfight wasn't healthy, if they still had any ammunition left to burn.

Little Wolf must be aware of that, but still he asked the question. "Go in now?"

"Better to wait a bit," Slade answered.

And the words had barely left his lips when a long figure ran into his field of vision, smallish even with the telescope. A single man, running as if he had a pack of hellhounds on his heels. He was bare-headed, Mexican, apparently unarmed. The bandoleers that drew an X across his chest pegged him as one of the Rurales.

Slade saw his pursuers seconds later. Two men who had kept their hats and weapons, neither face familiar to him through the spyglass. When they had a line of sight on the Rurale, both stopped dead and raised their guns, a pistol and a Winchester, taking their time to aim.

Both fired together, one or both scoring a hit that dropped the runner facedown in the dust. Dying, he wriggled like a stranded swimmer, while the shooters came to stand above him, studying their handiwork. After another minute, more or less, the pistolero fired a close-range head shot and the Mexican lay still.

"I'd say that settles it," Slade said.

"You recognize them?" Little Wolf inquired.

"No," Slade said, "but they're both gringos. If they aren't with Sabiano, who else could they be?"

The Cherokee responded with a silent shrug. He was right. There was an outside chance—one in a couple hundred thousand, say—that the Rurales had come hunting Sabiano's gang and stumbled on another one, by chance. Slade didn't buy it, but he couldn't absolutely rule it out.

The only way to know, for sure, was to go in and find out for himself.

Slade checked his pocket watch and said, "It's barely two o'clock. There's lots of daylight left."

Thinking about the walk from where they stood to Santa Bárbara de Esperanza. Something like a quarter mile with nothing that resembled cover, and a rifleman could pick them off before they even saw it coming. Slade thought they might as well put guns to their own heads, eliminate the middleman.

"So many dead," said Little Wolf, "they may not wait for dark to leave."

"You're right," Slade granted, but it didn't solve his problem. Even if they left their animals behind, two men on foot made tempting targets in the open desert. If they weren't cut down within the first few yards—say, if their enemies skedaddled out the other side of town—then they'd lose more time doubling back to get their horses and give chase.

"See this," said Little Wolf.

Slade raised his glass again, to find the gunmen dragging off their victim, one clutching each of the Rurale's feet. The body left a drag mark in the dust.

"They're taking time to tidy up," Slade said.

"Maybe they stay," said Little Wolf.

"Or hide their tracks, at least," Slade said. "It stands to reason that they'll be distracted, then."

"We try it?" asked the Cherokee.

"We might as well," Slade said. "But separate, circling around to east and west."

Little Wolf, already moving, said, "I'll see you later," and was gone.

"I hope so," Slade replied, but he was talking to himself.

19

Little Wolf had chosen the eastern approach to the village, so Slade took the west. A flash-flood channel covered him for roughly half the distance that he had to travel, jogging hunched over in sand marked by sidewinder tracks. Slade didn't see the snakes themselves, but did spook an old vulture picking stringy meat from a coyote carcass.

Nothing wasted in the desert, from a drop of water to a shred of dessicated flesh. Red ants would eat whatever Mr. Buzzard missed, and the coyote's bones would ultimately fertilize a cactus or a yucca plant.

That could be me, Slade thought, then put it out of mind. His nerves were wound tightly enough without another twist for worry's sake.

The last three hundred yards or so were open ground. He had considered crawling, then abandoned the idea. It wouldn't help much with concealment in the open—might even wind up attracting more attention—while it flayed his hands and knees before he ever got to Santa Bárbara de Esperanza. Hunching over was the best that Slade could do, and even that drove little needles deep into his lower back, until he straightened up and took his chances walking like a man.

The town was quiet after all that shooting. No raised voices, women wailing, horses whinnying. A dog barked once, but that was all.

Slade wondered if the little burg was used to sudden death, or if the battle had claimed more lives than he'd thought. Slade hadn't tried to count the shots that came in flurries, rising to gale force at one point, then subsiding slowly into silence. He'd seen one Rurale die, and took for granted that the rest were down as well. But what about the town's normal inhabitants?

One thing he was sure of: two gunmen, at least, were still alive. They'd fired the last shots of the day, so far, and hadn't ridden out of town since then. It seemed too much to hope that all of Sabiano's other men were dead.

In fact, Slade hoped they weren't.

When he reached the village outskirts, Slade considered it a fair accomplishment. He'd made a belly-buster draw against an inside straight and filled it, but the hand was still in play. He didn't know what the other players were holding, or even how many remained in the game.

Killer odds.

A narrow alleyway between two buildings offered shade and access to the town's main street. Slade took advantage of it and immediately felt as if he'd stepped into a kiln, surrounded by adobe walls that had been baking in the sun all day.

Out of the frying pan, he thought. *Into the fire.*

Burch Thornton helped Ned Worley drag the last Rurale to the spot behind the livery that Sabiano had selected as their body dump. He made it fifteen stiffs, including Monty Stofer and some Mexican who'd run into the crossfire in the plaza, thinking God knew what before a storm of lead ripped into him.

Stupid.

"These bodies will be ripe before you know it," Worley said. "Some of 'em smell already."

"Gonna draw coyotes," Thornton said. "And buzzards."

"Me, I'd just as soon not be here while they're chowin' down," said Worley.

"I'm with you," said Thornton. "But if Sabiano wants to stay—"

"He's crazy," Worley finished the remark.

"But still in charge," Thornton reminded him.

"Things change," said Worley.

"Oh? How's that?"

Ned shrugged. Replied, "People gotta look out for themselves. That's all I'm sayin'."

Thornton didn't bother answering that platitude. He couldn't argue with it, and he didn't want to chase it any further, in case Worley had a mind to tattle on him later. Anything could happen in a gang like Sabiano's, and another chance to flee had slipped through Thornton's fingers, lost beyond recall.

Worley took Thornton's silence as an invitation to keep talking. "Look," he said, "we've both seen Sabiano shoot. He's fast, all right, but—"

"But nothin'," Thornton interrupted him. "Just say whatever's on your mind, and say it plain."

Worley stared at Thornton for a moment, then opened his mouth to speak, but never got the words out. From the plaza, up ahead of them, another shot rang out and echoed through the village.

"Jesus!" Thornton said. "What, now?"

They had been walking down the middle of the street,

nothing in sight before or after the gunshot. As Thornton
pulled his Colt, he veered off toward the buildings on his
left for cover, leaving Worley to decide what he should do.
It wasn't any great surprise when Ned fell into step behind
him, jogging to catch up.

"You think they found another Messican?" he asked.

"The town's nothin' *but* Mexicans," said Thornton.

"Yeah, but—"

"Hush a spell and let me listen," Thornton ordered.

Dumb as dirt, Worley replied, "Okay. Sure thing."

Ready for anything, Burch Thornton crept along the
street with Worley on his heels, hoping the idjit didn't acci-
dentally shoot him in the back.

The plaza was deserted when Slade reached it, or appeared
to be. He lingered at the alley's mouth, hoping the shadows
there would hide him from a casual observer. One good
thing: the buildings he could see from where he stood
weren't big on windows, and the ones they had were shut-
tered, either keeping out the midday heat or holding secrets
locked inside. Whichever it was, anyone trying to spot him
would be forced to peer through narrow slits that would
keep their range of vision to a minimum.

Good for defense, up to a point. Lousy for spotting enemies as they approached.

Slade risked a look around the corner, left and right,
ready to pull back in a second if he saw someone nearby.
The village had no sidewalks, only dust up to the thresholds
of surrounding shops, and there was no one on the street as
far as he could see. No sign of Little Wolf across the square.

Slade wondered if the Cherokee was hidden somewhere
over there, as he was, watching Slade watch out for him. If
so, he gave no sign. Slade tried to think of reasons why he

wouldn't show, then dropped it when the list began to run long in his mind.

He could be there all day and night, waiting for Little Wolf to show himself. Instead, Slade knew he ought to make a move. The sooner the better, while he had the street and plaza to himself.

First step into the open, easing back the hammer on his Winchester, a round already in the chamber. Slade had barely cleared the alley when he heard a door scrape open, to his right, and saw a figure step into daylight.

The man was Mexican, but not your standard villager or campesino. He was short and wiry, thin-faced underneath a flat-brimmed hat, and wore twin pistols on his hips. He was about to light a cigarillo, when he cut a glance toward Slade and froze.

How long that moment lasted, Slade could never rightly say. It ended when the pistolero dropped his match and reached for both his guns at once, but Slade already had his Winchester on target, careful not to jerk the trigger when he fired.

The shot cracked out between them, and the gunman staggered backward, empty hands still precious inches from his pistol grips. He went down like a puppet with its strings snipped in the middle of a dance, raising a puff of dust on impact with the ground.

So much for sneaking up on Sabiano's crew.

Hoping that Little Wolf was somewhere close at hand, but not counting on it, Slade moved toward the open doorway where the gunman's body lay.

Little Wolf *was* watching Slade, from his position crouching atop a flat-roofed building at the southeast corner of the village plaza. He had found a ladder propped against the back wall when he got there, and with no sign of a tenant to oppose him, he had gone for the advantage of a bird's-eye view.

Slade had not spotted him, as far as Little Wolf could tell, but he was covering the lawman when their enemy stepped out into the street. He could have dropped the Mexican with his Sharps carbine, easily, but Slade took care of that and rushed on toward the entrance to whatever sort of building had disgorged the dead man.

A cantina or a brothel? Little Wolf was at a loss to say, and did not care, as long as Slade took care while entering. His gunshot would have sounded an alert to everyone in town, outlaws and peasant folk alike. How they responded, after all the recent killing, still remained to be observed.

Slade reached the doorway, fanned an arm across it as a test, and drew no gunfire from inside. A second later, he was gone, vanished into the building, out of sight. More shooting started then, pistols and Slade's Winchester, nothing Little Wolf could do from where he lay.

But then he heard the sound of voices issuing from somewhere down below him. Two men, not quite whispering, moving along the same side of the street where Little Wolf was stationed. They were moving close against the shop fronts, where he couldn't see or fire at them unless he stood upright and leaned over the low adobe parapet that edged the roof.

Making himself a target if they saw him first.

Instead, he scrambled back across the rooftop, to the waiting ladder. Clambering swiftly down its trembling length to reach the ground, he slipped around the east side of the building. By the time he reached the plaza, the men were fifty feet beyond him. Fifty feet closer to Slade's blind side.

He made a choice and shouted, nothing either one of them would understand. A curse, in Cherokee. Both turned as one to face him, pistols leveled, the surprise clear on their faces as they saw him. Switching back to English, Little Wolf said, "Drop them!" Sighting on the nearer gunman as he spoke.

He fired as both men raised their guns, his heavy bullet ripping through the first target's chest and slamming him away. The other gunman fanned two wasted shots as Little Wolf ducked backward, out of sight, and hurried to reload.

A footstep scurry as the other fled, and by the time he looked again, crouched low, the second man was gone.

Scowling, he set off in pursuit.

Sabiano de la Cruz was drinking mescal when the shooting started up again. He'd had enough already that he didn't flinch at the first shot, took time in fact to drain his fourth glass of the liquor made from the succulent agave plant. It stoked the fire inside him, as he rose to go and find out what was happening.

The first shot could have been an accident, or an expression of exuberance. His men fired weapons indiscriminately— sometimes at stray animals, or persons who offended them, who didn't?—but the concentrated firing that had started by the time he reached the plaza could not be so easily explained.

And when he heard the loud *bam* of a weapon larger than his people carried, something like a long-range hunter used, he knew they had a problem.

Sabiano left the private home he'd commandeered for privacy, old friends of his long-since-departed family, and turned toward the cantina. He took his time, because only a fool ran toward a gunfight when he didn't know how it had started or who all might be involved.

Crossing the plaza at an angle, Sabianio drew his right-hand pistol, left the other in its holster and his left hand free. He wished that he had brought his Winchester, but hadn't

thought of it, suffused with alcoholic confidence instilled
by the mescal, and couldn't go back for it now.

No matter.

Anyone he couldn't kill with twelve shots had to be invincible, so it was hopeless anyway.

Which, naturally, did not mean he wouldn't try.

He circled to the rear of the cantina, went in that way,
wondering if there'd been more Rurales in the hunting party
than they'd seen? Hard to believe they would have hidden
in the shadows while their comrades died, but anything was
possible. Maybe a band of reinforcements coming late, but
then, where were their horses?

Or, he wondered, could it be the gringo lawman and his
indio? If they had followed him somehow, from Agua
Verde . . .

Sabiano smelled the heady scent of gun smoke as he
entered the cantina through its back door, pistol cocked in
one hand, while his other slid along the rough adobe wall.
A few more yards to reach the barroom, through a curtain
made of cheap strung beads, but Sabiano paused there in
the darkness, squinting as he tried to scan the main room
and discover who was killing whom.

A figure staggered past the doorway, obviously wounded,
turning in the last moment before it dropped. He recognized
Tom Garrity, clutching his chest and spitting blood, Colt
dropping from his palsied fingers as he fell.

"Mierda!" Sabiano hissed and drew his second gun
before he vaulted through the rattling veil to join the fight.

Another man was drinking in the tavern when Slade entered,
after taking down his friend outside. The light was poor,
likely designed that way to make the *putas* more desirable,
but he could tell the drinker was a gringo. He'd set down

his glass but hadn't drawn a weapon yet, though it was plainly on his mind.

"Think twice," Slade told him. "I want you alive."

"For what?" the stranger asked. And, "Who'n Hell are you?"

"Jack Slade."

"Shit-fire! You're Thornton's marshal."

"Not his, in particular," Slade said.

"And not mine, neither."

As he spoke, the gunman kicked back in his chair, went sprawling, but still managed to produce his six-gun with a decent draw. Slade fired his Winchester and missed, before the pistol slammed a shot at him that whispered past his ear.

Slade hit the floor, rolled over as a second shot smashed glass somewhere above him, jagged pieces raining down. There wasn't much in way of cover, but he wriggled underneath a table while his adversary lurched upright.

Can't lose him now, Slade thought and realized that Little Wolf wouldn't be able to support his version of the shooting, or the last one. Slade would have to plead his case alone before Judge Dennison—or not, if he decided there was no point going back.

If he was was still alive.

First things first.

He saw the shooter making for a little gate that would've let him duck behind the bar. Slade fired a quick shot from the floor and heard it hit, a hard, wet slapping sound. His adversary staggered, then collapsed.

Thornton was cut off from the stable now, the Indian somewhere behind him, stalking him for some reason. Slade's Indian, it had to be. Hard to figure what the world was coming to, when he was hounded by a marshal without jurisdiction and a redskin he had never met, from Oklahoma Territory all the way to Mexico.

One thing seemed plain enough: Slade hadn't followed him this far with any thought of making an arrest.

The only way to shake the lawman and his Indian would be to kill him. And it stood to reason that he couldn't manage that while he was running for his life.

Huddled inside the recessed doorway of a smelly butcher's shop, Thornton decided that he needed help. With Worley down, how many of the gang were still alive? He started counting, finished with two fingers left to spare. Three men besides himself, out of the twelve who'd ridden onto Faith Connover's spread—how long ago?

It felt like years.

Worst damned idea he'd ever had, but there was nothing he could do to change it now. Live with the outcome, if he *could* live, and complete the job he'd bungled on the marshal's wedding day.

Which meant finding the others, fast, and pulling them together while they still had time.

He risked a look around the square and couldn't see the Indian. No way of knowing if the brave was waiting for him somewhere, out of sight, to drill Thornton the minute that he showed himself. Waiting would only tip the odds in favor of him getting killed, however, so he swallowed hard and set off running like a lunatic for the cantina.

Thornton heard a rifle crack behind him, almost stumbled from the panic of it, but he somehow kept his balance, ran on, waiting for another shot that didn't come. Loud weapon. Maybe some kind of a big-bore single shot?

Maybe his luck was changing, after all.

He reached the tavern, glancing back, and nearly tripped over a body lying in his path. Saw Miguel Fortunato's dead eyes staring past him and revised the count to three survivors, with himself included. He lunged across the threshold and collapsed on hands and knees for just a second, breathing hard, then scrambled to his feet again as gunfire hammered at him from the barroom.

"Are you dead, amigo?" Sabiano de la Cruz asked someone Thornton couldn't see.

"Not yet," a grim voice answered—and another shot slammed Thornton's ears.

Then, silence. Thornton waited, heard a scrape of footsteps in another moment, wondering if Sabiano had disposed of the lawman. In other circumstances, he'd have turned and fled, but there was still the Indian somewhere behind him, in the plaza.

Trembling and sweating like a fever victim, Thornton edged along the hallway, toward the barroom.

Finish it, a small voice in his head insisted. *Do it now!*

Slade stood over the corpse of Sabiano de la Cruz and waited for the first sweet rush of satisfaction to envelop him. When he felt nothing, not even relief, he told himself it was because he hadn't finished yet. As far as he knew, there were still two members of the outfit drawing breath in Santa Bárbara de Esperanza.

One of them, Burch Thornton.

How was Slade supposed to find him? And, while he was thinking of it, where was Little Wolf?

He hadn't heard the Sharps carbine, but that was easily explained by all the racket he'd been making in the tavern. Little Wolf could have dispatched a herd of deer outside, and Slade wouldn't have noticed it while he was fighting for his life.

And if the Cherokee had drawn a losing hand? What, then?

"Then nothing," Slade told Sabiano's corpse. "I finish up."

"You talkin' to yourself?" a voice asked from behind

him, bringing Slade around to face a smallish man with a large pistol in hand.

"It happens now and then," he granted.

"Done a bit of that myself," the stranger said. "It's good to know I ain't the only one around here who's gone loco."

"I'm guessing these were friends of yours," Slade said.

"We rode a ways together," said the other. " 'Friends' is stretchin' it."

"I didn't catch your name," said Slade.

The small man swallowed hard and said, "Burch Thornton. Reckon I'm the one you're lookin' for."

"One of them," Slade acknowledged.

"All that's left," Thornton replied. "You'n your redskin took the rest."

"You're not surprised to see me, then."

"Been waitin' for it," Thornton said, voice cracking. "Swear to Christ, I wish I'd never started this, but it's too late to change things now."

"I'll tell you what I told the others," Slade said. "There are two ways we can do this. One, you live a while and see what happens with Judge Dennison. The other ends right here."

"When I drop you, you mean?" The smile that Thornton forced looked like a death's-head grimace.

"If you're quick and accurate enough," Slade said. "You want to go that route, I guess we'll see."

A silent shadow loomed out of the hallway behind Thornton. Little Wolf leveled his Sharps and said, "He isn't quick enough."

Slade saw the gunman's shoulders slump, the muzzle of his six-gun droop. Thornton said, "Can you tell me one thing, Marshal?"

"Do my best," Slade said.

"Just how'n Hell you plan to get us out of Mexico alive?"

20

The main thing, Slade decided, was to steer clear of the Federales and Rurales on their ride back to the border. They were starting late from Santa Bárbara de Esperanza, leaving death behind them for the townsfolk to clean up, and dusk would catch them twenty-five to thirty miles from town if they were fortunate enough to get that far.

And they did, in fact, shaving an hour off their head start with a ruse that Little Wolf devised, taking a westward course when they left town, and only turning north again when they had put the village out of sight. When Mexican authorities arrived, as Slade knew they would eventually, maybe they'd be misdirected for a while.

And maybe not.

It was the only hand they had to play, and Thornton offered no objection, riding with his ankles bound beneath his horse's belly, while Slade led the piebald mare himself. They left his hands free, since he'd been disarmed and couldn't grab the reins—or leap for freedom, either, without swinging underneath the mare and likely dashing out his brains.

They rode that way until night overtook them near a copse of trees that told them water was available. Concealed within the thicket, they made camp and let the horses drink, while Slade tied Thornton to the trunk of a Chihuahua pine. He'd thought of picking a catclaw acacia instead but didn't want to lose sleep while his captive moaned all night from thorns prodding his back.

One out of ten in custody was sure to irritate Judge Dennison. Thornton had told them all about the tenth man, Perry Larson, who had left the gang immediately after the attack on Faith's place and could be most anywhere by now. Slade filed his name away, with a description, thinking he could start the hunt again as soon as he'd dropped Thornton off in Enid and completed his report.

The good news: Little Wolf had made his mind up to return and speak on Slade's behalf, concerning all the outlaws they had killed along the way, although he wasn't sold on going back to drudgery and hunger on the reservation. Slade made no attempt to counsel him in that regard, but knew he'd never take part in a search for Little Wolf, if his companion made a run for it.

Slade calculated that they'd ridden some six hundred miles since picking up the trail of Faith's attackers at the Crawford spread. An epic journey in itself, and it would nearly double by the time he made it back, if that was in the cards. If they spared the horses from a killing pace and met no obstacles along the way, Slade calculated that he should be home within ten or eleven days.

Which meant another full day's ride before they crossed the Rio Grande. With any luck, they'd spend tomorrow night in Texas and could light a fire, secure against arrest if nothing else.

"Reckon they'll hang me?" Thornton asked, while Slade was standing watch and Little Wolf was catching up on sleep.

Feeling no urge to spare his feelings, Slade replied, "I'd guess so."

"For the dead'uns."

"Right."

"Don't guess there's any point in saying I was there but didn't do the killing."

"That's up to the judge," Slade said. "He's got a book of rules to follow."

"So do you, supposedly."

"Meaning?"

"You ain't suppose to be in Mexico. Leastways, not actin' like a lawman."

"Anyone can make a citizen's arrest," said Slade.

"You ain't a citizen down here," Thornton reminded him.

"You're splitting hairs. I've got you. That's an end to it."

"How come you didn't go ahead and shoot me, back in town? I bet you wanted to."

"You'd win," Slade answered. "But I made a promise."

"To that judge," said Thornton. "But it didn't stop you with the others."

"They were fighting," Slade replied. "I didn't execute them. That's somebody else's job."

"But still, if it was me—"

"I'm not you," Slade reminded him.

"I only meant—"

"Shut up and go to sleep," Slade said. "We've got a long, hot ride tomorrow, starting early."

The next day *was* a long, hot ride, but they got lucky. They met no Federales or Rurales on their way north to the border—met no one at all, in fact, except a solitary peddler headed south, his wagon full of pots and knickknacks rattling loud enough that they could hear him coming from a quarter mile. It felt almost as if the sun had purged the landscape, cleared a path for them to reach the Rio Grande.

In fact, Slade guessed, it would've taken time from Santa
Bárbara de Esperanza to alert the law, then wait for troopers
to arrive. For all he knew, the dozen dead Rurales in the
village were responsible for all the law enforcement in that
corner of Chihuahua, with no reinforcements on call.

Crossing the river in a purple dusk, Slade felt the first
hint of relief since he'd awakened long weeks earlier, in Dr.
Abernathy's hospital. He had a feeling that they just might
make it, after all.

Then, thinking of the news that might be waiting for him
back in Enid, dread returned, as chilling as the river's current lapping at his feet.

Slade calculated they should be six days in transit between
rivers, from the Rio Grande to the Red, then he allowed a
seventh for whatever problems they might have along the
way. A state that large, it could be anything from sandstorms
to flash floods, even without the human interference factor
added in. He put his badge back on, that night in camp, and
hoped that it would see them through whatever confronta-
tions might arise, but you could never tell.

For starters there were nature's wild cards: rattlesnakes
and cougars, wolves and bears. It was a zoo out there, only
the cages lacking, but the predators you really had to watch
for traveled on two legs.

Their last time through the Lone Star State, there'd been
Comanche renegades at large, and outlaws were a constant
threat to travelers and homesteaders alike. Depending on
location, Slade had learned while he was drifting, gambling
for his living, certain lawmen in the area weren't far removed
from criminals, themselves. Besides all that, there might be
white men who got itchy in proximity to Little Wolf.

No problem, Slade decided. If he couldn't badge his way

through any problems they encountered, they were still well armed and disinclined to argue much.

Thornton, somewhat surprisingly, turned out to be no problem. Slade had half expected him to try something along the way, maybe work loose from being tied at night and try to make a run for it, but nothing of the kind occurred. The knots Slade used were tight, and double-checked by Little Wolf, but Thornton also seemed to lack the spirit for a break. He rarely spoke unless directly questioned, and showed little interest in their meager fare of jerky, corn dodgers, and anything that Little Wolf could bag in arid country.

Their best meal of the journey was wild turkey, shot when they were nearly halfway home, crossing the plains between Lubbock and Abilene. Slade wasn't much good in a kitchen, but he did all right with meat over a spit, and no one criticized him for the drumsticks being on the crisp side.

Half a day from the Red River, they met Texas Rangers for the second time. A different bunch, less surly than the others, but they all still looked askance at Little Wolf, seeming to think that Slade was nuts for riding with an Indian. Their leader asked if Thornton had committed any crimes in Texas, leaving Slade to say that he had no idea. Eventually satisfied that he was bound to hang in Oklahoma, they rode off in search of someone else—two Mexicans accused of stealing salt, whatever that was all about.

Slade made a point of crossing the Red River where they had before, at its Prairie Dog Town Fork. The water was a little lower this time, but not much. Slade kept an eye on Thornton, more from fear he might be swept away than that he'd choose the river-crossing as an opportunity to run for it. Leading a second horse while managing his own was awkward, but Slade got them both across in barely twice the time that Little Wolf required.

Their first night back in Oklahoma Territory, camping out, Thornton seemed restless. That was only natural, Slade thought, as they drew closer to his place and day of judgment, but aside from looking nervous, Thornton kept his feelings to himself. If he was praying for deliverance, he kept that quiet, too.

Despite an urge to question him, Slade left the prisoner alone. He didn't ask how Thornton felt about the lives that had been wasted on his whim to punish Faith for firing him, or if he thought the end result was worth it for a half-baked moment of revenge born out of petty spite. He didn't bother to inquire if Thornton had considered, even for a moment, that his own behavior had produced his firing and it was nobody else's fault.

It was too late for such considerations now. Thornton had muffed his chance to think about a move before he made it. Now, he'd have to pay the price, whatever that turned out to be.

And Slade would be there when Judge Dennison passed sentence. If it meant the rope, he would be there to watch when Thornton did his air dance and departed from this world.

The cold truth: he was looking forward to it.

On their last day out from Enid, Slade asked Little Wolf about the rez and whether he'd decided about going back. The Cherokee was slow to answer, maybe thinking Slade would be assigned to chase him if he ran, but he must've known that job would fall to soldiers out of Fort Supply.

At last, he said, "I don't like Agent Berringer."

"Can't say I warmed to him, myself," Slade said.

"He robs my people and your government," said Little Wolf. "They send him money for prime beef, but we eat scraps and gristle."

"Makes you wonder where the money went," said Slade.

"His pocket," Little Wolf replied, with firm conviction.

"On a deal like that, with money out of Washington, there must be records," Slade suggested. "And he'd have to buy the meat your people get somewhere close by."

"There is a rancher I have seen come visiting," said Little Wolf. "His name is Jackson. Fat, red hair, what there is left of it."

"Shouldn't be hard to find," Slade said. "I'll sniff around when we get back and see what's going on. Look for a place where I can get a crowbar in between them. My experience, thieves turn on one another pretty quick, if one gets the idea that he can save himself."

They rode a little while in silence, then, before the Cherokee asked Slade, "Why would you do that?"

"If they're criminals and I can prove it, that would be my job," Slade said. "Plus which, it galls me, big men kicking people when they're down."

"Red people," Little Wolf reminded him.

"That makes a difference to some," Slade said. "Not me."

"I said before, you are a strange white man."

"If that's the worst I'm called today," Slade said, "I should get by all right."

Little Wolf said, "You cannot change the way things are between our peoples."

"I suppose not," Slade replied. "That doesn't mean nobody ought to try."

Thornton broke silence, then, to ask, "You two some kinda blood brothers or somethin'?"

"Something," Slade agreed, without a glance back at his prisoner. Beyond that, explanation failed him, and he figured Thornton wasn't worth the effort, anyway.

"I had a little brother," Thornton said. "He caught diphtheria and died when he was barely two. Folks took it hard."

Slade couldn't think of a response to that, or reason out

why Thornton felt the need to mention it. A misplaced bid for sympathy, perhaps? A random thought that he might see his brother soon, in some version of afterlife?

Whatever Thornton had in mind, the reminiscence seemed to clear his mind of any thoughts worth voicing, and he lapsed back into silence. Slade was relieved to have him quiet, concentrating on the trail ahead of them and freeing up his thoughts for images of Faith.

Was she awake yet? Even still alive? He wanted to be back in Enid now, but simultaneously dreaded it. If there was bad news waiting for him at the hospital, Slade didn't want to hear it, but he couldn't put it off indefinitely.

One way or another, Thornton had to face his day in court.

Slade hated stopping when the sun went down that evening, but he had come too far to risk the last leg of his journey on some dumb mistake. They camped a half day's ride from Enid, in a grove of oak and red sassafras with a stream running through it, the best site they'd found in their travels so far. Slade wished that he could take it as an omen, but he'd given up belief in signs and wonders when he was a child and couldn't backtrack now.

It would require a miracle to change his mind, and what would that be? Faith awake and healthy, on her own two feet and smiling at him?

Maybe.

He'd believe it when he saw it, but as Slade took first watch for the night, he didn't count on anything. Faith *was* his miracle, and she'd been snatched away from him by men who cared for nothing but themselves. He'd settled up with all but two of them, and one might be forever out of reach.

The other was securely bound, almost within arm's reach. It would have been a simple, satisfying thing to cut his throat and watch him shiver like a grounded fish until his heart stopped pumping.

Simple, satisfying—and completely wrong.

Slade turned away from Thornton, toward their morning's destination, and surrendered his imagination to the night.

Coffee and corn dodgers at the crack of dawn. It wasn't much to ride on, but Slade's stomach couldn't handle any more. He surely didn't need caffeine to boost his nervous energy as they broke camp and saddled up. Binding Burch Thornton to his mare, Slade double-checked the knots to guard against eleventh-hour slipups. Making sure he wouldn't have to shoot his prisoner within sight of their goal.

Hard to explain, no matter how he dressed it up, and winging Thornton on the fly might be beyond him. Easier to aim dead-center and be done with it.

Enid lay northwest of their last night's camp, so they were riding into sunrise, more or less. At first, it looked to Slade as if the prairie was on fire, way off—then, later, giving birth to something like a dragon, formless in its radiance, rising to climb the sky. After last night, it didn't strike him as a hopeful sign.

It was enough, for now, that all of them had lived to see another day.

High noon was hot enough, but nothing in comparison to Mexico or southern Texas. Here, at least there was a breeze to chill the sweat of Slade's forehead and riffle through the hair along his collar.

Should've had that cut before I left, he thought. *And should've shaved this morning.*

Too late, now.

By Slade's watch, it was pushing one o'clock when Enid rose on the horizon, growing from a shape that might have been a far-off mesa to acquire specific forms of man-made structures.

"Guess we made it," Thornton said, with resignation in his voice. Nothing Slade felt obliged to answer. He ignored the prisoner, but kept a firm grip on the piebald's reins.

No one appeared to notice them at first, as they rode into town behind a teamster's wagon piled with wooden crates and kegs. They'd covered roughly half the distance to the jail and courthouse when Slade felt the ripples start to spread, people along the sidewalk stopping dead and watching them ride past. They were a minor spectacle, at least in part because of Little Wolf. Slade also caught a few surprised looks from some townsfolk who, he guessed, had thought they'd seen the last of him.

Arriving at the courthouse, Slade tied up their horses, freed Burch Thornton from his bonds, and marched him through a side door to the lockup. Ethan Tatum was the guard on duty, making no attempt to hide his shock at seeing Slade.

"I'll be goddamned!" he blurted out.

"Wouldn't surprise me," Slade replied. "I'm signing in a prisoner. Burch Thornton."

"Thornton! Well, I'll be—"

"Goddamned," Slade said, nodding. "You and me both."

"I'll take him off your hands," said Tatum. "Judge left us a standing order. You're to see him right away, as soon as you get in. *If* you got in, that is."

"I'll see him," Slade agreed. "But first, I need to stop off at the hospital."

That put a frown on Tatum's face. "You haven't heard?"

Slade felt a fist clench in his gut. "Heard what?"

"Miz Connover. She's been released."

"Released?"

Not dead and buried. Slade felt dizzy now. The courthouse seemed to tilt for just a second, then ease back to plumb.

"She's back at home?" Slade asked, when he could breathe again.

"No, sir," said Tatum. "Got herself a room at Grady's."

Enid's best hotel. Of two available, that was. Slade cocked a thumb at Little Wolf, told Tatum, "He's with me," and left without another word to either man. Walked past his tethered horse and two blocks farther on to the hotel, where he impressed a young clerk with the urgency of giving up Faith's room number.

Slade's heart was pounding as he climbed the stairs, two at a stride, to the third floor. Half deafened by his pulse, he felt as if someone had stuffed his skull with cotton. Forming a coherent thought was suddenly beyond him. Pacing off the hallway, Slade began to worry that he would be stricken mute.

He reached the numbered door, then spent a full half minute staring at it. When he knocked at last, Slade thought it was too loud but couldn't take it back. An urge to run came over him, but he was rooted to the spot.

Footsteps approached, and the door eased open to reveal Faith in a high-necked dress in cobalt blue. Her hair was down, seemed longer now than Slade remembered it somehow, and she was pale, as if she'd spent the past few weeks without a touch of sun.

"You're back," she said.

"I am."

Slade took a last step forward, reaching out for Faith. She stopped him with a palm pressed flat against his chest. Warm flesh, but Slade still felt a chill.

"Are you all right?" he asked.

"I'm better. Getting better," she amended.

"Good. That's good."

"I didn't think . . . nobody seemed to think that you'd be back," Faith said.

"I brought in Thornton," he explained.

Her eyes closed for a heartbeat, and a shadow seemed to fall across her face. "The others?" she inquired.

"They didn't make it."

"Oh, Jack."

"Listen, if there's something I can do . . ."

"There isn't. I can't do this anymore."

"Do what?" he asked her.

"Live in fear," she said. "You know it's been one thing after another, since we met. One or the other of us is in danger all the time. I'm glad you're safely back, but now it starts again."

"Faith—"

"No. I'm leaving, Jack. There's nothing more to say. I'm selling up and going home."

Slade didn't recognize his own voice as he asked, "Where's home?"

"Back East. Away from here."

She rose on tiptoes, brushed her lips against his left cheek, featherlight, then stepped away.

"Good-bye," Faith said. And shut the door.